About the Author

Fin C Gray was born in central Scotland but has spent his time between London and New York for the last twenty years. Now semi-retired, he invests in theatre and film. An avid traveller, Fin enjoys making trips abroad learning about cultures and customs. He is a graduate of the Manchester Metropolitan University where he was awarded an MA in Creative Writing with Merit in 2017. This book was the result of this degree. He is now working on his second novel and hopes to write full-time in the future.

For more information about his writing, please visit fincgray.com.

Duplicity

Fin C Gray

Duplicity

Olympia Publishers
London

www.olympiapublishers.com
OLYMPIA PAPERBACK EDITION

A CIP catalogue record for this title is
available from the British Library.

ISBN: 978-1-78830-406-1

This is a work of fiction.
Names, characters, places and incidents originate from the writer's
imagination. Any resemblance to actual persons, living or dead, is
purely coincidental.

First Published in 2019
Olympia Publishers
60 Cannon Street
London
EC4N 6NP
Printed in Great Britain

Dedication

For Anne, who always wanted this for me but never saw it, and for Michael who has supported and encouraged me throughout.

Acknowledgements

There are so many people to thank for making this possible. Firstly, I must thank Michael Melnick who offered so much encouragement and belief in me. Without him, this would not have been possible.

My class from Manchester Metropolitan University were a beacon of support throughout the creation of *Duplicity,* offering advice and continual encouragement. Heartfelt thanks to Helen Steadman, Dot Devey-Smith, Sue Smith, Bee Lewis, Nicola Lennon, Jane Masumy, Eleanor Moore, Zoë Feeney, Marita Karin Over, Susana Aikin and Kate Woodward. Your guidance and support came second to none.

Special thanks to Bee Lewis, not only for slapping me when I needed it but also for providing me with the title that had eluded me up until she handed it to me and saved me banging my head any further.

Derek Brown. Thank you for your friendship, your insight and your unequivocal critiquing both of this and other works I have subjected you to.

Without the many people who shared their knowledge of the Muslim faith and customs, the people I met in India and on the Pakistan border, the generosity of people on Facebook and Instagram who accepted and responded to my messages and constant questions, I wouldn't have been able to complete this novel. Thank you all.

Love seeketh not itself to please,
Nor for itself hath any care,
But for another gives its ease,
And builds a Heaven in Hell's despair.

'The Clod and the Pebble', *Songs of Innocence*
William Blake.

Prologue
Today, Friday

A mosaic of bodies... strangers... women, men, schoolchildren, teachers, businesspeople, lovers, friends. Excited chatter, stony faces, daydreamers, smartphone zombies. The buzz of humans is drowned out by the train rumbling through the tunnel. A voice clatters through the speakers, urging the crowds not to push and shove, promising that another train will be right behind this one. A tinny sound, like his old transistor radio with the volume turned up to max. For a second, he is a child again.

He sees commuters pressed against one another behind the carriage windows, suggesting this won't be the train for him. Bodies disembark, quickly replaced by the lucky ones closest to the platform edge, pushing and shoving, squeezing themselves in. Maybe they know. He won't miss this. He moves forward, now two rows of people from the platform edge. If the next train is full, these bodies in front of him might be lucky too. New travellers are already filling the space behind him, pressing against his back.

As the next train shudders to a stop, the announcer bellows out the same message as before. His voice sounds angry. Maybe it's just a wish to be heard above the noise of the train. Passengers spill out through the open doors, casting dark glances at those on the platform getting in their way.

He joins the push into the nearest carriage and manages to get inside this time. He feels sweat trickling down his neck and hopes the tattoo he has worked so hard to cover up stays hidden. A dishevelled old man sits mumbling to himself, the seats either side of him unoccupied. As he takes the seat next to the man, an acrid smell of urine and sweat hangs like a fog around the man. Despite the crowded carriage, there is space all around him.

His love had promised him he would see his mother again. He had promised that they would be together again for eternity. This short journey is going to be the end of what has seemed like an endless path. This pointless life is finally going to have meaning, purpose. *Are you watching, my love?* He smiles and closes his eyes, blocks out the faces in the carriage, imagines the face of his love. But instead, the ugly, hateful image of his father fills his brain. His smile dissipates, and his eyes snap open again.

'This is Charing Cross. Change here for the Northern Line and National Rail Services. Exit here for Trafalgar Square, the National Gallery and the National Portrait Gallery. This is a Bakerloo Line to Harrow and Wealdstone. The next station is Piccadilly Circus.'

The recorded voice sounds soft, almost reassuring, feminine, the antithesis of the platform announcer's voice. He looks at the people sitting opposite him. Some are reading papers, but most are studying the screens on their phones. One young man is staring at him, his eyes the same deep-brown as his beloved's. He fights back a long-suppressed desire rising inside him. The man is Indian, maybe Bangladeshi. He closes his eyes again and tries to remember the dark features of the men in the camp. The faces in his head alternate between his love's and that of the man sitting opposite him. Is the one he loves testing him?

He looks beyond the young man to the map. Two more stops. Just two more stops. Two more stops and his life will have meaning. His life will have purpose. There can be no going back. The final rush hour. He fingers the detonator in his pocket, traces the button, feels its rough indentation. The train stops. The doors open. Piccadilly Circus. One more stop. His heart beats faster. Destiny, moments away. Now, he feels the man's eyes on him again. When he returns his gaze, a different expression has seized his dark face. The imagined desire now replaced with one of recoil, fear – his eyes are wide and bulging, his pupils seem to consume all colour. The doors close.

He fingers the grooves of the vest beneath his clothes. A tight band of panic constricts his chest, and he breathes in deeply, fighting an intense nausea swelling inside him. He feels sweat pouring down his face and can't stop himself wiping it away. Streaks of make-up are visible on his palm.

'Long... deep... breaths.' That's how his love told him to push back any fear. 'When the moment draws close, take breaths from your soul,' his love said. 'Let Allah wash through your body and prepare you for your journey. Chant His name as you reach into your soul. *Allahu Akbar*. God is great. Let all doubts pass with each mention of His name. See nothing but Him. Think of nothing but Him.'

The man's eyes flit from his face to his waist again and again. His horror is visceral. Could it be the tattoo? Is it showing through the make-up? He looks down. A red wire is protruding from his pocket, the detonator button now visible. The man is now standing. He's shouting. His accent is foreign. Thick and rhotic – Middle Eastern, perhaps. Other faceless people leap up and start a frantic push down the carriage, scrambling away from him like frightened animals. The homeless man stays where he is, the wire clearly of no interest to him. He pushes it back out of sight nonetheless.

The recorded announcer is telling the passengers that the next station is Oxford Circus. Shouts and screams battle with the rumble of the train; panic is spreading like an epidemic. Someone tries to open the connecting doors. People push towards either end of the carriage, leaving him and the tramp in their own small space.

He stands up, his right hand in the detonator pocket. Somebody shouts, 'Don't! Please!'

As the train begins to slow down, he hears the sound of a child crying, piercing the jabber of noise pounding his brain. He looks to his right and sees a tall, blond-haired man moving swiftly towards him, focusing directly on him.

With his left hand, he pulls the knife from his waistband. Traces of dried blood still mark the top of the hilt. For a second, he remembers the semi-naked body covered in blood – and jabs at the air between him and the blond-haired man, who pulls back, both hands raised.

'Easy, easy,' the blond man says, inching forward again.

He points the dagger at the blond man's face then makes a slicing motion with it in front of his own neck. The man reaches for the emergency-stop lever, but he lurches towards him and stabs the man in the groin. Roaring with pain and clutching his wound, the blond man falls to his knees.

The train is drawing to a halt, and the female voice announces, 'The next station is Oxford Circus. Change here for the Central Line and Victoria Line. This is a Bakerloo Line...'

He reaches back into his right pocket, feeling for the detonator. The train is silent. The babbling has ceased. A sense of tranquillity sweeps over him. Someone has managed to open the connecting door, and the crowds pressing against the back of his carriage are pushing through, jostling one another, but he can hear no sound. His inner peace is complete. He looks to his right and sees the homeless man sitting there, impassively. He smiles at the tramp and sees the first light of the platform breaking through the dark of the tunnel. It is time. His thumb rests on the button in his pocket.

Without warning, the noise returns – the jabbering crowd releasing their terror again. He inhales deeply and, as the train screeches and grinds to a standstill, he looks upwards and bellows, '*Allahu Akbar*!' He presses down hard on the button in his pocket. The carriage doors open and the announcer's voice starts up again.

Incredulous, he watches the crowd of panicking people spill out into the mass of commuters. The tramp sits motionless, oblivious. Like him, this old man will be glad to be set free of this terrible world. He presses the button again. Again. Again. Nothing.

Commuters are pushing their way into the carriage, but freeze and turn around when their eyes make contact with his. He runs towards the open door, a spike of panic penetrating his chest. The platform is swarming with people pushing away from him in both directions. Two transport police officers are visible further back, forcing their way through the crowds, yelling at people to get out of the way.

The passage through to the Victoria Line platform is in front of him, so he runs, following those commuters trying to escape him, still frantically pushing the detonator button. This platform is awash with people too, many seemingly unaware of the danger he poses. The train comes rumbling through the darkness at the far end of the tunnel just as he trips over a bag someone is dragging behind them. He falls against three or four panicking women and sees them smash against the rails as his knees crack against the platform edge. His finger is still on the button as his body falls onto the tracks.

Chapter One
Then

Daniel wasn't set to go home yet. Jenny would be there already, and Mum wouldn't be back for at least an hour. He ducked down as he passed the house. No way was he going to let Jenny tag along and spoil this for him. Dad would kill him if he knew – and if Jenny knew, Dad would know too. There was nothing surer than that.

'Don't ever let me catch you going to that lorry park, son. Right? I'll whack your arse if I ever hear that you've gone there.'

When he'd asked Dad what was wrong with the lorry park, all he'd said was, 'Just do what I tell you, OK?' What could be so bad about it? OK, it was dusty, and his school uniform would get all dirty, but he could shake it off in their backyard, in the wind. Nobody would know. The dust blew over the road onto their house nearly every day, anyway. It could just have got on his blazer from the wind, couldn't it, if anyone asked? If Mum asked. Probably there was a lot more of it in the actual park, mind, so he'd more than likely have to shake it off.

Mum and Dad seemed to love moaning about the park. Dad even spoke to Black Jash, the owner of the café, about it and got angry with him. He was shouting a lot, something about it being the café's responsibility and that he should pay to get it tarmacked. Black Jash had shouted back at Dad. He'd got very red in the face. Daniel hoped that Black Jash would get the lorry park tarred over. Because then the tar lorries would come. Nothing smelled better than hot tar, and Daniel loved to step on it while it was still sticky. Not sticky enough to dirty up his shoes, mind. That had happened once when he was much smaller, and Mum had been mad at him. She said she couldn't afford any new shoes and that he'd have to go to school in bare feet. She was joking, but he had believed her.

Better than the tar itself were the big black lorries that poured the thick, black, lumpy stuff out. What a roar they made. And the roar would turn into a grindy, scrapy noise when the back started to rise and the tail-gate opened up. Oh, how he would love to pull the lever that tipped the tar out of the back. He'd jump out of the lorry as it tipped and watch the tar spill out the back, like some big metal robot mouth throwing up black sick.

And then there'd be road rollers. Rollers, with their hissing and banging, were probably even better than the tar lorries. Yeah, he'd rather have a go on a road roller than a tar lorry, any day. He could pull the thing that made the smoke whistle out of the chimney at the side of the cab and watch the roller flatten out the mounds of tar as flat and black as liquorice toffee.

Daniel lurked at the entrance to the lorry park, glancing in every direction, making sure nobody was around who might tell his Dad he was going in. A massive green artic was pulling up to where he was standing, sending clouds of gritty dust into the air, making a fog of the sunshine. He looked down at his blazer, and spluttered and frowned at the coating of grey now dulling the deep-maroon cloth. Oh, damn! He hadn't even set a foot in the place, and already grime covered his clothes. The lorry driver blared his horn and waved down at him. Daniel waved back, forgetting all about the dust.

As the green lorry pulled away, throwing clouds of dust in its wake, Daniel took a tentative step onto the forbidden ground, wondering how many trucks he might be able to count and which towns they might have come from. The best ones were the lorries that had foreign words on the side. They almost always had unusual loads, and he liked to imagine them rolling onto ferries heading to far away countries. The green lorry had the word POLSKA printed on the back. Tomorrow, he'd ask his teacher what that word meant. All the other words on the back were very long and too hard to read and remember.

Kevin, Daniel's best friend from school, had told him his father was a lorry driver and that he took his lorry on the ferry from Stranraer to Ireland twice every week. Kevin lived in Newton, five miles away, so his Dad never parked his truck here. Newton had its very own lorry park, and Kevin's dad didn't even mind him going into it and checking out all the different sorts that were parked there. Mind, the Newton lorry park had tarmac on, so it *had* to be the dust that bothered Mum and Dad so much.

As Daniel walked further into the park, all he could see were flurries of dust being whipped up by the wind. Not a single lorry in sight. Where could they all be? There were always loads of them on a Tuesday. He walked over to the café. Well, everyone called it a pub, but it sold fish and chips, so that made it a café too, didn't it? And kids were allowed to go in it – not like the big pub opposite the school. The man there shouted at any kids who even stuck their head round the door.

Outside, there was a blackboard sign tied to the door. Chalked in shaky writing were the words: CLOSED DUE TO POWER CUT SORRY. Daniel frowned and kicked a discarded paper cup at it. Just his luck. Now he'd have to go home and do his homework. Damn.

Kicking up his own clouds of dust, he headed towards the entrance again and grinned widely as a gigantic red truck pulled into the park. The driver was smiling back at him from his cab. Daniel waved, and the driver waved back and winked. The lorry drove all the way to the back of the park and turned around, before slowly reversing and stopping. Daniel stood where he was, listening to the faint rumble of the engine, and waited for the air to clear. After a few minutes, he saw the headlights of the lorry flash on and off.

He looked behind himself, pleased that nobody was around to see him there, then slowly started walking towards the red rumbling shape at the back of the park. The sun was bright behind the lorry, and he squinted, trying to see if the driver was still in his cab. He'd be in so much trouble if Dad found out, but this was more exciting than anything he could imagine. Maybe he'd get a chance to look inside this lorry. Maybe even sit in the driver's seat and hold the massive steering wheel. The biggest wheel he'd ever had a go on was Johnny Rae's tractor, and even *he'd* warned him not to tell anyone afterwards. It wasn't as if he was actually driving it or anything. Grown-ups just didn't make sense sometimes.

The headlights had flashed a couple of times more, and Daniel was getting quite close now, close enough to see the driver grinning at him. Daniel smiled back. This man looked awfully friendly and, if he made friends with him, he might even get a chance to go for a quick drive around the park. That would be ace. He could tell Kevin all about it at school tomorrow, as long as he swore him to death secrecy. Everyone knew that telling anybody a death secret meant certain death. Not just death, but a horrible death, as if being strangled by a boa constrictor, or run over by a combine harvester. Kevin would never tell anyway.

Mum always said, 'Never talk to strangers.' But not all strangers could be bad, could they? This man wasn't really a stranger, anyhow, because he was in the village lorry park. All the lorry drivers who came here usually came twice or three times a week, so this man would be no stranger to the village, would he? Black Jash would definitely know the man because he'd be in there a lot to eat his dinner, wouldn't he? The only reason the lorry drivers came there was to have a rest and have their dinner. That's what Kevin had told him. Sometimes they might have a nap in their cabs. Some lorries even had beds in them. If Daniel drove a lorry, he would sleep in the bed every single night. Kevin said some had TV sets. And Kevin also told him that some trucks had showers and baths and kitchens. He wasn't too sure about that, though. If they had kitchens, there'd be no need to stop at cafés, would there?

Daniel was level with the cab now, and the man was rolling down his window. He couldn't see the man's arm moving, so this lorry must have electric windows. That would make it quite a new lorry because the old ones didn't have electric windows, and the red paint on the cab was very, very shiny and bright. Maybe that meant it had a TV too. The man's arm was hanging out of the open window, and his arm had tattoos all over it. There were even tattoos of letters on his fingers. Daniel couldn't see these properly, though, because there was a lot of oil on his hands. The arm disappeared back inside, and the door started to open very slowly.

The man began to climb down from his cab, and he had quite a fat belly that was poking out of his T-shirt. His belly was very hairy, and he had a tattoo of Bart Simpson's head near his belly-button. He smelled a bit of sweat and, when he smiled, his teeth were yellow and stained. His big brown boots stirred up a lot of dust when he jumped onto the ground. Daniel smiled when the man ruffled his hair and pinched the end of his chin with dirty fingers.

'Alright, kidder,' he said. 'What you doing here, all on your own?'

'I came to see the lorries. There's usually a lot more here.'

'Well, you're lucky that I turned up then, aren't you, son? Otherwise, all you'd be seeing is dust.'

Daniel nodded, trying to smile, but he was starting to feel that something was wrong. The man had crouched down so that his face was level with his own. His breath smelled of rotten eggs, and his cheeks were all covered in red splodges and hair.

'It's your lucky day, son, because I'm going to let you see inside my lorry. I bet you'd like that, wouldn't you?'

Daniel looked up into the cab. The steering wheel was the biggest he'd ever seen. A large bag of sweets was on the dashboard. Then he felt the man pressing against his back. Maybe he shouldn't go into the lorry. Maybe this was the driver's first time here, and he was a stranger, after all. He looked towards the café and pointed to the sign.

'The café is closed today, mister,' he said. 'You won't be

able to get your dinner here today. That's why there're no other lorries here. Maybe you better try Newton lorry park. My friend Kevin—'

'I have sandwiches in there,' he said, pointing to his cab. 'I got sweeties and games too. Jump in, c'mon. You'll like it, son.'

The man wasn't smiling any more. He was pressing closer against him, and his hand was gripping one of Daniel's arms. Daniel looked towards the road, this time hoping that he might see someone he knew.

'I think I better go home. My Dad says I'm not allowed to come here, and I don't want to get into trou—'

The man didn't let him finish. He took a tighter hold of Daniel's arm and it hurt quite a bit. His grip was very firm, but the man was smiling again. It wasn't a nice smile, not a friendly smile. It reminded Daniel of the sort of smile the Joker might make at Batman. The man put his dirty hands under both Daniel's arms and lifted him up into his cab. It was huge inside, and there was a bed made up behind the seats. A strong smell of petrol hit him. There was a red tartan rug scrunched up on the passenger seat, and the rug had oil stains all over it. There were pictures of people with no clothes on near it. Daniel hadn't seen pictures like that ever before and felt sure he wasn't supposed to look at stuff like that.

'In you go,' said the lorry driver, throwing him in roughly. 'Your dad will never know.'

Daniel's face pressed into the smelly rug. He'd hurt his knee on something hard when the man pushed him into the seat. He heard the man's heavy boots pounding on the metal steps into the cab, and he started to cry.

Daniel had managed to stop crying by the time he saw Mum's car pull into the backyard. She was a lot later than usual. Just as well, really. Peeping from behind his curtain, he watched as Mum got out of her car. Jenny was with her and they were laughing about something. Why had Jenny not been at home, as usual? Why was she with Mum? And where had they been? His blazer was on his bed, and he gasped a little when he realised that he'd forgotten to shake off the dust. He stuffed it under his bed and went to the bathroom to check himself in the mirror. There were dark streaks on his cheeks where tears had made tracks in the grime. He turned on the tap and rubbed soap and water onto his face.

'Danny, are you up there?' Mum called from downstairs.

'Yes, Mum, I'm just in the toilet.'

Daniel scrubbed his face with the rough washcloth and patted down his hair. His throat hurt really badly and he could still taste that horrible taste, no matter how much he gargled with water. There was still blood oozing from his skinned knee, and it stung when he dabbed at it with the cloth. When he got downstairs, Mum was in the kitchen, peeling potatoes.

'Hello, love,' she said, smiling. 'How was school today? Have you got any homework for tomorrow?'

'It was OK, Mum. I've only got spelling homework, but I know all the words, anyway.'

'Alright, love. You go and make sure you know all the words, and I'll call you when tea's ready. I'll test you after we've eaten.'

Daniel turned around and started to head into the dining-room.

'Danny?'

He stopped dead, a feeling of panic rising in him again. Did she know? He turned round again, slowly.

'Tuck your shirt in, there's a good boy. You look like you've been sleeping in a hedge.' She laughed.

Daniel heaved a great sigh through a growing need to cry again. 'Sorry, Mum,' he mumbled, tucking in his shirt. He rushed to the stairs before she could call him back again.

Back in his bedroom, he pulled the blazer from under the bed, opened his window, and shook it as hard as he could, whacking it against the windowsill. Jenny was in the yard with her skipping rope.

'What you doing?' she called up to him.

'None of your bloody business,' he called back to her.

Jenny threw down her skipping rope and gave him a look of pretend shock. 'I'm telling Mum you swore at me!'

Daniel slammed his window shut and hung his blazer on the back of the chair at his desk. He sat down and took out his spelling book. The words blurred in a rush of horrible thoughts, along with the tears that were forming fast. He gulped and gulped, but the pain in his throat wouldn't go away. Never, ever, ever, as long as he lived, was he ever going back to that lorry park. He hated lorries now. He never wanted to see another lorry again.

Chapter Two
Today, Friday

If anything calls for more wine, it's 'Hallelujah'. Of course, Jeff Buckley's is the only voice that sounds right singing it; Tom can't stand hearing any other singer attempt it, not even Leonard Cohen, even though it is his song. The other thing is, these days, it just doesn't sound right without a glass of wine in his hand, and he has to feel at least a little tipsy too. So he gets up and presses pause on the remote before throwing it on the sofa. Two candles on the coffee table in front of him flicker and darken, but the light in the room doesn't diminish as the sulphurous glow from the lamps in the gardens bathes the living-room. Shadows from the shivering trees dance across the walls of the flat. Tom hears Big Ben chiming three bells. Three in the morning already?

Steadying himself with the help of the chair backs in the dining-room, he spies an unopened bottle of red wine on the kitchen counter. He glances at the two empty bottles beside it. It's Thursday night, after all, and who's counting? But where is the bloody corkscrew? It should be with the fucking empties, shouldn't it? His tabby cat miaows and rubs his purring body against Tom's legs.

'Hello, Rufus. You hungry, buddy?' He bends down and tickles the cat's throat, before Rufus pads urgently towards the laundry room at the end of the long hallway. Rufus glances back, standing by the laundry room door.

'I'm coming, daftie!'

When he gets there, he notices the empty food dish beside the litter tray. Then he sees the corkscrew on the countertop next to an unopened tin of tuna, Rufus's favourite.

'What a good cat you are, showing your old dad where his wine opener is. Let me get you some dinner, puss.'

As he heads towards the kitchen again, Tom thinks he hears a rustling sound. He stops and listens at the front door. It's more than a rustling – it's someone pushing on the door. The handle is moving too. Bloody cheek! It's three in the morning. Better not be one of the porters. He presses his ear to the wood before opening the creaking double doors and peering out into the marble hallway. There is no sign of anyone. The service lift in front of him is on the basement level, so he steps outside the flat and checks the residents' lift at the other end of the hall. Although he can't quite make out the glowing digits on the display, he can see it doesn't show '3' for his floor. There isn't a sound anywhere. He can't be bothered to check the stairs and heads indoors again. Probably imagined it all, anyhow. Rufus gives a brief backwards glance as Tom walks into the laundry room, then continues munching his tuna. Tom picks up the corkscrew and winds an uneven path back to the sofa via the kitchen, where he collects the unopened wine bottle.

As Tom sips the freshly poured Cabernet, Jeff Buckley's voice fills the room. Tom puts his bare feet up on the coffee table and gazes towards the flickering candles and the silver-framed photograph that he'd taken from the mantelpiece earlier that evening. In the picture, his wife sits on their old sofa, flanked on either side by their two children. Broad smiles beam from a happy, colour-faded past. Tears pool in Tom's eyes.

He and the ghost of Jeff Buckley sing together before Tom collapses on the cushions, spilling red wine all over the leopardskin fabric, sobbing. If he needs any reason not to drink alone, this song is it, and he knows it, but it's about as addictive as the wine is to him. His sobbing dissipates as sleep gradually comes to him, sending him deep into dark forgetfulness. He is hardly aware of Rufus jumping onto his heaving chest, nestling his head into Tom's furrowed neck. Purrs mingle softly with erratic snores and grunts.

A soft jingle from the front door causes Tom to stir from his slumber. 'Hallelujah' has long since faded out, replaced by a low hum, something Tom wakes up to more often than not. Again the bell sounds, making the cat scamper onto the floor. He tries to force his eyes to open as Rufus scampers to the alcove and begins to miaow plaintively.

'What's up, buddy?' Tom stretches his arm, feeling for Rufus just as the bell breaks fully into his consciousness. 'What the f—'

The bell rings again. This time, it seems louder.

'What the fuck? Who the fuck is that?' Tom lifts his head and tries to focus. 'Rufus?'

He forces himself up on one arm and blearily studies the new red wine map on the sofa. No! Not again! Fuck! He looks at the clock on the mantle, rubbing his short, grey-stippled hair, and he stretches his legs back to the floor. Tom stands up and places the toppled wine glass back on the coffee table.

'Rufus?'

He looks around, sees all the candles are out, and looks out of the windows towards the river and the London Eye. A moistness in his crotch slowly enters his consciousness, and he looks with disgust at the dark wet patch around his groin and screws up his nose at the sharp smell of urine. You fucking tramp! The bell rings again and, as he begins staggering into the hall, he peers towards the Victorian coiled bell quivering on its wire. Rufus is nowhere to be seen. Probably hiding under the bed again, scaredy-cat that he is.

Tom shoots a vicious look at the door. It'll be some lost drunk from the hotel. Every fucking night, he seems to get some idiot who is lost, looking for their room. He's just in the mood for giving him a piece of his mind, and he approaches the door shouting, 'Who's there?'

There is no response. He scrabbles for the key in the lock and turns it awkwardly. A twist on the handle makes no difference, and he remembers he has to release the security catch. Again, he shouts, 'Who's there?' Two firm bangs on the door make him jump. He pulls the catch. The door is heavy as he pulls harder, feeling it give as something pushes it from the other side.

'Wait!' he shouts.

Tom squints at the young man before him who seems to be averting his eyes from him. He is shorter than Tom, with a long scruffy brown beard that tapers to a point at his chest. Long hair covers the collar of the heavy dark coat he wears, and he has a thick metal ring in his nose as a bull might have. A tattoo of a snake, its fangs gripping his right nostril, covers his right cheek, the winding tail curving beyond his chin, twisting down his neck, disappearing behind the beard. Tom blinks at the dull chain linking the nose ring to a grey metal hoop in his left ear.

'Can I help you?' Tom is trying to focus on the dull band of yellow and red silk poking out from under the young man's coat, leading a path to scruffy cut-off jeans revealing his shins and sandalled feet.

'A'right?' A dank acrid smell hits Tom at the same time as the voice connects with his brain, and their eyes make contact.

'Daniel? Daniel, is that YOU? Is that you?' He looks into the boy's large green eyes. The eyes are his answer, but he waits for it anyway.

Tom rubs his hands together, and an involuntary shudder shakes his shoulders. His feeling of drunkenness leaves him as he leans his head forward, trying to focus. Is this a dream? His hands fall to his wet crotch. No words will come. Could this really be his son? The essence of the man standing before him bears no relationship to the memory of his boy, his firstborn. It has been so long since he last saw him. He blinks away tears.

'It's Dani now.'

Yes, this is Daniel. 'Come in, son, come in!' Tom puts his hands on his son's shoulders. The boy shrugs them off as soon as they make contact.

'Where the hell've you been? I hardly recognise you,' says Tom.

Daniel shrugs again. 'Been travelling, Tom.'

'Tom? Can you at least call me Dad? However much you resent me, I'm still your dad.'

'Whatever.'

'Come in, will you? Let's not stand here in the doorway.'

'You're drunk.' Daniel looks him up and down and adds, 'As per usual.'

'Daniel, it's four in the morning. OK, I've had a drink. So what? It's the weekend, isn't it?'

Daniel scowls at Tom. He throws his backpack behind him in the hallway, eyeing the walls with a frown, scrunching up his nose, giving movement to the snake. 'You've tarted the place up.'

'I'd only just moved in when you last saw it. That time when you came with that friend of yours, Vikram or something, wasn't it? Anyway, magnolia was never my colour, was it?' Tom sweeps his arms towards the walls and smiles.

'Waqar, idiot! He was my best friend.' Daniel gazes at the deep-red Venetian plasterwork. He scowls again and gathers phlegm in his throat and makes as if to spit.

'Don't even think about it! What do you mean *was* your friend? Have you two fallen out? Shame, I liked him.'

'He was the best friend I ever had, or ever will have. He died.'

'Died? God, no! He couldn't have been more than twenty-three. How awful. What on earth happened to him?'

'A car accident. He was twenty-five,' says Daniel, looking at the floor. He pauses and wrings his hands. 'I miss him.'

'Where, when? Was he driving? Did a car hit him? God, Daniel, it's just too awful.'

For the first time, Daniel's expression seems to soften; there is a vulnerability hidden under his façade of anger. Is he close to tears?

'I don't want to talk about it.'

'Daniel, I'm so sorry. That's just dreadful.'

Daniel's face hardens again, as if some switch has been flicked inside him. 'Shit happens.'

'Are you staying the night? You can stay as long as you like. It would be good to catch up with you, find out what you've been up to.'

'I'm here for tonight... OK?'

'You're always welcome here. You know that.'

'Yeah, OK.'

Rufus pads up to them, purring, pushing himself against the boy. Daniel kicks him away. The cat screeches and scuttles back to the sanctuary of Tom's bedroom.

'What was that for?' Tom wants to kick Daniel – show him how it feels. 'He misses you. He's YOUR cat, after all!'

'YOUR toy, more like. You've kept it trapped here all these years. Let it free. Who the fuck are you to say who or what belongs to anybody?'

'Daniel—'

'Dani! I told you!'

'For fuck's sake, you lumbered me with the damn cat when you couldn't be bothered to look after him any longer. What did I ever do, Daniel? Why are you angry with me? It's been the same ever since Mum died.'

'I'm not angry with you.' He turns away from Tom. 'I've got a lot on my mind. It's been a rough few months.'

'OK, let's start again. Are you hungry? It's late. Do you want a shower? Can we maybe just sit down and talk, sort things out between us, after you've cleaned up?'

'Maybe we can talk when you're sober...'

'Danie... Danny, I don't think I've... Seeing you at the

door knocked me sober. Yeah, I've had some wine, but I'm perfectly compos mentis. To be honest, I feel more sober now than I've ever felt. It's been nearly three years. I've pretty much been going out of my mind, wondering if you're alive or dead.'

'Fuck, Tom. I wrote to you, didn't I? I told you I needed time. I needed space. How much clearer could I have been?'

'I deserve better than that, don't I? You have a phone. And there's the flat, which I pay for, if you remember! You have—'

'Look, forget the emotional blackmail, OK? Forget telling me all you've done for me and what a cunt of a son I've been. I just need to stay here tonight, alright? It's no big deal. I can go now if that's what you want. I've lived independently of you for long enough. One more night won't change a thing.'

'I'm sorry. Of course you can stay. Of course I don't want you to go.' Tom feels an inexorable sob rising in his chest. It explodes, spattering over Daniel. He searches around for a tissue, covering his face with his hands.

Daniel turns away again. He sucks up some phlegm into his throat and spits on the floor before heading to the living room. Tom goes to the kitchen and pulls some paper towels from the holder and wipes his face. He yanks some more from the roll and returns to the hall to scoop up the mucus from the parquet floor. Through the archway, between the dining room and living room, he sees his son sitting on the sofa with his back to him. He starts to walk towards him but, instead, changes course towards the study. The heavy panelled door needs a good shove, so he pushes his weight against it.

This is Tom's favourite room and, as he looks around at the fine books and art, he manages half a smile. He releases the brass catch on one of the high shelves in the centre of the room, revealing the fake section of books that disguise the fold-down double bed. The bed slowly descends into the space below and the study transforms into a bedroom. As he pulls bed linen from a cupboard, he becomes aware of a strong, now familiar, foreign body odour in the room. He turns around and sees Daniel there, looking around the room with a growing sneer.

'You could've fed an entire village in Pakistan for a year for what it must have cost you to kit this room out.'

'Pakistan? What do you know about Pakistan?'

'I know it's a piss-poor country created by rich British bureaucrats like you.'

'Oh spare me the lectures, please, Danny. You'll be comfy enough here tonight then, won't you?' Tom starts to walk away.

'I'll be happy kipping on the sofa,' Daniel says, 'as long as it's not the one you've pissed all over.'

'There are fresh towels in the guest bathroom. Try and get some rest. We can have a better chat in the morning when you've had some sleep. Goodnight.' Tom walks through the door, but Daniel pushes past him.

'I need my backpack.'

'I can get it for you.'

Daniel ignores him and picks up the backpack, throwing it into the study. He goes back in and slams the door behind him. Tom can now feel the dull drag of alcohol pulling him back down as he takes small, careful steps to his bedroom. He scowls at his unmade bed, and his eyes turn towards the open door and the key in the lock. Bad memories start to break from a long-closed chamber in his past, back into his present:

memories of having a guitar smashed in his face, of being trapped in his own living room by his son, of having a brick lobbed at him through his bedroom window, of being pushed downstairs. Best to lock himself in. No point taking any chances, the way Daniel is tonight.

He lurches at the key and twists it around, not sure whether the lock has engaged or not. All he wants to do now is sleep and block out the day. An open bottle of sleeping pills lie on his bedside table. With no pause for thought, he tips some into his hand. Two, three or four blue pills blur together in his palm and he pops them into his mouth, swallowing them down with a glass of stale water from the night before. Finally, he pulls off his shirt and climbs out of his damp trousers. The bed seems to ripple and swivel before him as he collapses onto the unkempt sheets, wearing only his sodden underpants. As Tom starts to fall into a deep, drugged, drunken sleep, Rufus appears from under his bed, jumping up on him and snuggling down on his warm heaving chest.

Across the hall, Daniel pulls a colourful chequered mat from his rucksack and lays it on the floor of the study. He removes the silk, which is wrapped around his torso like a bandage. Underneath, he wears a ragged pair of denim cut-off jeans. From the pocket, he pulls out a mobile phone and searches for the compass app on it. Using that, he faces east. He winds the greater part of the unravelled silk around his head, leaving his skinny, hairless frame exposed. A gap in the waist of his shorts reveals a ceremonial dagger, sheathed in cheap leather. He looks down at it and touches it for a brief few seconds, and then he goes to the bathroom in the hall and washes himself.

Cleansed, he returns to the study and, kneeling on the mat, he places his hands either side of his knees and drops his forehead onto the chequered surface. He closes his eyes and begins to recite the *Isha* prayer: '*Allahumma inna nasta'eenuk, wa nastahdeek…*'

When he has finished, he goes to the door that leads to his father's bedroom suite and gently pushes it. The door into his father's grand bathroom is open and the lights are on. With narrowed eyes and a twist in his mouth, he casts a long gaze around the room, despising every polished granite surface, as if each is an intended insult to everything he holds true. A seething hatred compels him to empty his bladder into his father's huge Jacuzzi bath.

Now, he takes slow, cautious steps towards his father's room, his prayer mat hanging limply in his hand. Why has he brought it with him? The door gives in to his push, and the key falls onto the carpet. Revulsion almost overcomes him as his eyes meet his father's semi-naked body, one leg hanging over the edge of the bed, the other obliquely stretched towards the bare French windows, signposting the Thames outside and the privileged view. Again, he spits. Tom lets out a loud, drunken snore and pulls his leg back onto the bed. Daniel leans over him and hisses '*Allahu Akbar*' into his face, dropping the prayer mat to the floor. His father does not stir.

Daniel lies down beside his father. He doesn't know why. It is something he feels he has to do. It reminds him of the day his mother went to *Jannah*. A distant thread of lost love tries to snake inside him. He resists it as body warmth leaks from one to the other. Something presses at his brain: love, memory, nostalgia? Again, he resists it. All that matters now is his promised destiny. Nothing can interfere with that. A sense of love still persists. A love for Tom? Fight it. Stop it. Do not let it break your resolve. Waqar's love is what he craves. A writhing snake slithers from his face into his psyche. The snake on the box. Waqar's mother's pewter box. The box that protects the promise of love.

As Daniel lies there, Rufus moves off Tom's chest and clambers onto Daniel, tail tall and upright in a feline hello. Daniel tickles the cat under his collar and feels the vibration of his deep purr. Loved cats, wooden cats, twist and writhe inside him, becoming snake-like, taking him back to lost days – days of innocence. Beautiful days of knowing nothing but truth. Again, the synapses click shut and his better brain stops the interference from getting through, like whatever it is that blocks the radio frequencies in Pakistan.

'Lucky you weren't born a Pakistani cat,' whispers Daniel, stroking Rufus. 'You'd not have much to purr about if you were.'

Rufus removes himself back onto Tom and settles down on his chest again.

Daniel takes hold of his father's limp left hand and sneers at the wedding ring on his finger before wrenching it from him. His mind is now set on his task. This worthless bastard must die. Then he walks towards the French windows and steps out onto the balcony. He makes as if to throw the ring out into the darkness, but stops himself. The ring on Daniel's little finger, a smaller version of the one he has just yanked off his father, won't allow him to destroy its partner. He tosses it from one hand to the other. He wants to throw it as far as he possibly can. Tom's ring is a lie, a false symbol. Again, something prevents him. Mum gave that to his cunt of a father. She didn't know any better, though, did she? He looks again at his own ring. Tom gave that to her. Should he throw both rings into the darkness? He can't. Not one, or the other. The link must remain. One cannot exist without the other. Both, or neither. Each ring means something different, but his mother hammers at his brain. He throws his arm back, ready to send his father's ring into dark solitude. He stops himself. Instead, he places it on the bedside table next to Tom.

Tom looks peaceful as Daniel withdraws the dagger from his jeans. The sheath remains there, and the metal of the blade catches the light of the lamps outside and the blue of the London Eye. Cool air blows into the room, and the blade glints as he presses its sharp edge into the sagging folds of his father's neck.

Chapter Three
Then

'Tom, I love you, you know that. But really?' Ewan said.

Tom scowled at the man in front of him, draining the last drops from his pint. A work friend, at best. When Ewan left for his new job, that should have been it. He somehow seemed to think he was still relevant to Tom. But without work, there was no real connection between them.

Tom looked him up and down. Why did all the ugly, pointless bastards seem to land on their feet? But Tom hated the fact that he was struggling at work without him, the man who'd been his lowly junior at Armstrong's. Sinking more than struggling, if he was honest. He fumbled in his pocket for his wallet and rummaged between the flaps before throwing it on the table.

'I'd get another round in, but I'm a bit strapped, mate,' he said, the words catching in his throat. What had he done wrong to be beholden to this fucking waste of space?

Ewan rolled his eyes, picked up their empty glasses and went to the bar. Wispy ginger hairs were doing their best to disguise the dome of his head, as he walked away from Tom.

Tom felt his phone buzz in his pocket. Alison most likely. Well, she could fuck off. Almost before the buzzing had a chance to stop, the phone buzzed again, a text this time. He pulled it out:

NEED TO TALK TO YOU. CALL ME, PLEASE.

Tom thrust the phone back into his pocket and waited. A few moments later, Ewan returned with two fresh pints. Tom pulled his towards himself and took a long gulp.

'You're welcome!' said Ewan.

'I'm serious, Ewan. I just want out. It's nothing but debt, misery and despair for me. You're lucky, mate. You escaped.'

'Lucky? Me? Bugger off.' He sipped his pint. 'OK, the new job pays a bit more than I was getting when I worked with you, but every extra penny goes towards the bloody divorce. If it ain't broke, don't fix it, mate, believe me. Ali is fantastic, and you dote on those little uns, I know you do.'

'Well, Dan isn't so little anymore; he's nearly ten and a miserable little shit with it.' Tom glanced at Ewan's glass, making sure it was nearly empty, before taking another large gulp from his own. 'I've got bills coming out of every orifice.' He pressed on, although it felt wrong. Did Ewan even care? He was at least trying to look sympathetic. 'Ali nags me from the second I wake up until the second I fall asleep. Both kids are fucking nightmares. Sometimes I just want to get a cheap camper van. I'd be off quicker than you could finish that pint, I promise you.'

Ewan's sympathy seemed to be dissipating, and he rolled his eyes again, but Tom ignored him and stared blankly through the grimy window.

'How many times have you given me this camper van fantasy?' he said, sighing. 'Why the hell don't you just do it? Stop rattling on about it and grab your dream by the balls. Then at least I can laugh when you come back, begging for what you already have.'

'You know what? I'd be singing all the way to the Channel Tunnel, never to be seen again. Just imagine – me shagging my way around Europe and then everywhere else the wheels'd take me. No more worries. Freedom.'

'Honestly, Tom. You've been saying stuff like that ever since I've known you. When it comes down to it, you love Ali. Fact. You're never just going to pack up and leave.'

'I'd trade the whole lot for freedom. Freedom and a wad of cash.'

'Good luck with that,' said Ewan, barely able to stifle his laugh. 'Believe me, getting out of a marriage doesn't come cheap.'

Tom shifted his weight in the chair and looked squarely at Ewan.

'If we could just make ends meet, things might be different. I was never cut out for this. The pipe and slippers game just isn't my thing.'

'Tom, every Christmas do Armstrong's ever had, you and Ali were the most loved-up couple there.' Ewan furrowed his brow, looking earnestly back at him. 'Every time Meg and I had a night out with you both, she'd say that she wished we could be more like you two. God, she drove me mad with it. You need to stop feeling sorry for yourself.'

'We should never have had the kids, and that's the truth. If it were just Ali and me, I'd be a lot happier. She wouldn't be a full-time nagging machine, for a start.' Tom couldn't look his friend in the eye anymore. He studied his nearly empty glass. 'It's all kids and bills with her. She was never like that before they came along. I tell you now, if my numbers came up, the first thing I'd do is ship them off to boarding school and fuck off somewhere warm with or without Ali.'

Tom felt his phone buzzing again and pulled it from his pocket. He turned the screen for Ewan to see.

'See? It's constant!' he said. 'Bloody hell, mate, I dream about it. I pray for it. Just a windfall from somewhere to sort out my life. There's nothing, and I mean nothing, I wouldn't do to get off this fucking hamster wheel.'

'Believe me, mate, money isn't gonna solve all your troubles, not even a fraction of them. Money brings as many problems as it takes away,' said Ewan, reaching for Tom's arm.

Tom shook it away. 'Yeah, *you'd* know.'

'Mate, you seem to have an inflated idea of what I'm bringing in these days. At my new place, I'm only a few grades higher than you are at Armstrong's. If I could have a fraction of what you have – lovely wife, kids, I wouldn't be sat here, that's for sure.'

'So, I'm a bad father now, am I?'

'For fuck's sake, Tom. Grow up! Listen to yourself. The whole world doesn't have things better than you. And yeah, moaning about your kids here in the pub, when all I wanted was to discuss a few things that might have interested you, maybe you aren't such a brilliant human being.'

Tom stood up and drained the little left in his glass. Fuck him!

'Two poxy pints after work. Hardly painting the town red, am I? Why the fuck did you want to meet for a drink tonight, anyway? Catch up, or simply gloat?'

'I'm beginning to wonder.'

'See you around, Ewan,' Tom said, pulling on his coat.

Outside, the pavements glistened under the streetlights. Tom's phone buzzed in his pocket as he walked to his car. His belly tightened with each new vibration as he forced it further down in his pocket and felt for the off switch. A car alarm in the distance seemed to be keeping time with the buzzing in his pocket. He gazed up at the sky and shouted, 'Not my car, please!'

But, as his car came into view, he saw the driver's door ajar, and the window smashed in. When he looked inside, his briefcase was gone. Where the sound system used to be, the dashboard was a gaping rictus, wires drooling from the mouth. Tom banged his fist on the roof of the car. Fuck! His phone buzzed again. He yanked it from his pocket, ready to hurl it into the drab night. But wait. What was this? Ewan's name on the screen. He rejected the call. All the other missed calls, twenty or so, were from Alison, of course. There was also a raft of texts from her, the most recent said:

PLEASE COME HOME.

As he was about to delete it, a ding of another voicemail. 'Why won't these bastards leave me alone?'

Ewan. Probably just more abuse that he didn't want to hear. There were five voicemails from Ali too, as well as random missed calls from work. He stuffed the phone back into his pocket. Everyone was out to get him.

Pulling down his coat sleeve, he brushed the broken glass off the driver's seat and sat down heavily. Was there even any point in reporting this? The insurance wouldn't pay out unless he did, and fuck knew he didn't have any spare cash to deal with this. He looked at his phone again, chewed on his lip, tapped the screen. May as well hear what Ewan had to say. He put the phone to his ear, deleting all of Alison's voicemails until he got to Ewan's message.

'Tom, I'm sorry things didn't go well with us in the pub. I can see you're stressed out. Maybe this'll help, and this is why I arranged to meet with you before... anyway, the thing is, my firm wants you.' There was a long pause. Was that a sigh? '...That's really why I asked to meet up. The pay's a lot better than you're getting at Armstrong's. There's a car with it, and you'll have your own mandate. Call me back, please. I need to talk to Austin tomorrow.'

Tom tossed his phone onto the passenger seat, a smile pushing its way to his mouth.

'Thank you, God! About bloody time, but thanks!'

He pressed his forehead against his knuckles, mottled from gripping the steering wheel. You'll see, Ewan. I'll be the main man again. Tom tightened his eyes against the tears, forcing their way from a place he couldn't fathom. Man up!

The yard lights came on as he drove in. Alison was waiting for him at the back door. Her face was pink. Had she been crying again? He got out and walked over the cobbled yard towards her.

'Look, I'm sorry,' he said, splaying his palms in front of him. 'Things got out of hand at work, then Ewan called me. You know what a gasbag he is.'

'Just come inside, will you?'

She turned and went indoors without waiting for him. Had she not noticed the smashed window on the car? Typical. Always so wrapped up in herself. Fuck it, should he just get back in the car and drive away?

Alison was in the living room, sitting on the sofa, staring into the fire that was blazing in the hearth.

'Ali, what's wrong?'

'I don't know how to say this.' She was still gazing into the flames. Tom wanted to read her face. Turn around, show what you're thinking!

'I've got a dozen missed calls from you,' he said.

'And you didn't answer one.' She paused, seeming to wait for a response from him, then, 'Where have you been?'

Was something wrong with one of the kids?

'Where's Daniel and Jenny?' Tom put his hand on her shoulder, but she shrugged it away. 'Look, my meetings ran on; my phone was on silent. You know I can't have it ringing during meetings, Ali. Hey, guess what? I have good news, for once.'

'Dan's in trouble at school again, but that's not what I wanted to talk to you about—'

'Don't you want to hear it? I tell you I have something good for once, but still, you don't want to listen. Does everything have to be so fucking negative with you?'

'Your news can wait.'

'Why not? What the fuck is up with you, Ali?' Alison turned to look at him, her face puffy, eyes red.

Tom's chest tightened. He scowled at her and went to leave the room. He wasn't dealing with whatever it was now. Always fucking something.

'Tom, wait.'

He turned to face her again, fighting the impulse to spit out the invective pulsing in his brain. What for? So you can have yet another go at me? Another final demand? Another shitty

47

letter from school? For fuck's sake— Just say what's on your mind and let's get it out of the way, OK?'

She was staring into the fire again, but now her shoulders were shaking. He waited for her to speak. Nothing.

As he turned to leave the room again, he heard her ask him, 'Are you having an affair, Tom?' The words made him stiffen. What the fuck? He felt his face redden. He turned around, his heart pounding.

'No! Why would you even ask something like that?'

She was looking away again. What was she thinking? What the hell had brought this on? God, she couldn't want to talk about— could she?

He moved closer to her, bent down and touched her still quivering shoulder but she shrugged him away again. She was like an animal caught with nowhere to go.

She turned to face him, her face wet.

'Tell the truth, Tom,' she said, her voice weak. She sounded defeated.

He fell to his knees in front of her. Why couldn't he stop himself being so shitty all the time? He wanted to hold her but daren't. Whatever it was controlling his fate loved to play these games, didn't it? He felt exposed, forced into a position unnatural to him.

A cold silence separated them both, and the roaring fire gave him no warmth. Tell the truth? What was the truth?

'Ali, I'm not having an affair. What would even make you think that?'

The silence had been broken, but her silence made it new. Speak, for the love of—

For the love of what? At least Ewan had come up trumps.

48

Wouldn't this be the payoff he'd gambled everything on?

'Why would you think I was having an affair?'

Of course he wasn't having an affair. He knew it. She didn't. Yet. He never thought he'd have to stand up and explain it all, not after all these years of sharing their lives. Wasn't it a given? Weren't his special times outside the marriage an unspoken truth between them? Was he going to have to come out and say it all in plain speak now?

'I'm going,' he said. This wasn't the time. Or the place. 'Pull yourself together, Ali. Then we can talk. You can tell me what put this nonsense into your head.'

What the fuck had put this in her head? Had he been careless? Had someone seen him coming out of the bloody hotel on Monday in his jeans and tee-shirt and gossiped? Ali wouldn't listen to tittle-tattle, would she?

As he headed to the door, he looked back at her. Alison stared back, eyes as hard as slate. 'Don't,' she said.

Tom sat down in front of her. 'OK, let's have it then.'

Alison started to look uncomfortable, squirming where she sat. 'You know I had some itching…'

'Yes, and you got some cream—.' Tom felt his face burn hot again.

'Well, it wasn't clearing up, and I started to get other symptoms.'

She now crossed her arms tightly and gazed at the floor. 'So, I went to see Dr Palmer…'

Tom felt a boulder fall into his stomach. He clasped his hands together to stop them shaking.

'He called me back this morning. My test results show I have chlamydia.'

'Chlamydia?' How? How could it be? He didn't have any symptoms. Anyhow, he had been so careful.

'Are you having an affair?'

'How many times? No!'

'Tom, it's a sexually transmitted disease. There's no other way to catch it. I haven't had sex with anybody but you. Ever. Dr Palmer says you'll need to be treated too.'

Who the fuck could've given him that? That kid in the sauna? How long does it take to show? What the fuck was it, anyhow? God, no. He didn't want to see that judgemental bastard, Palmer. He'd be doing a cartwheel over this, wouldn't he?

'I don't have chlamydia. I've no symptoms. I'm not even sure what it is. Palmer must have got it wrong.'

'He's sure that's what it is, Tom. Some people can carry it asymptomatically. You're clearly one of those.' Her eyes were locked on him now.

'Ali, I don't know what to say.'

'Just tell me, whoever it was, that it's over, please.' Her hands were like claws digging into the cushions.

Tom felt as if he was going to collapse. He wanted to run from this, make it so it never happened. Tears began to flood from his eyes. Was this the end of their marriage? But surely – my god! Hadn't she known all this time? Was he going to have to speak the words? He couldn't lose her. Why the fuck had he said those idiotic things about his marriage to Ewan in the pub. He knew it, and Ewan knew it. He couldn't live without her. He knew that. It was the stress talking. Ali was the love of his life. He simply couldn't lose her. Wiping his eyes on his sleeve, he took a deep breath.

'Darling… I thought you knew it…'

He studied her face. Surely, she knew? All he got back was her blank stare. 'I'm not having an *affair*. You're the only woman for me.'

'So, a one night stand? Is that what you're saying?'

'Ali, you're the only *woman*.'

'Tom, who gave it to you?'

'I don't want to lose you. Please try and understand. I'd never hurt you. I can't help the way I am.'

'Are you saying… it was a man?'

A bleak dawn was breaking over her face. It twisted her mouth as it grew. With it, the panic in Tom was spreading like brushfire.

'You mean you just didn't know? I'm so sorry, Ali. I thought you understood me.'

The words were echoing in his head, hollow, empty.

'There's always been that other side to me. I honestly thought you knew… You know how much I love you, right?'

Alison stood up and made for the door. The sound of her retching as she rushed through it made him flinch.

Tom followed her to the bathroom, but she'd locked the door. He could hear her vomiting.

'Ali, let me in, please.'

After a few long moments, she replied.

'Go away, Tom. I don't want to see or hear you. Go wherever it is that you go.'

'Please, Ali…'

'Go,' she said. 'Just go.'

Chapter Four
Then

Tom lingered at the door of Ewan's office, watching him through the glazed panels, packing his belongings into one of those plastic containers he'd seen so many of the other company employees use. Did Armstrong's provide these for purpose? Probably not. Staples was just a few streets away, wasn't it? Anyhow, being top level now, he should know, shouldn't he? But he didn't. Yet. Everything comes to he who waits. Wasn't that the truth? Hadn't he waited long enough? He'd waited forever, and there were things he needed to prove: to Alison, to himself, ultimately to Danny and Jenny. Not to the world, though. The world could fuck off. It would be his, soon enough.

Through the glass, he saw Ewan place a framed photo of the two of them into the box. The one where they both tied for 'Employee of the month'. Oh, Ewan. Oh, Ewan. This was intended, right? Not anyone's fault – all of it decided already. Tom withdrew his whisky flask from his pocket and took a swig before he dared venture into Ewan's office. Well, the office he inhabited for now, anyhow. Today was the day of farewells; there had been many, but this goodbye would be the hardest, almost bittersweet. Almost.

OK, time to bite the hand that had fed him, at least the hand that thought it did. Ewan had to have known. It was all meant, wasn't it? Tom had known. He'd known all along if he was honest. And he had been honest. Honest with Alison, honest with Ewan. Everything was out in the open now. Time to move on. Claim the prize.

'Alright, Ewers? Sorry that it's come to this…'

Ewan looked up from his box and turned to scowl at him.

'Happy, Tom?' he said, turning his back on him and gazing out of the window.

Tom could feel his throat tighten. He was losing a friend, a supporter, someone who had really looked out for him in the past. He wished there was some other way, some way to salvage something from this. Maybe there was still a place for him here. Think, Tom. Try!

'C'mon, Ewan. It was inevitable, wasn't it? How many times did I ask you to move over to my department and avoid all this?'

Tom sat down in Ewan's chair and swung from side to side. Ewan turned to face him again, sighing deeply.

'Bugger off, Tom. I told you – remember? Get into Marketing and Research, didn't I? Actually, if you think about it, it was *me* who invited you into the firm.' Ewan turned away again and continued packing things into the box.

'Anyway, it was Austin who wanted me back, wasn't it? You needed me. I stepped in at the right time. You were floundering. That's how it was, wasn't it?' Tom's sympathy for Ewan was fast dissipating.

Ewan didn't look up this time. Tom even wondered if he was going to speak, but he still lingered in spite of the freezing silence. Was there some way back from this? The squeaking from the chair seemed amplified as he swung back and forth in it. And he stopped, making Ewan's silence complete. Should he just go and leave him to it?

'Tom, you're delusional. Fact. Always self-centred, always after the next best thing. Were we even friends once?'

Ewan didn't cast Tom even a glance as he spoke. Tom stood up, turned around and left, closing the door quietly behind him. Fuck you, Ewan. I did everything I could to keep your job safe. Fuck you.

Tom marched back to his oak-lined office. Moira sat meekly in the ante-room, at her desk, hardly daring to raise her eyes from her screen. He glared at her through the open door.

'Everything alright, Mr McIntyre?' she asked, her gaze never straying from whatever she was looking at.

Tom ignored her, thumping down into his chair. Hands on his head, he began kicking the edge of his desk. Have I done the right thing here? The phone rang. When he picked up, Moira told him Alison was on the line.

'Put her through,' he said brusquely, pressing the speaker button. 'Hello, darling,' he said, wringing his hands.

'Hi, Tom…' Alison was hesitant. Then wasn't she always, these days? 'Danny's been pulled up again…'

Tom took a deep breath. What was he supposed to do? He pulled the bottle of whisky from his lower desk drawer and poured some into the near-empty glass, beside the pile of files that had been glaring at him all morning.

'He'll be OK, darling… It's just a phase. I'll talk to him when I get home, I promise. I'll be home early tonight.'

Silence.

'Ali… tonight, can we… It's getting on for eight months now. Can we at least…' Tom glanced at the expensive looking red bag, its black tissue paper rustling under the fan above his desk – he'd sent Moira to get Alison's favourite perfume first thing this morning.

'Come home, Tom. We'll talk properly then.'

'But…' Tom could hear Daniel and Jenny arguing in the background. 'OK, darling, I'll be home by six.'

'Thanks,' she said and hung up.

Tom felt tears welling in his eyes and brushed them away. What was wrong with him? Ali would be OK; it'd just take a bit of time. Was it Ewan's predicament that was preying on him? Fuck no! That piece of shit? The complete traitor? Hadn't he done his absolute best for him and got shit in return? Ewan could go and fuck off and what did he care if he got another job or not. He'd ballsed it up here. His role was gone. Anyone could see that. Did he have to always point out the faults in this place?

God knew he'd turned the company around. The balance sheet proved that. He'd been rewarded for that and before long, he'd get rid of a few a lot higher in stature than poxy Ewan, too. If Tom knew one thing, he knew how to turn things around. Armstrong's loved him for that. Tom was on the way up and, with no doubt, the whole damn thing would be his. Property was his game and he knew how to play it.

Tom pulled the gift card from the red bag and picked up his pen. What should he write? Mustn't sound trite. She wouldn't be expecting this. He scribbled quickly on the card:-
I smell this, I think of you, I want you. You are the only one for me. Always will be. Always Yours. Tom x. He stuffed it back into the bag and picked up his phone.

'Moira, I'm leaving early tonight. If Austin asks, I've gone to inspect the Wilton site, OK?'

'Absolutely, Mr McIntyre. See you tomorrow.'

As Tom drove into the yard, all the house lights were dark, including the yard lights. Six-thirty? Why? No fucking welcome, as usual. When he tried the back door, it was locked. Charming. Could he do nothing right? Well, they'd get the silent treatment from him, when he got in. There'd been quite enough unpleasantness thrown his way today, and he wasn't up for any more. Let them feel his wrath for a change. Sick of kow-towing to the world. Fuck them all. Had they no idea of what he was dealing with at work? Well, why would they? No-one spoke to him at home anymore. He almost threw the red bag into the bin but instead looped the corded handles around his wrist and dug in his pocket for his keyring.

Before he could put his key in the lock, using his phone to light the way, the door opened. Alison stood there, smiling. Had she had her hair done? She looked different.

'Hello, Stranger,' she said, stepping to one side to let him in. 'Can't remember the last time we saw you before ten p.m. on a work night.'

Daniel was right behind her, smiling his gap-toothed smile.

Tom felt disarmed, all his anger dissipating into the new light shining on him.

'Hey, Danny,' he said, reaching for Alison's arm.

He felt an almost imperceptible twitch as he got hold of her wrist, but it evaporated quickly and the smile reaching his lips was impossible to resist.

'Hello, you two,' he said, grinning. 'Where's Jenny?'

'Oh, Jenny's in trouble... again!' said Daniel, a conspiratorial smirk on his face, glancing toward his mother.

Alison, however, with just one look, wiped the smile from her son's face and he sidled back to his room, wordless.

'Oh dear,' said Tom. 'Somebody wanted to pull the wool over his dad's eyes, didn't he?'

'Danny can wait, Tom. We have more important things to talk about, don't we?'

Tom sensed a resistance in her. Why was she blowing hot and cold? He leant into her and placed a soft kiss on her neck.

'Let's wait until the kids are in bed,' she said.

After dinner, once the kids were packed off to bed, Tom lit all the candles, making the sitting room shimmer. He'd poured a large glass of red wine for himself and a tall glass of sparkling water for Alison. As he turned on some soft music, she appeared wearing the peach-coloured chiffon dress she knew he loved to see her in. Soft fronds of the material clung to her as she perched herself in the doorway.

'Well, hello,' she said, deep red lipstick glistening on her lips, long unseen makeup on her face. That unmistakable scent of Opium perfume filled the room.

It was so long since he had seen her look this beautiful and he had to stop himself rushing forward to hold her.

'You look amazing,' he said, tentatively pulling her towards him. 'Does this mean that I'm forgiven, at last?' This was what he wanted most of all. Her forgiveness.

'Small steps, Tom. Small steps. It'll take time, but let's just say, I'm coming to terms with it all. You're still you... I still love you.'

Tom felt tears pooling in his eyes. He put his glass down as he brushed them away.

'That's brilliant, Ali,' he said, taking her hands. 'It's more than I had dared to hope for after all these months, but I'm just so grateful that you can see a future for us. I've been going out of my mind... I've been stupid.'

Why had he been so self-destructive? He really was stupid! Would he really be better off on his own? It was time to face up to things. Repair the damage. Be a man!

'I've had a lot of time to think about everything, and I know you can't help the way you're... what do I want to say? Made? Maybe I wish you'd told me though, told me before...' Alison's face was soft, beautiful. The anger and hurt had all disappeared.

'It all crept up on me. I wanted to tell you. I seemed like it was an unspoken truth between us. It was so hard for me to talk about with you... some days I felt like it would spell the end for us. If that were ever to happen... I just couldn't face that. Darling I...'

Alison rested her head on his chest, breathing heavily.

'There's no end for us. It was never an end. What could end mean anyway? The kids? The house? Our friends? Just change. That's what it means. Change. We're in this for the long haul,' she said, her words muffled. 'We can work this out. It'll just mean... a few... adjustments...'

'Don't worry,' he said, running his fingers through her hair. 'I've put all that behind me. I'm going to be the man you want me to be, the one you fell in love with.'

'I'm not asking that of you. You *are* the man I fell in love with and *still* love, in spite of... all I ask, Tom... no more secrets – just be honest with me. In all these years of being together, of being able to talk about anything, of trusting no one more, the hardest thing was finding that I had no idea about something that was such a huge part of you.'

'I'm yours, Ali. That's the truth. Always have been. Will be forever. Forever! I mean it. I couldn't mean it any more.'

Alison smiled a weak smile. 'I know, Tom. I know you. At least *mostly* I do. It'll take more than an odd fling, male or female to rock us. Don't you think so?'

He could tell she wasn't wholly convinced, but at least it was a starting point. That was something to work with, wasn't it?

'Can we, d'you think…?'

'Yes,' she said, her eyes not meeting his. '… I think so.'

Tom smiled before he pulled her towards him. A smile of relief. Not everyone needed to know everything. Alison was happy now, so nothing else really mattered. Fuck you, Ewan. This was his strength. He was good at keeping the little people at bay, out of the loop. Ewan was proof of that. Everything he wanted was his. The world was his. It was. All the battlements were strong and functional again. His. Bring it on. He'd fuck her tonight, and the world would be the way it should be. The way it was meant to be. *His* world. God, what a master he was! Easy come, much less easy go. Wasn't that right? C'mon Ewan, c'mon Ali, c'mon world. He'd played the game long enough, hadn't he? The time was his. The world was his. Finally. Thank the gods, or whoever, whatever it was looking out for him.

Tom smiled again as he took Alison's hand and led her towards the bedroom. Pulling her onto the bed, he pressed his tongue into her mouth. That's what she wanted, that's what she liked, wasn't it? Kissing her face and neck, he felt her kick off her shoes. 'Hang on,' he said and got up, going back to where he'd left the bottle in the living room. The glass was winking at him, coaxing him to fill it up. He filled it up, he obliged and brought it back to the bedroom, along with a second bottle, just in case. Alison was already undressing as he returned.

'C'mon,' she said, 'time waits for nobody. It's been too long!'

Sharp rays of sunshine poked through the curtains and he rubbed his crusty eyes, wondering why she hadn't pulled them to. He nudged her. Nothing. Raising himself from the bed, he yanked them shut and dumped his body back onto the bed, elbowing her as he turned to face the wall.

'Tom?' Alison said, placing her arm around his naked chest.

'Fuck, Ali, how many times do I have to say? Shut the fucking curtains, why don't you?'

'They're shut,' she said through a yawn, squinting at the window. 'Go back to sleep. It's Satur...'

Tom hunched himself up on one shoulder, piercing her sleeping face with his eyes. He shoved the duvet towards her and forced his legs to the floor.

'Bitch,' he said quietly, getting to his feet.

As he stood in the ensuite, peeing, he wanted to go back into the bedroom and shake her. Show her how he really felt. Always bloody right, always comfy up there, on the moral high ground. A wave of nausea rose up from his belly and he dropped to his knees, cupping his face in his hands as he gazed into the toilet bowl. Get me out of here! It was a scream. It was palpable. No one heard it but him. Returning to the bedroom, he pulled the duvet back and wrapped his cold arm around her, feeling her flinch ever so slightly. Tom felt his body tense as the room started to shrink and enclose him. Did he really want this anymore? His brain throbbed and threatened to burst. He turned to face the wall again. He should have walked away when he had the chance.

His phone vibrated twice beside the near-empty wine glass on the bedside table. A quick glance at Alison to see if she had noticed, but she remained still, her back to him. Raising himself on his elbow, he drained what was left in the glass and picked up the phone. Two texts:

ANDY_GD – ENJOYED WED MATE. HOPE YOU DID TOO

ANDY_GD – FREE TODAY? WANT A REMATCH?

He didn't have to think twice:

SURE, MATE. WHEN U FR

But the bedroom door creaked open, and he placed the phone face down on his table. Jenny stood there smiling at him.

'Danny and I have made breakfast,' she said.

'Thanks, love,' he said, 'I'll give Mum a shake, and we'll be right through.'

Tom tapped Alison on the shoulder. She turned to look at him, her eyes half closed and bleary.

'It's Saturday,' she mumbled. 'Go back to sleep.'

'The kids have made breakfast,' he said. 'C'mon, get up. They're waiting for us.'

He reached over, pulled her towards him, kissing her neck half-heartedly. 'They've made an effort for a change, c'mon, we need to make some effort too. Show them we're solid. They need reassurance.'

'OK,' she said, rubbing her eyes. She got up from the bed and pulled her dressing gown on, smiling at Tom as she headed towards the door.

'I think I smell burning. I best go and help them,' she said.

'I'll be through in a sec,' said Tom, picking up his downturned phone.

His fingers felt for the keys as he watched her leave the room. He finished off his text and pressed 'send'.

SURE, MATE. WHEN U FREE? THIS AFT?

The reply was immediate:

ANDY_GD – GR8! 4 PM? MY PLACE AGAIN? CNT W8!

Tom put his phone face down again and turned towards the picture of him and Alison on her bedside table. Where was that? Morocco? Before the kids came along, anyhow. God, we were so happy then! Oh, my darling, I'm such a shit aren't, I? What was he turning into? She was everything that was important to him. How could he even consider jeopardising that? A pervading sense of shame washed over him, and he felt tears welling. I'm sorry!

His phone buzzed with another text. He picked it up. It was Andy again. The message was blurred through his watery eyes. It didn't matter anyway.

He pressed REPLY:

SORRY, SOMETHING'S COME UP.

Then he deleted all the messages and blocked the number. It was time for change. Time to be a better man.

Chapter Five
Then

Tom stared in disbelief at the screen on his desk. 'Fucking hell! I've done it!'

He took his calculator from the desk drawer and punched in some numbers. A broad smile spread across his face, and he threw his head back, laughing. Now the mortgage payments on the new house wouldn't be a problem. In fact, he wouldn't even need a mortgage. His secret wish had been answered and then some. A better life would be theirs. Just let this work and then he'd take whatever came to repay the spirits for their benevolence. He looked at his watch. Where was she? He'd been trying to call Alison all day – when had she ever not picked up when he called her? God, he had to tell her this news. It was going to change their lives forever, and the look of joy and surprise on her face was all the reward he wanted right now. As he picked up his phone to call her again, his office door clicked open. Tom swung round in his chair, sensing her presence and grinning. Alison had no smile for him. Her blue eyes were wide and frightened, and her face was flushed; she was on the point of tears. Tom felt his grin dissolve, and he stood up.

'What's up, darling?'

Her lips trembled. She lunged towards him, her arms extended, with hot tears streaming down her cheeks. He pulled her to him and cupped her head against his chest as she sobbed deep breaths onto his shirt. Caressing her long brown hair, he whispered into her ear, 'C'mon, Ali, what's wrong?'

She pulled away from him, taking both his hands in hers, squeezing them. Their eyes locked, but all he could see in the glistening blue of hers was fear.

'I've just come from Dumfries General.' Her voice was shaky.

Panic began to rise in Tom. What on earth could be wrong? She'd seen Dr Palmer that morning – an infection in her right breast, she'd thought. It had swollen up overnight, and she felt sure that it was an inflamed gland – something simple, something antibiotics would put right. She'd had those all the time when she was breastfeeding, and quite a few times since. There was never anything that wasn't fixable in a week or two. Maybe the tears were because she was being laid off from her job. Well, that wouldn't matter now that...

'They think it's cancer,' she whispered. 'I had every test under the sun this afternoon. They say it's aggressive. I have to go to Edinburgh for further assessment on Wednesday. They think the biopsy results will be through by then, but they don't seem to be in any doubt, anyway.'

Tom stepped back. The words were like hammer blows. Tell him she was having an affair. Tell him she was leaving him. Don't tell him this. Please, not this. He closed his eyes and pressed his thumbs against the lids. The familiar white nebulous map of eternity formed on his retinas. He wanted to scream. He wanted to run away from it. He wanted time to reverse and prevent this moment from ever happening. Unsay those words, please! He sucked in a deep breath, grasping for a response.

'It'll be OK, darling. They'll get rid of whatever it is. We'll get through this. They've caught it early, thank God.'

Had he said that? Fuck, Tom, get a grip. Alison forced a weak smile and sat down.

'You know, when you didn't call me, I just guessed it was something and nothing – the usual – nothing to worry about,' said Tom.

'Dr Palmer phoned the hospital as soon as he finished examining me. Yes, he thought there was probably nothing to worry about too. But, of course, it was best to be sure. Being told to go straight to the hospital and being seen by a consultant as soon as I got there, gave me my first clues. I just didn't want to worry you. There was no point until they had more idea of what I might be facing.'

They drove home in silence. As they pulled into their courtyard, she pulled on the sleeve of his jacket. 'Let's not tell the kids until we know the full picture.'

Tom smiled at her. 'Let's not tell them at all. It'll be fine. When it's all over, they'll be none the wiser. We'll beat this, Ali. Me and you. We'll beat this.'

They walked hand in hand through the back door and into the kitchen. It was a mess. There were empty packs of ham and cheese strewn around, with bread hanging out of its wrapper, mayonnaise smears all over the worktops, and an open mustard pot. Empty crisp packets were littered here and there, and the sink was full of dishes and cutlery. Toast crumbs and other detritus crunched on the tiles under their feet.

'Please don't have a go at them,' Alison pleaded.

'With what we're facing, nothing else matters.' He shrugged.

A feeling of defeat permeated through Tom. His jaw dropped as if some invisible scaffolding had collapsed and the structure had given in. He took hold of her waist and pulled her close to him, his fear tarnishing the air, mingling uncomfortably with hers, leaving him helpless. They walked through the dining room, still holding on to one another, and when they reached the stairs, there was the garbled noise of two TV sets fighting the blare of one another.

Tom shouted upstairs, 'Daniel, Jenny!'

There was no response, so he went halfway up the staircase and shouted again, more loudly. The sound stopped on one of the TVs and a door opened.

Daniel's voice cut through the noise from Jenny's TV. 'Hi, Dad.'

'I'm going to make dinner. Have you already eaten or will you join us?' asked Tom.

'Yeah, I'm starving. All the mess in the kitchen is all from fatso next door.'

'OK,' Tom replied, trying not to sound angry. 'Please ask your sister if she wants to eat with us. Sorry we're late home.'

'OK, Dad. See you in a minute.'

Alison squeezed Tom's arm and smiled up at him. 'I love you.'

Daniel came bounding downstairs, kissed his mum on the cheek, and headed straight for the kitchen. Tom watched him scoop up the litter on the worktops and tidy up the general mess before he turned on the oven. Then he took a casserole from the fridge.

'I've got a surprise for you,' said Daniel, grinning from the kitchen door. Alison smiled widely.

'Oh, really? That's nice. Do tell.'

'I've made dinner for us tonight,' he replied.

Tom had his back to his son, pouring himself a glass of wine. Turning around, he smiled and said, 'That's great, buddy, what've you made? We're totally whacked. You really couldn't have given us a better surprise! Thanks.'

Daniel beamed. 'Yeah, we made lasagne in domestic science at school today. Mrs Bryce said mine turned out best of the lot. Why are you so late tonight, Dad? Mum, you're always home first. Where have you been?'

Tom noticed his son eyeing his wine glass suspiciously, and he put it down. Try and keep things normal. Drinking during the week wasn't a habit of his.

'It's been an odd day,' said Tom. 'There was me thinking it was Friday, too. A glass of wine will be perfect with your pasta, mind you. Mum and I just had an errand to run.'

'OK, I've put the oven on,' said Daniel. 'It'll be ready in half an hour. I'll set the table.'

Daniel returned to the kitchen, leaving a bemused Tom and Alison staring at one another.

'Well, this is a first,' said Tom, raising his glass to Alison.

She smiled. 'He's growing up. Be nice about it when you try it, please.'

'I'm always nice!' Tom stuck out his tongue and pressed his thumb against his nose, wiggling his fingers, before slugging another mouthful from his glass. 'If only you liked wine too. I can't think of a better time than tonight for you to start an excellent habit.'

'I don't like the taste and I never will. You know that. Get me some orange juice, please. I'm going to change. I want this day gone.'

When Alison returned in her dressing gown, Jenny and Tom were sitting at the dining room table. Daniel had set the table, and he'd put napkins at every place, with a glass of water and a bread plate next to each setting. He was busy placing a roll on each plate. Soft music was playing in the background, and Tom recognised the opening chords of 'Hallelujah'. He and Alison exchanged knowing glances.

'Sit down, Mum. Dinner is about to be served.' Daniel bowed, waiter-like with a white tea towel folded over his arm. He winked at his father and headed to the kitchen, oblivious to Jenny's scowl chasing his back. Tom reached over and tapped Jenny's shoulder.

'Behave, you,' he said. 'I want no squabbling this evening, OK? Mum has had a long, hard day.'

'Sorry, Dad,' said Jenny.

On Wednesday morning, Tom woke up at six thirty a.m. He threw on a pair of jeans and a jumper, pulled on his dressing gown over the top and walked through to the sitting room. The curtains, only partly closed, allowed a dull streak of the grey morning to split the room in two, one shade of bleak only slightly lighter than the other. He pushed them further apart and gazed out at the darker clouds fingering the bare branches of the trees. Morning news chattering from the television washed over him, and he pulled at the cord of his dressing gown, wondering what to do next. Daniel came bustling in and plunked down next to him on the sofa.

'You're up early, Dad,' he said, digging his elbow into Tom's side.

Tom laughed. 'That's good, coming from you! What gets you up at this time?'

'I'm always up before you,' he replied, 'I'm just usually upstairs waiting for the day to get going.'

Tom put his arm around him. 'We should hang out more often, then. Morning is my lonely time.'

Daniel put both his arms around Tom. 'Don't be daft, Dad. There's no need to be lonely with Mum and me here. And if you really crave company, there's always fatso upstairs. She could win Olympic gold for Britain if they introduced a mindless-prattling category.'

Tom laughed. 'I know that, son. Thanks. And stop bad-mouthing your sister, please. You want some breakfast?'

'Do bears shit in the woods?' said Daniel.

Tom laughed again, poked his son in the stomach, and headed to the kitchen. Alison had come through from their bedroom too and followed him. She put her arms around his waist and nuzzled her head between his shoulder blades.

'Morning, my darling,' he said, cupping her hands and pushing them to his chest.

Rufus and Jasper came trotting after them, purring and rubbing themselves against their legs.

'Breakfast time for the moggies,' murmured Tom.

'My appointment is at ten thirty on Friday at Edinburgh Royal. Will you be able to drive me? They said I might need collecting if they start treatment right away. That private insurance you talked me into may be useful now.'

Tom released himself from her arms and turned round.

'They're starting treatment as soon as this? God, Ali, I thought it was just an assessment then. Of course, I'll drive you.'

Hours of tests, poking, prodding, mammograms, MRIs, biopsies. It was nearly five o'clock, and it felt as if they'd been there forever. Poor Alison looked wrung out. Every test had her crying or wincing. As Tom sat holding Alison's hand, the surgeon's words knotted in a jumble in his brain, 'aggressive tumours, lymph nodes, metastasis, mastectomy, chemotherapy, hair loss, vomiting, radiotherapy,' all of them with meaning, but none that seemed to belong or apply to them.

'Mrs McIntyre, Mr McIntyre...'

They both looked round, glad to be released from the surgeon's gaze; he may as well have been wearing a black executioner's cap. A pretty nurse with short blonde hair stood smiling at them.

'My name's Fiona, and I'm going to explain your treatment today. Follow me, will you?' Her voice was a soft Scottish brogue, and she looked easy to trust.

'I'm having treatment today?' asked Alison.

The surgeon stood up and handed a folder to the nurse.

'The sooner we start treating these tumours, the better chance of success we will have,' he said.

Tom felt hopeless. This man exuded pessimism. Everything he'd said conveyed an implicit understanding that success was the least likely outcome of whatever treatment they might try. He was like some harbinger of doom. Tom was glad to escape his office and follow the smiling nurse. Alison gripped his arm and he felt her fear course through him.

Fiona led them through bright white corridors, pungent with hospital smells, to a small anteroom that led through to a much larger room, separated by a glass partition. Through the glass, other women sat on high-backed armchairs, with tubes running into their arms from bottles on stands. They all seemed interconnected, all linked by a common dread. Alison didn't belong here. This was like being trapped in a horrible dream. If only there were a way to wake himself up from it.

Fiona explained all the side effects that were common with the chemotherapy drug that was about to be administered. Alison seemed to be resigned to it all until the nurse mentioned hair loss. That's when she started to cry and burrow her face into Tom's chest.

'How likely is that?' he asked Fiona, looking at the women behind the glass; most of them were wearing bandanas or ill-fitting wigs on their heads.

'Ninety-nine percent, I'm afraid,' she said, her smile gone. 'This is a potent drug. But the hair always grows back, and this medication has a fantastic success rate with the sort of cancer Alison has.'

Tom closed his eyes and kissed Alison's thick, lovely curls. He felt her push into him. Her hair still had the sweet smell of ripe apples from the shampoo she used. Inhaling deeply, he pulled her head against his chest.

'It'll only be temporary, darling,' he said.

Alison slept for most of the long drive home. Tom tried to lose himself in the music he was playing, but the horror of the day just churned in his head. Yesterday's bright future had crumbled into meaningless dust. He hadn't even mentioned his windfall to Alison; it held no joy for him any more. He turned the radio off. Had he to pay this debt just for wanting something better for them all? This was too cruel. Take it all back. This was too high a price to pay. The debt was his, not hers. Fuck this.

Jenny was ten paces behind Daniel, sauntering into the yard as their parents' car turned in through the gates. Daniel stopped and waited for them to get out.

'Where've you been, Dad?' His quizzical look turned to one of concern as he watched his mother pull herself out of the passenger side. 'What's up, Mum?'

'Your Mum...' Tom looked at Alison then back at his son, '... is not feeling very well. Let's get her inside and make her a cuppa, OK?'

Daniel opened the back door and made straight for the kettle. Alison walked over to him, lethargically, and put her arm around him.

'Thanks, Danny,' she said, her voice cracked and weak. 'Don't worry about me. It's just a bug. I'll be fine.'

Daniel returned an unconvinced smile. 'Go and sit down, Mum. I'll bring the tea through. Do you want anything to eat?'

'No, love, thanks. If you don't mind, I'll leave the tea. I just want to lie down.'

Chapter Six
Today, Friday

Daniel wakes up in the fold-down bed in the study around eleven a.m. His eyes scrunch against the sharp rods of sunlight pushing into the room. As he turns over, he feels the shove of the dagger's jewelled handle against his bare ribs. Pulling it from beneath him, he looks at the thick, semi-congealed smears of dark blood on the wide blade. He reaches for the silk, still around his head, and cleans the dirty metal before returning the knife to the sheath, which remains nestled in his waistband. Then he wraps the stained silk around his body again and stands up. He listens at the door and, encouraged by the silence, pulls it open.

Daniel goes into the master bedroom and retrieves his prayer mat from the foot of the bed, averting his eyes from the bloody mess on his father's bed. Sunshine fills the room, but he feels a chill from the open French window. He closes it, then takes the large brass key from the lock on the bedroom door and pulls it shut, before locking it from the other side. He places the mat into the main hallway and recites the *Fajr* prayer. The dark, shiny red of the hall resonates in his brain. Blood. There has been too much blood in his life already. He walks to the front door, takes the key and leaves, locking the door behind him. The stairs are the best option again. None of the nosy bastards on the desk will see him that way.

Moments later, he is on the street. He grins at the concrete behemoth of the Ministry of Defence building, with its row of armed military guards outside, and turns away from it to Embankment tube. There are lots of uniforms in the street and around the entrance to the station, but he pays them no heed. Passing his Oyster card over the reader, he pushes past the tourists with their wheeled bags, his eyes eagerly searching for the Northern Line escalator. A feeling of breathlessness overtakes him as he bounds onto the train, which is sounding warning beeps that the doors are closing. Fumbling for his inhaler, he studies the map above the seats and is relieved to see he is on the right train for King's Cross.

As soon as he arrives there, he pulls out his phone and opens his texts. Scrolling down to JOHN LONDON, he opens the text thread and begins typing.

LAKKY: @ KINGS X. R WE ON?

He waits a few seconds, and a vibration accompanies the reply:

JOHN LONDON: YEAH. U KNW WHR 2 COME? DOORS OPEN. ITS ON TABLE

LAKKY: OK B THRE SOON.

JOHN LONDON: LVE YR SIM ON TABLE. THRS A FRSH 1 4 U IN PACK.

LAKKY: YES I KNOW.

Daniel follows the map on his phone to an address in Northdown Street. He presses the button for Flat C on the grubby panel next to the dull-blue door, which is adjacent to a halal butcher's shop. A long entry buzzer sounds and he pushes the door, which opens with a click.

The hallway smells of stale food. Junk mail and discarded

cartons litter the floor. Daniel walks up the sticky steps to the second floor and sees that the door of Flat C is slightly ajar. He looks all around the landing and, when he is satisfied he is alone, pushes the door open. The small dark vestibule of the flat is dingy and damp. A solitary bare bulb throws weak light into the windowless space, but it is enough to let Daniel see the brown paper package. It lies conspicuously on a white Formica table, the only piece of furniture in the hallway. He stops and listens for a few seconds, but can hear nothing, so he throws his SIM card on the table and snatches up the parcel, before running downstairs and out into the street. His heart is pounding and he suddenly feels conspicuous, which makes him wary. Keeping his eyes firmly fixed ahead of him, he marches quickly back to the tube station.

He sits on the train with the package on his lap. Later, what is inside will be wrapped around him, and the people on that train won't be as lucky as these here now. The carriage is full, and he stands up to let an elderly lady sit down.

'So considerate, dear,' she says, taking the seat.

Daniel studies the others in the train. There are people with luggage, a skinny man chattering to himself, families with young children, twenty-somethings, elderly couples. A random slice of society going about its day. Who will he see on his chosen train – waiting to enter eternity without even knowing it? Some will join him and Waqar, and many others will get the destiny they deserve. Maybe some will thank him – glad to be released early from this terrible world. Among that group will be abusers, kiddy-fiddlers, liars, cheats, thieves and drunks. People like Tom will be there. Like Tom, they will perish and suffer. Like Tom, they will get what they deserve.

Soon, he is back at Embankment, heading the same way he had left, through the hotel to his father's flat in the adjacent building. The key turns easily in the lock, and he walks into the silence of his father's flat. Daniel heads directly to the study and throws off his coat, yanking at the silk around his body, discarding it on the floor. Picking up his rucksack from the bed, he pulls out a shirt and a large padded jacket and lays them flat on the bed. Now he opens the package with reverence. Inside, he finds a khaki vest with long cylindrical pouches of explosives all around it. There is a pocket detonator hanging from a long red wire. He places the straps over his bony shoulders, cautiously feeding the wire underneath the vest. Carefully, he clips the detonator into the right pocket of his jeans and covers the explosives belt with his thick twill shirt before taking a heavy woollen pullover from his rucksack and putting that on over the shirt. He walks into the bathroom and examines his reflection in the full-length mirror. These clothes make him look so much bigger.

He smiles and begins plaiting his long greasy brown hair. He piles the dark plaits in a neat pile on his head and presses them down with a thick woollen cap. In the mirrored cabinet, he finds a pair of scissors and uses them to snip away most of his long beard. One of Tom's fancy airline toilet bags lies in one of the cupboards, and he fishes out the shaving kit from it. Removing the beard takes a long time, and he has to soap his face and go over it many times before it is completely gone. There are lots of small nicks all over his face. It's been many months since he has shaved and he admires the snake, fully revealed for the first time since the tattooist finished it.

He is late for the *Zuhr* prayer and he knows that he will miss the unity of reciting it with the rest of the Muslim world in this time zone. This will be his last formal prayer on this earth. If he has the presence of mind, he will recite the *Asr* prayer in his head on his final walk towards eternity. Waqar had told him to say each salat as long as his body was whole. Reciting the prayers makes him feel close to Allah but closer still to his beloved Waqar. When he has finished the *Zuhr*, he rolls up his mat and lies beside it on the bed as he watches Waqar's video again and again. This is his way of making his love a part of his final journey and keeping him strong in his mind as he fulfils his task.

Turning the camera on himself, he films his own message to Waqar, telling him that he is resolved to do what he has to, and that he now knows the peace that Waqar promised would come to him. Waqar will know this without him having to do this, but he wants to leave a record of his love for him on earth as Waqar had done for him. Let the world know that what he will do will be for love, as well as for Islam. When he is finished, he immediately deletes it. He has no need to explain himself to the world that he is leaving. It is a stupid idea and he reproaches himself for even considering it. He allows sleep to come to him, trusting that the peace he has found will remain with him.

It is 3.42 p.m. when he awakes, and he starts to worry that he will not be ready in time. The peak of the rush hour is the time prescribed to carry out his task. His tattoo must be hidden and he digs deep into his rucksack where he finds the paper bag containing make-up compacts, concealer sticks and foundation. He remembers for a second how embarrassed he felt buying these from the small Indian pharmacy, and the odd looks the young girl there had given him.

Returning to the bathroom, he opens a concealer stick and applies thick flesh-coloured cream to his face and neck. The snake begins to disappear and, as he spreads layers of foundation and pats on powder, he feels as if the chrysalis is beginning to crack open. When he has used nearly all the make-up, the tattoo is gone. Examining his reflection in the mirror, he sees a face that is not his. A waxwork version of his younger self stares back. Now he is almost ready. The pupation is almost complete.

Back in the study, he plugs earphones into his ears and puts on the thick padded jacket before taking a last look around. It's going to be a bit warm for the August weather, but it won't be for long. The discarded silk still lies on the floor, and he glances briefly at the backpack, which he has laid on the bed again. He pulls out a picture, a copy of the same photograph that still sits on the coffee table in the living room, and he kisses the image of his mother. He places the picture beside the prayer mat on the bed and stares at her face for several minutes. *See you soon, Mum.* Now, he kicks his bag into a corner and closes the door.

With slow, deliberate steps, he walks through the hall to the front door, dragging his hand across the glossy red smoothness of the polished plaster, and casts one last glance backwards to the large open arch of the dining room and the long-resented view beyond. He strokes the comical wooden cat that sits on the hall table beside a large vase of white lilies. It bears a silver collar engraved with I SAW THIS AND

THOUGHT OF YOU. ALL MY LOVE, ALWAYS, T XXX.

This is the cat that Dad gave to her that Christmas. The Christmas before she died. He pauses as though checking himself. *Forget it! Forget it all. That life is gone. Nothing else matters. Allahu Akbar.* He lays the cat on its side before locking the door behind him and posting the keys through the letterbox.

Back on the street, the MOD building and its guards cause him no mirth now. He walks towards the gardens in front of his father's building, his jaw firm, his eyes blank, and he sits down on a bench. Daniel looks at his watch and then up at the sky. The only other person he can see is an old tramp huddled on a bench on the opposite side of the lawn, scratching his crotch as he guzzles from a paper-clad bottle. Daniel takes out his phone and turns the camera on his face, pressing the record button. This final message to the world must be given outside with the sun on his face. In a soft, determined voice he begins.

'The message I carry to the British and American governments, and all other oppressors of Islam, is that there is no God but Allah. We will chase you from every corner. We will drink your blood. We know there is no better blood than the blood of the oppressors of Islam. We will not leave you alone until we have quenched our thirst with your blood, and all the children of Islam will quench their thirst with your blood. We will not rest until you leave the Muslim countries. My actions now will show this. God is Great. *Allahu Akbar*!'

Without playing it back or checking it, he uploads the video to YouTube, then drops his phone behind the bench into a pile of dead foliage. He removes his Oyster card and puts it into his jacket pocket before discarding his wallet behind the bench. Taking a deep breath, he heads out of the gardens towards the station.

Chapter Seven
Then

Faceless polystyrene heads sporting many colours and styles of hair stared blankly from the shelves all around the room. Alison sat beside Tom on a small sofa at the far end of the showroom; she seemed to be concentrating on her shoes. Was she trying to stop her hands reaching to check her hair? There had been clumps of her curly brown locks in the shower that morning. As he put his arm around her shoulder, he saw a small tuft of hair fall to her lap. She quickly brushed it off her skirt and onto the floor.

'We're going to have to tell them,' she said, her voice flat.

'I know, darling. Daniel is already worried something is wrong. Can we try and put it off for a wee while? Fuck, maybe the chemo will stop being so harsh on you.'

He went to touch her hair, but she pushed his hand away.

'The doctor said hair loss was unlikely with this latest drug, didn't he? Dr Ramage even said it was the least likely side effect. You've not even been nauseous… Can we not just wait?'

Alison's face hardened, and a piercing flash of anger met his eyes. He looked away. How could he see her like this? He was making a bad situation worse for her. Get a grip of yourself, Tom.

'You're fooling yourself, Tom. We need to tell them.

That's it. The longer we leave it, the worse it will be.'

Tom looked at the faceless heads, looked back at Alison, looked at his shoes, looked at the walls and looked through the window into eternity before standing up. Why destroy the kids' lives before they had to?

'Stop it!' he said, trying his best not to shout. 'At least think about it! For fuck's sake, don't give in so easily!'

Why was he like this? She didn't deserve to be spoken to like this. Not by him – not by anybody. She was doing her best not to cry; her mouth was starting to quiver.

'Darling, I'm not giving in. Believe me,' she said. 'I'm just saying the kids need to know. When you can't hide things… well, you have to admit… defeat—

'Defeat?'

'I didn't mean defeat in the way you're saying it. I'm just saying we need to tell them. God knows, we need to tell them before they guess. Yes?'

Tom sat down again, grasping for control, wishing to kill the conversation and move on to some other nothing kind of chat.

'OK,' he said firmly. Taking her hands, he said more softly, almost in a whisper, 'OK. OK.'

Now, they sat in silence, Tom twisting his wedding ring around and around, Alison squeezing his knee. The door behind them clicked, and a small cough followed it. They both looked round, and Tom managed to force a smile at the squat, balding man making his way into the room.

'Hello, you two. I'm Robin. I'm here to help.' He peered at them through thick, round glasses. 'Now then, is there anything here that takes your fancy, madam? We have lots of styles and colours. What's your usual look? I'll bet you anything we can get something very close.'

Tom and Alison exchanged glances. Tom felt his irritation bubbling into something stronger. He stood up.

'Anything she likes? Anything she likes? Likes? Do you know why we're here? And call her Mrs McIntyre. You could at least try to personalise this damn thing.' Tom's face reddened and he felt his chest tighten. Alison pulled at his arm, and he sat down again.

'Sorry,' he said, drawing her towards him.

Robin put his hands behind his back and walked further into the room. He hunkered down, almost kneeling in front of them. He was wearing a black suit with a dark-green tie that hung loosely at his collar. Tom looked at him face on and scowled. Robin's right hand reached to his tie and twitched at it. This idiot is nervous, probably new to the job. What the fuck is he doing dealing with people in these horrible situations? He yearned to pull him up by the lapels and spatter invective into his podgy, pockmarked face. Robin stood up again, shifting from foot to foot in front of them, twiddling his tie, wide eyes gazing earnestly at them.

Leaning in towards them he said, 'My dears, I know exactly why you're here. My heart goes out to you, believe me. I'm here to help, to try and make things right.'

Tom felt a growing desire to tell him to fuck off. Nothing was going to make this right, least of all this sweaty nonentity in front of him. He stood up again, struggling against an impulse to hit Robin.

Brushing himself down, he said, 'She's losing her hair, OK? She wants to look like everyone else, look healthy, look normal. She wants our kids not to be worried. We want this over and to be out of here as soon as possible. Can I be any clearer?'

'Tom. Stop it, please!' Alison's eyes were glistening, threatening to let go of held-back tears. Tom's face fell, and he felt his throat tighten. God, this is me. It's not the cancer, it's not this oaf in front of us. It's me. He sat down beside her again.

'Sorry,' he mumbled, refusing to look at the assistant. He fixed his gaze on his wife. Shame now replaced his anger. He felt stupid and small. All he seemed able to do was upset her and make things worse.

'Mr McIntyre, Mrs McIntyre... I'm sorry. This is awful for you both and it doesn't help that I'm new at it. I don't want to make it any worse. Bear with me a second, please.'

He picked up the phone from the table at the side of the sofa and dialled. 'Agnes, bring in some tea and biscuits please, quick as you can.'

Jenny was waiting for them at the back door as the car drew up. It was already dark, and insects were flitting around the yard lights as Tom got out of the car.

'Where've you been, Dad? I tried calling both mobiles but got no reply from you or Mum. What's for tea? I'm starving.'

She nodded at the bag that her father was clutching. 'Frasers? Have you been all the way to Dumfries? What did you buy?'

Tom looked at his daughter standing there, her dark-brown hair carelessly caressing her shoulders, her deep-blue eyes untroubled. There was a sense of normality about her that he wanted to soak up and let spread over them all.

'You've never been shy about raiding the fridge, Jenny. Nothing for you in the bag, that's all you need to know. Give us a chance to get in, at least.'

Tom cringed at the unintended curtness in his voice. He'd apologise to Jenny later, make her understand. He'd already taken away her mother's positivity, and now he was doing the same to his daughter. He'd have to dig deep and find some of his own. God knows from where!

Alison got out of her side of the car slowly, seemingly oblivious to the scowl forming on Jenny's face. Tom aimed a warning look at his daughter. She turned her back on them and went indoors.

'We'll all sit down after dinner and tell them what's going on,' said Alison.

Tom shrugged and clicked his key fob to lock the car and held the back door open for her. In the small utility room that led into the kitchen, he pulled her to him and said, 'Can we not wait? Just a little bit longer? Let's just see how things go after the next chemo session—'

He felt Alison's hand tighten on his arm, and he turned to see Daniel standing there in the kitchen, waiting in the darkness. Tom flicked the light switch on and, as their eyes met, he saw the look of accusation on his son's face, made harsher by the spotlight that bathed his features. Daniel turned and ran into the dining room, slamming the door behind him. When Tom turned back around, Alison had thrown her head back, and her eyes were scrunched up, her mouth tight.

'We don't have a choice now.'

Tom dropped the bag to the floor and the wig half fell out,

looking like a bad joke. He pulled her to him. He wanted her close and pulled her nearer, but she pushed him away.

'I'm sorry,' he said.

She was already walking away. 'I'm going to lie down for half an hour.'

He tried not to notice the bald patches on the back of her head as she wearily pushed on the dining room door. They hadn't been there this morning, had they?

This was all happening way too fast. He was losing control of his world, and he didn't have a single idea how to handle anything anymore.

Tom looked around the kitchen at the mess littering the surfaces yet again. And it wasn't just in there. In the dining room, coats half hung over chairs, and schoolbooks spilled out of discarded bags on the table.

Marching to the front hallway, he stopped himself from shouting upstairs to Daniel and his sister, and glanced back to the door to his and Alison's bedroom, which was slightly ajar. Alison's feet were visible at the end of their bed. He turned around, headed back out into the yard, and got into his car.

The radio came on as he turned on the ignition and the engine started. He pushed the gear stick into reverse. He needed to escape from this, drive away, keep driving, never stop. He looked over his shoulder as the car started to move backwards, but quickly pushed his foot on the brake and turned the engine off again. Darkness was taking a tight hold of the sky, turning the house into a shadow; the only light visible now came from the kitchen window. He laid his head against the steering wheel and closed his eyes. What on earth was he going to do?

At first, Tom was hardly aware of the tapping at the window beside him. As it grew more insistent, he lifted his head and saw Daniel staring back at him. He rolled down the window, blinking at his son. His brain throbbed with dark thoughts that were sparring with one another.

'You've been sat here for over an hour,' Daniel said. 'Come inside. Mum's worried and we need to talk, don't we?'

'I'm... I'd no... sorry. Sorry, Daniel, I just needed to think, needed some quiet. No idea that it had been that long. I'll be right in.'

Daniel turned and went back indoors without waiting for him, but turned the yard lights back on. Rain – a thin drizzle at first – gathered momentum and seemed to hammer the metal of his car, another admonition, urging him to go inside. Tom watched rivulets streaming down his windscreen for a few moments before he pushed his door open. He was soaked through, even in the few seconds it took him to run inside the house.

Alison, Daniel, and Jenny were sitting around the dining table. They sat in silence, but all heads turned to him as he appeared in the doorway.

'Give me a couple of minutes,' he said, pointing at his wet clothes. 'I'll get out of these and be right back.'

When he returned, they hadn't moved. All three sat in mute expectation. Jenny looked anxiously at him as he sat down opposite them. Daniel fixed an angry stare on his father.

'Daniel, I know you overheard us as we came in and I'm sorry. We didn't mean for you to find out that way.'

Daniel folded his arms, his mouth thin and tight. Jenny

looked at her brother and then at her parents, a fearful look on her face.

'What's going on?' she said. 'You're starting to freak me out.'

'Mum's got cancer,' Daniel said, flatly, '...and Dad was all for keeping it from us.'

'No, she hasn't! You haven't, Mum, have you? You're lying, Danny! Mum, he's lying, isn't he? Dad?'

Alison took Jenny's hand and clasped it tightly. Daniel didn't take his eyes off his father.

Tom said, 'We wanted to wait until your mum had finished her treatment. We wanted to—'

'How long have you known?' Daniel now stared fixedly at his mother.

'About eight weeks,' she said. 'I've had two sessions of chemotherapy.'

Jenny's voice quivered. 'Are you going to die, Mum?'

Alison now took both of Jenny's hands in hers and said, 'The treatment is working, darling, and with help from you, your brother and your dad, I'll beat this. I'm sure of that.'

'I don't believe you,' said Daniel, tears streaming down his cheeks. He stood up, pointing his finger at his father. '*You* should have told me. This wasn't your secret to keep!' He turned his back on them and marched out of the room and upstairs.

'Danny, come back please,' Tom called after him.

The sound of Daniel's footsteps continued on the stairs. Alison stood up and kissed Jenny on the cheek.

'I'll go up and talk it through with him,' she said. 'Jenny, love, talk this over with your dad, please.'

Chapter Eight
Then

Tom sat in his office, staring at his computer screen without registering anything that was on it. He glanced at his mobile and smiled weakly at the picture of Alison grinning back at him. Restlessly, he rose and wandered to the window. The sky was dark, with deep-purple clouds, and the pavement was alive with people going about their lives.

The day had dragged, and it felt like late evening even though it was barely four o'clock. He paced back and forth in front of the window, his mind no longer registering anything outside. Returning to his desk, he picked up his mobile and stared at the screen. Still no missed calls or texts. Alison must know he'd be worried. He pressed the call button and waited. The call diverted to reception.

'Thornton and Spears, how may I direct your call?'

'Tom McIntyre for Alison McIntyre. I was calling her direct line.'

'Oh, Mr McIntyre, how are you? Hang on, I'll try her other extension.'

'*L'autunno*' from Vivaldi's *Four Seasons* filled his ears as he waited and he tapped his fingers on his desk. The music stopped briefly.

'Still trying, sir. Bear with me.'

More music, then Alison came on the line sounding

flustered. 'What's up, Tom? I'm busy here. I have another call on hold.'

'Just wanted to see how you were on your first day back.'

'I'm fine. I wouldn't be here if I wasn't.'

'I know what you're going to say, but you don't have to be there, you know that. They said you could have as much time off as you want. I wish you'd just come home and rest.'

There was a brief silence on the line.

'Tom, we've been through this a thousand times. I need something to keep me sane. The kids are at school all day, and you're at work. It's horrible being home on my own, at least I'm of some use here. Anyway, you keep telling me cancer hates positivity. I can forget about it here. I'm happy to be here, working. I feel normal.'

'Can you at least finish early?'

'Tom, get back to work, please. I'm run off my feet and more than happy to be so. I'll see you this evening.'

'OK, darling. I'll pick you up around five thirty.'

'Six. We agreed.'

'Six it is then. See you later. I love you.'

'Love you too. Bye.'

Tom sat down and tried to concentrate on his emails. He groaned when he saw the flood of unopened ones that were there, and every few seconds another would appear on the list. The phone on his desk started to ring. Hadn't he told Moira to field all his calls? Cursing her incompetence, he picked up the phone and barked, 'What?'

'Mr McIntyre, I'm sorry... I know you said you wanted no calls today... but—'

'Spit it out, Moira. I'm busy.'

'Your daughter is on the line, and she says she needs to speak to you urgently. She sounds upset.'

'Alright, put her through.' The line clicked.

'Hello, Dad, it's me.' There were tears in her voice.

'I know, Jenny. What's up?'

'It's Daniel,' she said. 'He's drunk.'

'Drunk? Did you say drunk? How? He's fifteen, for God's sake. How did he get drunk?'

'I dunno, Dad. There's an empty bottle of vodka in his room and he's been sick all over his duvet. He's passed out now, but I'm worried. Tanya from school told me that you could drink yourself to death. I couldn't call Mum, especially when she's just started back at work.'

'I'll be right home. Not a word to your mum about this, OK?'

'And, Dad…'

'What?'

'He's hiding something under his bed. I don't think he's—'

'Jenny! Enough. I'll be home soon.'

He grabbed his jacket and keys and raced out of his office without a word to his secretary.

Tom shook his son and tried to lift his limp body by the shoulders. Daniel groaned, pulled away and turned over. Tom picked up the empty bottle of vodka. There was another bottle, almost full, protruding from under his bed. As Tom reached for it, he noticed a raft of pictures and articles printed from various websites pushed further back. He knelt down, pulled a few of them out and grimaced at them before pushing them as far under the bed as he could. A thick, acrid stench of vomit hung in the room, making Tom retch. He went downstairs and filled a basin with hot water and disinfectant, inhaling the clean vapours, trying to erase the sour smell that was clinging to him.

He placed the bowl beside Daniel's bed and wrestled the pungent duvet from under him. Putting him in the recovery position, he pulled the cover from the duvet and scrunched it into a ball with the vomit inside. He sponged the duvet with the hot disinfected water and tried to dab it dry with some kitchen towel. It took him a few attempts to get a fresh cover on it, and he threw it over Daniel, who was now snoring loudly. Daniel looked almost peaceful as Tom picked up the vodka bottles, scanning the room for any other evidence.

When he went back downstairs, he found Jenny sitting at the dining table pretending to do her homework.

'That smells gross,' she said.

Tom ignored her and went straight to the utility room by the back door. He stuffed the duvet cover into the washing machine with some detergent and set it going, and then he hid the vodka bottles in the bottom of the outside bin. His brain pulsated against his skull, which seemed to be tightening around it, and he fought a powerful desire to scream. Back in the dining room, Jenny looked at him expectantly.

'So what are you going to do, Dad?'

'Nothing. And you're not going to say anything, right? Go and tidy up the kitchen and make some strong coffee. Call me when it's ready. When Mum gets home, Daniel is feeling poorly and has gone to lie down, OK? I'll need to go and pick her up soon.'

He went back upstairs and tried to rouse his son, placing a cold, wet flannel on his face. Daniel stirred and rubbed at his face as if trying to erase a mark. Tom stood up and opened the window and was glad to find the putrid smell was dissipating. He placed a fresh flannel on Daniel's face and knelt down beside him.

'Stop it!' Daniel's arms were now flailing, and he hit Tom in the face. Tom grabbed both his wrists.

'C'mon, Daniel, wakey, wakey. We need to get some black coffee in you.'

'Leave me alone.'

Tom persisted and eventually got him to sit up a bit in bed. He called down to Jenny to hurry up with the coffee, and she appeared with a pot and a cup.

'You're a disgrace,' she said.

'Fuck off, munter.'

'Daniel, that's enough. Jenny, thanks for making the coffee. I'm sure your brother will thank you in the morning. Now downstairs, please.'

Jenny set the coffee pot and cup on the bedside table and said, 'Charming!'

Chapter Nine
Today, Friday

Robert grimaces as he walks towards the porters' desk. He glances at the clock on the wall above the chair where Benny the night duty porter is softly snoring. It is 5.45 a.m. Slamming his bag on the counter, he throws the access flap up and kicks the small half-door against the wall. The CCTV monitors flicker in protest, but Benny doesn't stir, so Robert picks up the glass of water beside the sleeping man and throws it at his face. Benny splutters and jumps to his feet.

'What the fuck!'

'This is the last time, Benny. If I catch you sleeping on the job one more time, you're out. You understand?' Robert points an angry finger at him.

'I literally just fell over for a few seconds, boss. It's been a long night.'

'Heard it all before, Benny. Now where's Carlos?'

'Oh, he's doing the rounds, you know. I did the first half of the shift then took over the desk. We alternate each night – you know that.'

'OK, call him on the radio and tell him he can clock off. You can stay and polish the brass until Vince gets here at eight,' says Robert, turning his back on him.

'Aw, boss, it's been a long night. You usually let us both—'

'Just do as you're told, Benny, and stay where I can keep an eye on you. I'm going to check the overnight CCTV.'

Robert hands Benny the radio and throws a duster at him, then goes to the small kitchen behind the desk area, turning the kettle on before returning to Benny's vacated seat. He frowns at the two computer screens in front of him. The one to the right is labelled HOTEL LOBBY ACCESS AREA and the other has RECEPTION AND STAIRWELLS printed on top. Robert can see Carlos walking down the stairs on the second monitor before he appears at the front desk. Carlos walks through the open half-door and reaches for his coat on the hook behind Robert.

'Thank you, Mr Robert, for letting me go home early,' he says, smiling.

Robert returns his smile and waves him away as he sets both monitors to rewind to the start of the previous night's shift. He grows bored of watching the comings and goings of the residents and confused hotel guests who have taken a wrong turn, and heads back to the kitchen area to finish making his coffee.

Returning to the monitors, the screens show human traffic is dying down and the time stamp has moved on to 1.35 a.m. He sips his coffee, keeping one eye on the screens while he clicks fast-forward on both. Nothing very much happens most nights after two a.m., and he yawns as he watches no motion on the screens, apart from the intermittent sight of Carlos with a broom, occasionally carrying rubbish bags down to the basement.

Suppressing another yawn, he clicks fast-forward, hoping to speed this task out of his day. He plans to delegate this responsibility to Vince in future. Allowing the yawn to escape, he slumps back into the chair. He begins to sympathise with Benny for giving up on such a dull evening and calls him back to the desk, telling him to get his things and go home.

'G'night, boss,' says Benny, heading away from the desk. But before he has the chance to walk more than a few steps, Robert calls after him.

'Hang on a sec, Benny...'

Robert now sits upright and peers more closely at the image he has frozen on the screen.

'C'mere a minute and have a look at this,' he says.

Benny sighs and wanders back behind the desk, positioning himself behind Robert. The time stamps on both screens show 4.05 a.m. and gradually creep back as Robert rewinds the video feed. There is a figure moving backwards from one screen to the other, as Robert increases the rewind speed. Benny takes his spectacles from his pocket and puts them on, squinting at the monitors as Robert sets the play speed back to normal, with the time now showing 3.55 a.m. on both screens.

'Look at this, Benny.' Robert points to the screen labelled HOTEL LOBBY ACCESS AREA. 'In a second, you'll see someone appear from there.'

They both peer at the screen and Benny lets out a small gasp as a man wearing a thick, dark overcoat and a hat comes into view from the hotel corridor. He has a long beard and is carrying a backpack. The man stops outside the service lift and presses the call button, appearing to be looking all around as he waits for the doors to open.

As they watch him enter the lift, Robert says to Benny,

'Try and see what floor he gets off on. I can't make it out.'

'He's gone to the basement, boss,' replies Benny. 'I can see the down arrow clearly. He definitely went down rather than up...'

'How come you missed this last night, Benny? That was four a.m. Who was manning the desk at that time and who was doing the patrols?'

'Erm, I think I was on the desk, boss, but maybe I was making a cuppa when that guy came in. I got no idea who that is.'

Robert rolls his eyes. 'Well, look at the second monitor. At about 4.07 a.m., you'll see him appear again and make his way up the residents' staircase. How long does it take to make a bloody cup of tea, for Christ's sake?'

Benny watches intently as the man appears again, this time hatless, revealing long dark hair. The man seems to look directly into the camera before ascending the stairs adjacent to the reception area.

'He's got summat on his face, some tattoo or summat, it looks like. He don't look familiar, boss. I don't think I seen this guy in the building before.'

'I've told the residents' committee at every bloody meeting for the last three years that they have to extend the CCTV to the other floors here,' said Robert. 'If any of the flats have been burgled, Benny, you're out of a job. I can't believe you missed this. What the fuck do you think you're being paid for here?'

'I'll go and check every single flat right now, boss. I'm so sorry about this. I won't leave until I've checked every last one.'

'Too damn right you won't,' says Robert.

As Benny makes his way up to the first floor, Robert studies both screens, letting the film advance at regular speed, desperate to catch another glimpse of the curious stranger. He picks up the desk phone and starts to dial the hotel reception next door, but puts the phone down again before it starts to ring. There would be nobody sensible to talk to at this hour. He would have to wait until the duty manager came on at eight a.m. Robert continues to study the CCTV footage until he sees himself appearing at the desk before he threw the water over Benny. He wishes he hadn't done that now. He can't erase any of the feed now that there is something that might need investigating.

'Why you looking so glum, Rob?'

Robert looks up and sees Vince standing before him. He looks at his watch and says, 'Christ, Vince, I had no idea it was that time already! Come in, put the kettle on. There's a lot to tell you.'

'Righto,' says Vince, hanging up his coat. 'Just let me put my uniform jacket on and I'll be right with you.'

Just then, Benny appears, looking weary.

'Hellfire, Benny! Shouldn't you be back in your coffin by now? It's light outside, you know?' Vince grins at the old man.

Benny shrugs his shoulders and says, 'You don't wanna know, mate, you don't wanna know.'

'Enough chit-chat, Benny,' says Robert. 'What did you find?'

'Nothin', boss. Not a bloody thing. I've checked every single door of every last flat in this place, and not one has any sign of forced entry. And you know them security locks can't be picked. God only knows what that creep was doing in the building. Anybody's guess, if you ask me.'

'And you checked the basement too?' asks Robert.

'Yes, boss. None of the storage lockers've been touched, and all the bikes are where they should be. It's a friggin' mystery.'

'It's a mystery, alright,' says Robert. 'And the biggest mystery of all is this: where is that fucking scrote now? There isn't a single trace of him leaving the building, not by the stairs or either of the lifts. You sure you checked everywhere? The bin stores? The emergency exits? Are the doors to the roof secure?'

'I ain't checked the bin stores, but yeah, the roof doors are all locked and have no sign of tampering, and all the emergency exits are alarmed.'

Robert turns to Vince. 'Go with Benny and check every floor and every bin cupboard together. Don't miss a single square inch. I'll go next door and go over the hotel CCTV as soon as Nadjib comes on duty and takes over the desk. Ralph should be on reception next door in a few minutes. He'll help me go through the hotel footage. I hope to hell we can see something of this guy leaving. Then maybe we can put this thing to bed. Benny, fill Vince in on everything as you go.'

Ralph smiles at Robert as he approaches the hotel desk.

'Morning, Robert,' he says. 'We don't often see you here first thing. I've only just come on duty.'

'Yeah, mate, morning. It's been a busy old morning for me so far. There's been a strange-looking geezer wandering around our building in the early hours. As far as I can tell, he got in through the hotel, so I was wondering if I might have a glance at your CCTV.'

'Sure thing,' said Ralph. 'Come through.'

Ralph waves to his colleague to cover his post as Robert follows him through the door behind his desk. There, Robert sees a much more sophisticated set up than he has next door.

'I know I keep saying it, Ralph, but I bloody wish I had even half of what you got here.'

'What time frame are you interested in, mate?'

Robert tells him when he'd first seen the man. Ralph types '03:45' onto the keyboard and presses a few other keys. The bottom row of ten screens all jump to that time, simultaneously.

'That's impressive,' says Robert.

Two of the screens show either end of the street outside, including Robert's building. The others display each of the entrances to the hotel, the lobby, restaurants and the connection passage to Buckingham Court. Ralph presses some more keys, and each screen starts to move forward. The screen definition is much clearer than Robert has next door. He keeps his eye on the two screens showing the street.

When the time moves forward to 3:56 on all of the screens, Robert spots the man on the street near the main entrance to the hotel.

'Pause it! That's him. Can you print that picture? It's so much clearer than the one we have on our monitors,' he says.

'Sure thing,' says Ralph, pressing more keys.

The feed starts to move on all screens again, and the figure keeps walking past the main entrance, then pauses at the double doors that give access to the restaurant lobby and from there to the residents' corridor leading to Buckingham Court. Robert watches the figure look all around before he pushes the doors open and enters.

'Those doors are normally locked after the restaurant and bar close,' says Ralph. 'I'll have to have words with the night manager.'

Robert keeps watching the man on the screen, studying his every move. The man walks confidently through the lobby to the door that leads to the residents' passage before he opens it and disappears.

'You need a residents' key fob to open that door, don't you?' says Ralph.

'Usually,' Robert says. 'But the panel's been knackered for weeks. I did ask Benny to lock it at night until things gets fixed. Hardly any of the residents use it anyway, unless it's raining. I'll get back onto the firm when I get back next door.'

'Looks like we both need to up our security measures,' says Ralph.

'Let's have that printout, please, Ralph. I want to ask around my staff and see if anyone has seen this guy before.'

Ralph pulls a few sheets of paper from the printer and hands them to Robert.

'I printed a few different shots of him. Unfortunately, there are no close-ups, but at least you have some head-on and profile shots of the guy.'

'Thanks, mate. I appreciate it.'

Robert takes the printouts and heads back to his building through the passageway. This intruder has to know something about the building. Not many people, beyond the residents, know of this particular route into Buckingham Court.

Back in reception, he tapes the images of the man around the CCTV monitors. Benny is still at the desk, looking sheepish. Robert ignores him and sits at the computer desk, adjacent to where Vince is sitting.

'Nadjib has just called in sick, Robert,' says Vince. 'That'll leave us short- handed. I can do a double shift if you need me to.'

'Bugger,' says Robert. 'Thanks, Vince, I appreciate that. I'll take you up on it, if you're sure?'

Vince nods and Robert turns to Benny. 'Go home and get some sleep, Benny. But I want you back here at three p.m. sharp. Vince'll need a break if he's doing a doubler, and you can work through to tomorrow morning. I'll get Carlos to give you an hour's break around midnight.'

'Right, boss.' Benny hangs up his uniform jacket and pulls on his anorak, heading out of the building, looking miserable.

'Keep a close eye on those monitors, Vince. I'll have to leave you on your own for half an hour. I have a meeting with the chairman of the residents' committee about the gutter repairs. I'll keep it short.'

'I'll do my best, Robert, but you know it gets busy after nine – post and all that.'

Robert leaves, mumbling, 'Just do your best.'

Vince keeps his eyes on the screens through all the comings and goings of residents and doesn't even get up when the postman comes with that day's mail at around 10.45 a.m. *Where the fuck is Robert? Half an hour, my arse!* Vince could do with a break. His eyes are starting to sting. A cuppa wouldn't go amiss, either. Just before eleven a.m., the lift doors open and old Mrs Heath wheels herself out in her wheelchair. Vince grimaces.

'Morning, Vincent,' she chirps. 'Help me down the ramp, will you? There's a good fellow. Mr Heath is at his club.'

'Certainly, Mrs Heath, one second.'

He dials Robert's mobile, but gets his voicemail. Slamming down the phone, eyes still on the monitors, he gets up. It can't be helped. He goes around the desk and out into reception where the old lady sits smiling.

'No speeding now, Vincent,' she says, her eyes twinkling.

'Slow and steady as always, Mrs Heath. You're in good hands. Give me a moment to flatten out the revolving doors so we can get you through.'

By the time he has her out on the street and has reconfigured the doors, it is 11.23 a.m. He sits back at the displays, cursing Robert.

Robert returns just as Big Ben strikes twelve thirty p.m.

'Half a fucking hour?' says Vince. 'I've been run off my feet here, I'm bursting for a piss, I haven't had anything to eat and I'm going cross-eyed watching this thing.'

'Sorry, Vince, sorry. The chairman just wouldn't shut up. Of course, he pays my wages, as he loved to keep telling me every time I tried to leave. Go have a break and get some lunch. See you in an hour.'

Vince gets up, waving his arm at the chair in front of the consoles. 'All yours,' he says.

As Vince heads towards the front doors, he turns and sees the desk is unmanned. Robert is making himself a cup of tea or something in the back. *So much for keeping our eyes glued on the CCTV.* He snorts and pushes through the revolving doors to the street. What a load of old bollocks this all is, anyway.

Chapter Ten
Then

Tom put the phone down and turned towards Alison. She was lowering herself into the sofa with the help of the Zimmer frame; she had resorted to using it all the time now, even though there had been an angry scene with the Macmillan nurse where Alison had screamed at her to take it out of her sight. That was the day the nurse had brought it round for her, promising it would make things a little easier.

'This disease is turning me into an old-age cripple,' she cried to Tom after the nurse had gone. Tom hated seeing the twisted pain in her face every time she pulled herself up and down with its help.

'I'm afraid it's bad news, darling,' he said.

'I don't need any more bad news, especially not this close to Christmas,' she replied. Her voice was cracked and weak.

'I know, darling,' said Tom. 'This is only a fly in the ointment, not bad news as such. That was the builders; they've had to push back the completion to early February. The house won't be ready before then.'

Her eyes glimmered under the tears that were forming fast. Tom sat down beside her and put his arm around her.

'But they promised we could move in the first week in January. I don't think I can… I wanted to see you and the kids in there before… Oh, Tom. It's too cruel.'

'Don't be silly, Ali,' he said. 'It's just a few weeks later. The weeks will pass by quickly. We'll be in there before you know it.'

Alison seemed to crumble beside him. She looked small and helpless, and the wig that had slipped to one side of her head made her look like a damaged doll.

Tom straightened it up for her and pulled her closer to him. She winced and pulled herself away.

'Shall I get you some painkillers?'

'Call the nurse,' she said. 'I think this is going to take a morphine shot to get rid of it.'

She'd never asked him to call the nurse before. Not once. Was this set-back with the house making her feel the pain more? He picked up his mobile and was about to dial when she let out a hoarse cry of agony. Her face was grey, twisted and tainted with suffering.

'Darling, I'm calling an ambulance!'

Alison grabbed his wrist, and he felt her nails digging into his skin. 'No!' It was a shout that came out like a weak rasp. 'No, Tom. The nurse. Just the nurse.'

It felt as if he was losing her. Tom dialled the district nurse's line. He was grateful when she picked up almost immediately.

'I'm less than ten minutes away, Mr McIntyre,' said the soft, reassuring voice. 'Press a cold cloth to her face in the meantime. That's a good way of confusing the pain. Wrap a bag of ice and place it on top of the cloth. If you have no ice, frozen peas – anything light from the freezer – will do. I'll be there as quick as I can. Don't worry.'

Tom put down the phone.

'She'll be here soon, darling. I'm just going to get a cold flannel for your face—'

'Stay, Tom!' Her voice was racked with pain.

Tom could feel his control leaving him. Panic coursed through him and he tried his best not to show it. He took her hand and squeezed it gently. Her face twisted in a way he'd never seen. Alison always did her best to hide her pain. She denied it to herself, and she denied it to him and the kids. He'd heard her crying behind the bathroom door, the taps running at full pelt. He'd seen her grimace every three weeks when the nurse had prodded and poked the veins in her hands, searching for a viable vein to insert the cannula for the brutal chemotherapy drugs. How much of her pain had he missed all these miserable months? Had he denied it to himself as she had to him?

Alison looked so much older than her years. Forty years old, and the Zimmer she used didn't look out of place. Her skin was dry and flaky; what were once laughter lines were now deep, pitted crevices in her face. Her rosy cheeks were gone, replaced by skin like dry, cracked clay. And her hair: beautiful, brown, shiny and lusciously curly, now just a few tufts of grey fluff. Although the nurse had told them it would grow back quickly after her first round of chemo, it had never had a chance. An angrier, aggressive form of the cancer took hold and the doctors put her on another, more vicious drug just weeks after the end of the first sessions. There was so little left of the face he loved so much. Now her personality was gradually disappearing too. The woman he loved was creeping further and further into the distance. There was nothing but this terrible disease between them.

'I'm glad the kids are out,' whispered Alison. The pain was even stealing her voice from him.

'Yes,' said Tom. 'I hear someone at the door. That'll be the nurse. You'll feel better in a moment, my darling.'

Daniel and Jenny burst into their parents' room. 'Merry Christmas!' they shouted. Alison raised her head weakly.

'Merry Christmas, you two,' she said, raising a smile that didn't quite make it to her eyes.

Tom sat on a chair by her side.

'Merry Christmas,' he said. 'How about you both make us a nice pot of tea? We'll come through in a few minutes and open the presents.'

Daniel looked at them suspiciously, then took his sister's arm. 'C'mon, you,' he said. 'I'll make the tea, and you can burn the toast.'

'More like you'll stew the tea, and I'll make perfect, golden-brown, buttery, gorgeous toast,' laughed Jenny, tugging at Daniel's hair.

They both went out, arguing good-humouredly.

Tom stood up and went to the dining room where he switched on the Christmas tree lights. When he returned, Alison was trying to get up. He picked up her dressing gown and draped it around her shoulders. She reached for the Zimmer, hoisted herself up and began to move slowly towards the door. Every step she took made her face tighten.

'Tom, darling, get me two of those pills on my table, will you?'

She swallowed them back before Tom reached her with the water glass. Then she took a gulp of water and began her slow journey to the dining room. Daniel appeared from the kitchen carrying a tray containing a pot of tea and two mugs, one with a prancing reindeer on it, the other with a grinning Santa Claus. Jenny followed behind with a plate of mince pies, each topped with a sprig of holly.

Daniel had put some Christmas music on and 'Hark the Herald Angels Sing' tinkled into the room.

'Well done, kids,' said Tom, ruffling his son's hair and stroking Jenny's cheek. 'A perfect Christmas breakfast.'

By the time Alison made it to the living room, Jenny was already there, expectantly holding a misshapen parcel wrapped in bright-green paper.

'Open this one first, Mum – it's from Dad,' she said. 'You're going to love it.'

Alison sat down, and Jenny placed the package on her lap. 'Will you help me, love?' asked Alison.

Jenny ripped off the paper and held up what was inside; it was a life-sized cat made of the most beautiful striped *bocote* wood. Around its neck glistened a silver Tiffany chain from which dangled a shiny silver medallion that rested on the cat's chest. There was something engraved upon it.

'Read it for me please, Jen, will you?' Jenny held the cat close to her mother's face.

'It says, "I saw this and thought of you. All my love, always, T xxx."' Alison looked up at Tom, her eyes full of tears.

'Thank you, darling. I love it.'

'Cats at Christmas seem to be the right thing,' said Tom. 'Where are the moggies, anyway? I thought they'd be here to wish us all Merry Christmas. It is kind of their birthdays, after

107

all.'

'Both asleep on my bed,' said Daniel. 'Rufus brought in a dead robin and laid it at my bedroom door. Clearly, he didn't want Christmas to go unobserved.'

Jenny laughed. 'How very Christmassy. I had a dead shrew outside my bedroom. Probably a present from Jasper. At least Rufus made an effort.'

Tom laughed, and they all looked to Alison for her reaction, but she wasn't smiling. Her face was locked in pain. She was staring beyond them.

'I'm sorry, everyone,' she said. 'I'm not feeling too good. I'll just go and lie down for a while. Maybe take some painkillers. Tom, darling, help me up please.'

'Aw, Mum,' said Jenny. 'You haven't even opened *our* presents yet.'

'I will, love, once I've had a lie-down. I'll have more energy for it then.'

Tom gave Jenny a look that said 'no more' and gently helped Alison up to her Zimmer frame. He looked back apologetically at his two children as he followed his wife slowly out of the room.

Back in their bedroom, he helped her struggle into bed and he reached for the pills on her bedside table.

'Tom, darling,' she said, her voice barely audible. 'I don't think they will take this pain away. Call the nurse again, will you?'

'Are you sure?'

He could see she had no fight left in her. She could hardly form any words. 'Take these for now,' he said, pressing the pills to her lips. He held a beaker of water to her mouth to help her swallow them down. 'At least they might make a dent in it until the nurse gets here.'

It was midnight. Christmas day was over, and the district nurse was about to leave. This was her third visit of the day. She took Tom's hand.

'Mr McIntyre, I don't think she has long.'

Tom couldn't stop himself bursting into tears. He hadn't allowed himself to think of the unthinkable all through Alison's illness. To hear it said like this, out loud, was comparable to being stripped of every defence. She was always going to get better. None of the consultants or hospital nurses had talked in terms of time frames, and neither he nor Alison had been able to bring themselves to ask the question. Whether or not this had ever been a question in his mind, it was being answered. He didn't want the answer. He hadn't asked for it.

'The next few weeks are going to get harder, I'm afraid.' She had placed her arm around him now.

Stop talking, please. Just go.

'I can organise a Macmillan nurse to be around during the day. That way, she'll never be in any discomfort. Marie Curie nurses can help closer to the end. They can stay all through the night. You never need to panic, that way. Shall I arrange that for you, Mr McIntyre?'

Tom stood away from the nurse, pulled a paper tissue from his pocket, wiped his eyes and forcefully blew his nose.

'Can't I just call you when I need you?' he said.

'Of course you can call me. Call me anytime. But it will be better for Alison if you have someone right here when she needs them. If I'm on another call, it could be half an hour, longer even, before I get to you. Like today — the whole festive period is always very busy. Better for her and better for you and the kids if we get a Marie Curie nurse here to keep an eye on you all. They really are lovely, and you won't even know they are here.'

'Let me think about it,' said Tom. 'Can I call you tomorrow?'

'Of course, Mr McIntyre.'

'Tom. Call me Tom, please.'

'Yes, Tom. Call tomorrow. It won't take me long to organise someone. Just let me know.'

Tom watched her drive away in her little grey car. He closed the door and rushed back to Alison. Falling to his knees, he burrowed his face in the blankets around his wife's chest.

Tom looked at his watch obsessively. It would be New Year's Day in less than an hour. Margaret, the Marie Curie nurse, sat knitting on a chair in the dining room, just visible through the open door to their bedroom. Daniel lay on the bed beside his mother, gently stroking her face. She wasn't there any more. Muddled words had preceded longer periods of unconsciousness, until her body had suddenly tightened two days earlier and then there were no more words. Not from her. Only heavy, laboured breaths and no sense of the person behind eyes that rarely opened.

Jenny popped in every hour or so, but hadn't appeared since around ten o'clock. She'd probably fallen asleep upstairs; the poor thing was exhausted. Daniel only left his mother's side to use the bathroom. When Tom lay down in search of a few moments of sleep, Daniel would take his place in the chair at the side of the bed. Margaret continually brought them drinks and made sandwiches that usually stayed uneaten. Alison had a drip attached to her, unable to eat or drink now. The bedroom smelled like a hospital room. It smelled of death.

Alison's breathing became harsher and seemed to get worse every few minutes. It sounded as if she was struggling to breathe.

'Margaret, will you come, please? I'm worried,' said Tom.

She came immediately. 'She's not in any distress,' she said, feeling for Alison's pulse. 'I don't think it will be very long now. I'll just be outside if you need me.'

'But her breathing... she looks like she's struggling for every breath. It sounds like she's in terrible distress.'

'Tom, believe me, please. She isn't aware of anything. This is her body slowly shutting down. The worst is over for Alison, I promise you. I know it's hard to listen to this laboured breathing, but it's only the body labouring, fighting to stay alive. Her mind is totally unaware of any of that.'

'Can't you do anything? Give her something?'

'No, Tom. She's in no pain. There's nothing I can do to change her breathing. It'll be over soon. She's getting ready to go. Now, I'll leave you to say goodbye as a family. I'll come back in when you're ready.'

Tom watched Daniel sobbing into the pillow beside his mother. He held her hand. Tom took both their hands in his and kissed them. It was New Year's Day, just a few minutes after midnight. Each breath now sounded like a watery rattle that wasn't able to let any air into her lungs. Tom began to wish it was all over and that she would be set free from this misery.

At ten minutes to one, her breaths grew less frequent and

the rasping from her chest seemed louder with each one. A longer period of silence intervened every few minutes, and they both believed she had gone each time that it happened. Then the silence persisted, and there were no more sounds from her wasted body. Daniel lay beside her on the bed, crying quietly, and he put his arm around her waist.

Tom stood helpless by her side, gazing at the two of them. He touched his son's warm hand and said, 'She's gone.'

Daniel raised himself up and hugged his father tightly and, through their joint sobs, said, 'What are we going to do without her, Dad?'

'I don't know. I just don't know.'

Was this the first time he was admitting defeat to his son? The thing was, he just didn't know. He had never allowed himself to imagine life without his wife, his love, his best friend. What could he say to himself, far less Daniel?

'We're going to help each other through this, son,' he said. 'We've got each other. At least we have that. We will find some way to get to the other side and live again. She would want us to do that.'

Chapter Eleven
Then

Sympathy cards lined every surface that had any space in the room. Crosses, angels, doves, flowers, swans – the ways to express sorrow seemed to be endless. Tom wanted to throw any with Christian crosses in the bin, but Daniel had stopped him. He'd told him it didn't matter that Tom had no religious belief, that he must allow people to express their sympathy in a way that meant something to them. Tom had wanted to argue that the sympathy was for them and that people should show respect for their beliefs, but he had quickly realised that he wasn't sure what his son believed. He'd lost touch with him over the period of Alison's illness, although in the days following her death, he had felt close to him again. He had felt supported and loved by him. But the truth was, Daniel and Jenny had become more or less shadows to him.

Tom stood looking out of the window at the grey sky and the bare trees that were made less bleak by the light coat of frost they had taken on. He was wearing his best black suit and a black silk tie that he'd bought when he was shopping for Christmas gifts. Had he been thinking this was its purpose when he'd chosen it? Subliminally, maybe. Alison was never going to die, not really. Something was always bound to come around to prove it had all been a mistake and that she was going to get better. Some drug would come on the market that would deal with her form of cancer and fix things. Until it didn't.

In the reflection of the glass, he noticed his tie was squint. Alison would have spotted that way before he had and straightened it up for him. Life was going to be like that now. What Alison would have done. What Alison would have said. What Alison would think of this or that. Ghosts had many ways of haunting a person. Tom wanted Alison to haunt him. He wanted to feel her with him every second of every day.

Things will get easier. This mantra was what every other person he spoke to liked to chant at him. He hoped things *would* get easier, that he would be able to think about her and smile. Even laugh, maybe, like they had done so often together. Those memories would always make him laugh, wouldn't they? He'd always have those to hang onto. Nothing made him feel like smiling, never mind laughing, right now. Right now, all he wanted to do was drink himself into unconsciousness and blot everything else out. He walked to the drinks cabinet, poured himself a large glass of whisky and quickly swallowed it back. Another one would help him cope with this awful day.

Tom had just poured himself a third glass when Jenny came into the living room wearing a black pinafore. Her hair was tied back, and she had a tiny bit of make-up on her lips and cheeks.

'Will I do, Dad?' she asked.

'Yes, you'll do. Your mum would be very proud of you.'

He pulled her towards him and hugged her tightly. Looking beyond her, he saw Daniel standing in the doorway. He wore a black suit, the one he'd worn to the last school Christmas party the year before. It had been too big on him then. Now it fitted him perfectly. That time, he'd worn a sparkly blue bow tie. Now, he wore a thin straight black tie. His short spiky hair seemed glued down by some glossy varnish, making it all seem flat. He hardly looked like his son. He made Tom think of the young man who had come to finalise the service arrangements with them.

'Well, look at you,' said Tom.

Daniel shuffled slowly into the room. His cheeks were pink and his eyes were rimmed with red, making them look swollen. He had obviously been up most of the night crying. Tom let go of Jenny and went over to him, pulling his son's skinny frame towards him. He felt Daniel stiffen and pull away.

'You reek of booze,' Daniel said, screwing his face up.

'Sorry, Daniel. I… needed a bit of help to get me through today. I'll go and brush my teeth again.'

Tom left them in the living room and went to his bedroom. The bed was a scrum of blankets, and a pile of pillows covered the side where Alison had always slept. Someone had told him to do that; then if he woke up during the night, he would have a sense of her being in the bed beside him. He'd even scrunched her dressing gown beside the pillows to give a sense of her smell. The truth was, he never woke up during the night. Wine and sleeping pills saw to that. Whisky in the morning was a bit of a departure for him, but circumstances dictate behaviour, sometimes. He couldn't get through today, meet everyone, stand at the graveside and listen to the eulogies without some variety of chemical help.

Swiping most of the pillows onto the floor, he went into his bathroom and gazed at himself in the mirror. If Daniel looked bad, he looked exponentially worse. People would feel real sympathy for this wreck of a man, that much he was sure of. He threw cold water on his face and pressed a towel against his eyes. The mouthwash bottle was close to empty, but he swished the dregs from the bottom of it around his mouth for as long as he could before he started to gag. A big squeeze of toothpaste on his brush would do the rest of the job, and he brushed mindlessly, feeling slightly light-headed.

'Dad, are you OK? You've been in there for ages. We'll have to get ready to go soon.'

It was Jenny's voice.

'Yes, love. I'll be right out. Go and tell your brother I'll be through in a minute.'

Tom splashed more cold water on his face and pulled a comb through his hair. There was more grey than brown now. He'd have to get used to getting old. Used to getting old on his own. He'd have to get used to a whole different life. A lesser life. A diminished existence. The future had been grim for so long now; surely it would be easier to take on this new, inferior life? Probably. He sprayed on some aftershave as extra insurance and went to join Jenny and Daniel in the living room.

Daniel sat on the sofa, his head in his hands. Jenny was staring out of the window.

'What time are the cars due to arrive, Dad?' she asked.

'In about twenty minutes,' said Tom. 'Danny, are you alright?'

'Dad, are we still going to move to the new house?' asked Daniel.

'Yes,' said Tom. 'I've exchanged contracts on it and this place will go to completion in two weeks.'

'But Mum never even got to see it. She won't know where

we are.'

'Son, don't you remember that she saw the foundations and the plans? You and Jenny came with us that day. She helped choose all the fittings and fixtures that are going to be in there. Every tile, every worktop will have some of her personality in it. You'll see, when we move there. She knew exactly where we are moving to.'

'I couldn't tell you how to get there from here, right now,' said Daniel. 'Like me, she was only there once, and the whole estate was a building site. It's only had its official street name for a month or less. It's a completely new part of the city.'

'She knew the area very well, Daniel, and she knew what the street was going to be called right from the day we decided to buy it.'

'Can't we stay here, Dad? I'd rather stay here.'

'No!' shouted Jenny. 'I hate it here. So did Mum. She hated that lorry park, she hated the dust, she wanted to move away from here and so do I.'

Tom sat down beside Daniel and put his arm around him.

'Mum would have wanted us to move to the new house, son. She was sad that she would never see it finished, but she wanted us all to move there and be happy. She would be sad if she thought we had given up on what was a dream for all of us.'

'This is the last place she ever lived. I don't want to leave here.'

'You'll just have to get used to it,' said Jenny, her voice hard. 'This place is sold, and that's that.'

'Jenny's right, son. We can't break out of the contracts now. More importantly, Mum wouldn't have wanted us to.'

'You two have made up your minds. So that's that,' said Daniel. 'Anything can be changed if you want it enough.'

There was a knock on the front door. 'The cars are outside, Dad,' said Jenny. Tom stood up.

'C'mon, Dan. It's time. We can talk about this later.'

'You still stink of booze,' said Daniel.

It looked like a picnic hamper, only coffin-shaped. It was what Alison had wanted: no frills, no fuss, simple wicker. At least, that's what Tom remembered. From time to time, when they were young, they'd talked about what they wanted to happen after death in broad terms – when death was no more than a distant concept, when it was something they didn't have to consider until they were old, until they would have come to terms with it.

It had never come up when she was ill. The whole subject of death had never come up. It was avoided, frankly. All he could remember was that there was to be no church, no religious service, no fuss. Thankfully, Alison, in her final weeks, had told Daniel the details of everything she wanted, everything apart from the type of coffin. God only knows how the poor boy was able to listen to her tell him those things. He had cried as he told his father everything she'd said and, of course, Tom had broken down too.

So it was to be a humanist funeral, and Alison's body would lie in a woodland setting with no gravestone; the only marker for her grave would be a cherry tree that was to be planted directly after the burial. Cherry trees were Alison's favourite, and she loved the blossom that appeared every May. When the time came, Tom would be buried there too and a second cherry tree would keep Alison's company.

Tom listened to Angela, the celebrant, as she welcomed everyone to the service and explained the order of ceremony. After that, everything began to blur together, and the music and the eulogies passed over him as he descended deep into his darkest thoughts.

Had he brought this on himself and his darling wife and children? Hadn't he fantasised about wealth and freedom, and imagined a life where he could do what he wanted? Who had heard these thoughts and taken him at his word? It was simply a notion – a fantasy. It had never been a pact or a deal, at least not one where the repayment of the debt had been explained or imagined. Why would he have agreed to lose so much for so little gain? Be careful what you wish for. Tom had been careless in his wishes. Everything was in his grasp, just as his hold was slipping on the world that was most important to him. One wish granted, but with a diabolical price tag. Worse than that, he could not escape the feeling that somehow this wasn't a repayment. This was actually his coveted freedom being granted. Freedom to follow his nature and do what he liked, unbound. The irony was that the idea of it was far more appealing than the actuality.

He became aware of an elbow nudging his side. It was Daniel.

'It's time to carry her to the woodland burial area,' he whispered. 'This is the two minutes' silence for the god botherers to pay their respects.'

Was the ceremony over? Had he missed everything?

It was cold in the chapel. It stood centrally in the conventional part of the cemetery, surrounded by monuments and headstones. It looked more like a community centre, but for the arched windows, and was commonly used for both religious and non-religious funerals. No stained glass, thankfully. Tom shivered in his seat.

Four of Tom's friends had already taken their positions around the coffin, and Daniel took his place at the front. Jenny stood next to her brother, her face wet with tears. Tom squeezed her arm and took his place beside his son, and the undertakers helped the group put the coffin onto their shoulders. Music played, a song Daniel had chosen. It was 'The Scientist' by Coldplay. The words crept into Tom's ears, and he began to sob. She had been so slight at the end; it felt as if the coffin was empty. The rest of the congregation followed them, each carrying a white rose, and they slowly wound their way through the cemetery to the archway that led to the woodland burial site.

When they reached Alison's grave, the sky seemed to darken. Light rain began to fall as the funeral directors showed everyone where to stand. Angela said a few words and directed the bearers to lower the coffin into the grave using the cords they had been given. As the last cord dropped down into the grave, the assembled party began throwing their roses on top of the casket. Angela handed a single red rose to Tom. He kissed it and dropped it on top of the white flowers that completely covered the wicker.

'Goodbye, my darling,' he said.

Jenny took one of his hands and Daniel the other, and they gently led him away from the graveside.

Chapter Twelve
Today, Friday

Benny brings a cup of tea and places it in front of Vince, who is still studying the monitors. Robert has been on the warpath since Vince came back from lunch.

'Not much going on, Benny. Been no movement on either screen for twenty minutes or more. This guy has got to show up on one of the cameras one way or another. He can't just disappear into thin air.'

Vince takes a sip of the tea without taking his eyes off the screen.

'Want me to take over?' says Benny, half-heartedly. 'I know Robert wants the CCTV closely watched until we see this character.'

'In a bit, Benny. And he wants our eyes glued to the screens, never mind close watching. If we miss this guy, there'll be hell to pay. So if you take a stint, no tea, no piss, no fly fags. You're already in the bad books.'

'Don't I know it?' says Benny. 'Alright if I have a quick fag now then, Vince? I'll take over after that.'

Vince looks at his watch. 'Sure, Benny, take a break. I'll stay at this until four-thirty. You can take the hour after that. I want to take another scout around the basement, make sure all the door alarms are intact.'

'We already done that, Vince, but fill your boots, if it

makes you happy.'

Benny is already walking to the front doors, pulling a pack of cigarettes from his pocket.

This is the most boring fucking day that Vince can ever remember. One unusual person seen in the building, no signs of any problem anywhere in the building, yet he has to watch the bloody screens when no other fucker seems to care, Robert included. Maybe he'll just go through to the back and make himself a cuppa – see what Robert thinks of that. Good for the goose and all that. Vince can't do that, though. He's not going to let Robert talk to him like he does to Benny and Carlos. The only person he seems to like is fucking do-no-wrong Nadjib.

Buckingham Court's lords and ladies swan back and forth on the screens looking oh-so pleased with themselves. Let them try a few days in his one-bedroom in Brixton. See how they like that. Then let them lock horns with his shyster landlord. That'd wipe the self-satisfied grins off their mushes. But hang on! Someone odd has just appeared on the screen showing the feed from the link corridor to the hotel. It isn't the man that he saw on the earlier feed. This guy is much bigger, with no beard. No tattoo. Looks well out of place here, though. Wait a minute! Those manky sandals. Those skinny bare calves. That's him! Has to be!

Vince abandons reception and runs to the revolving doors, pushing his way through, causing it to spin faster than it was meant to. He looks left then right, but there is no sign of the man. The Ministry of Defence building gives off its usual sense of foreboding, and he feels sure that the man will have headed away from there and towards Embankment tube, so he begins running in that direction. He arrives quite out of breath and looks despondently into the crowd of people rushing to and fro, many dragging bags on wheels behind them. There is no hope of finding him here, so he pulls his phone from his pocket and dials.

'Good afternoon, Buckingham Court. Robert speaking. How may I help?'

'Robert, it's Vince.'

'Where the fuck are you, Vince? Two residents were at the desk waiting when I got back, and nobody on the desk. You were supposed to be watching the fucking monitors!'

'I didn't get the chance to tell you. I saw the guy leaving the building on the CCTV through the hotel. I gave chase but I lost him, I'm afraid.'

'Bloody hell! OK, Vince. I rang the Old Bill at Charing Cross when you were out, but they gave me short shrift. Said if there was no evidence of any offence, there was nothing they could do. Basically told me that we're paid to ensure the building is secure and that I should deal with it internally...'

'Alright,' says Vince, frowning. 'I'll be back in a bit.'

It seems this guy is long gone, so Vince goes to the little stall opposite the tube station and asks for a cup of coffee. Lighting a cigarette, he takes a long drag while he waits for it to be ready. The taxi rank has several black cabs waiting for customers. Vince sees the driver at the front of the queue is waving at him, and he goes over.

'My word, Vincent Cooper! Ain't seen you for donkeys. What you been up to, Vincey-boy?' says the cab driver.

'Alright, Alf. Long time no see, pal,' Vince says, smiling. 'Same old, same old. Apart from today, that is. Had a suspicious character in my building earlier and saw him leave a few minutes ago. Quite tall, big. Heavy dark trench coat and hat. Way overdressed for this hot weather. Shifty-looking. You didn't see somebody like that running into the tube, did you?'

'Nah, mate. Sorry. Been watching the entrance for any punters, but didn't see anybody like that. Just the usual tourists and work slaves. What's he been up to? Robbing the flats there?'

'No, no, Alf, nothing like that. At least not as far as I know. Just didn't look right, that's all. I better be heading back, or I'll have the boss on my case.'

'OK, mate, well don't be a stranger. See you at the Dog 'n' Duck, Sunday? You've not been in for ages. Old Bert's been asking after you.'

'Yeah, maybe. I'll see. Better go, mate!'

Vince throws his coffee cup into a bin and starts walking back to work. As he gets closer to the gardens on the river side of Buckingham Court, he notices a lone figure sitting on a bench near the entrance gates.

'Bloody hell! That's him.' Vince pulls his phone from his pocket and begins to dial Robert, but cancels the call before it goes through. He decides to move closer to the man to try and see what he is doing. After all, the police will just brush them off again unless he can find out whether this character is up to no good or not. There is a gap in the fence just behind where the man is sitting. Vince knows this is the way the down-and-outs and drunks get into the gardens when the gates are locked after dusk. He positions himself behind some bushes where he can just about see the man, and, when he hears him speaking, a shudder of dread runs through him.

'We will drink your blood… will not leave you alone until

we have quenched our thirst with your blood, and all the children of Islam will quench their thirst with your blood. We will not rest until you leave the Muslim countries. My actions now will show this. God is Great. *Allahu Akbar*!'

Vince shudders as he watches the man stand up and throw his phone behind the bench. He crouches down to avoid being seen and watches him walk towards the park gates. Then he pulls his phone from his pocket and dials '999'. As he tells the emergency operator what he has overheard, he can see the man crossing Northumberland Avenue towards Embankment tube.

'Keep your distance,' the operator says, calmly, 'but try and keep him in sight if you can. I'll alert local units and British Transport Police.'

Vince follows the man and sees him walk into the crowds that are milling on the pavement outside the station. He begins to run, hoping to keep him in sight, then realises that he is giving his commentary into dead air – his phone has lost its signal. The man is now waiting in line behind others swiping their passes to get through the turnstiles. Vince pulls at the arm of a uniformed London Transport official near the entrance and points at the man ahead of them.

'That guy!' He waves his finger wildly at the man and, in a suppressed shout, 'Stop him! He's a fucking terrorist.'

'Calm down, sir. Please.'

Vince runs towards the man he has been following as he is about to pass through the turnstile, but the guard pulls him back.

'What's the problem, sir? What makes you suspect him?'

Vince relates what he has seen and heard in the gardens and watches the expression change on the guard's face.

'Come with me,' the guard says pointing to a door by the ticket kiosks. 'We have to act fast.'

Vince finds himself in a room full of TV monitors, and he can see hordes of people on the screens, making their way up and down escalators and moving around on platforms.

'These screens here show the platforms of the lines that operate from this station.' The guard waves his hand over a bank of monitors. 'Keep your eyes on these screens and see if you can pick out the guy for me. He's bound to be down on one of the platforms by now.'

Vince narrows his eyes and tries to make sense of the sea of black and white pixelated bodies in front of him.

'I'm sorry, mate, it's gonna be impossible to—'

Vince begins rapping excitedly on the screen that is labelled BAKERLOO LINE, NORTHBOUND. 'That's him! I think that's him, anyway. I'm sure that's the hat and coat he had on.'

The train is drawing into the station on that platform, and Vince can see that the man is getting on it.

'OK,' says the guard, picking up his radio.

Vince can hear him chattering frantically into the mouthpiece as he watches the train pulling out of the station.

'Suspicious IC1 male heading north... Bakerloo Line... all-stations alert... Transport Police Terrorist Unit...'

Vince looks at his watch. 'I have to get back to work,' he says to the guard.

'Just let me have your details first, sir. Thanks for alerting us to this. Let's hope it all comes to nothing.'

'Where've you been, Vince? I was nearly sending a search

party out for *you*.'

Robert is standing in front of the porter's desk, looking stony.

'It's a long story, Robert. Let's go in the back and have a cuppa. I've got a lot to tell you. Benny can watch the desk for twenty minutes, can't he?'

Vince tells Robert all he has seen and heard in the gardens and what happened later in the tube station.

'The thing is, Robert, and I can't quite put my finger on why, but there was something very familiar about that guy's voice. He was saying these frightening words, but the sound of his voice kept reminding me of someone, someone I feel I know, but I just can't get my brain to fathom it.'

'How could you know his voice, Vince? I mean, we've all seen him on CCTV, and you've seen him up close, in the flesh. You'd surely put the voice and the face together and come up with the answer.'

'That's the trouble,' says Vince, 'that voice didn't belong to his face, or at least the bits of his face I could see. It was almost like he was imitating somebody I know.'

'I think your memory is playing tricks on you, that's all.'

'No. It'll come to me. I know it will. I'm going to review all the CCTV footage, if it's OK with you, Robert. I'm hoping something will click if I watch it again with the voice still in my head…'

Vince sits down in front of the consoles and rewinds the saved footage to four a.m. He watches the grainy figure come into the building via the access door of the hotel. The man, bearded and sinister, enters the service lift and Vince notices that the arrow is pointing down. So he went to the basement level. What could Buckingham Court have to do with someone who is planning a terrorist attack? None of this makes any sense. Vince had searched the basement himself. There had been nothing taken or disturbed, as far as he could see.

The time counter is now moving faster with Vince's increased pressure on the button, and when it gets to 11.10 a.m., he sees the man on the video feed, so he lets it drop back to normal speed. That must've been when Mrs Heath pulled him away from the desk. The shady figure appears again, his back to the camera, leaving the same way as he had entered. He is only on camera for a few seconds, and there is nothing about the image that helps Vince connect the voice with the person. He increases the speed of the video again and watches various residents and members of staff moving back and forth, their lives speeded up. Then, at 12.51 p.m., he sees the man again, this time face on, and this time he doesn't use the service lift. This time, he walks to the stairwell, right beside the porter's desk, carrying a bulky parcel under his arm. Vince's eyes widen. The man had walked in right under their noses – no, not his nose, bloody Robert's nose when he was out for his sandwich – and there, he walks upstairs to the residents' floors, as if he damn well owns the place.

Vince rewinds the short piece of footage again and again, staring into the eyes of the suspect, hoping they would reveal his identity. He keeps wishing those eyes would tell him who the voice belongs to. The hat and the beard cover most of his features, but surely the eyes would tell the truth. However much he rewinds and pauses, that revelation doesn't come, and he gives up and continues to fast-forward. Nothing of interest shows up on the screen until he reaches the point of the film that he'd witnessed in real life, which caused him to run out into the street and pursue the man.

Here, the figure is again much larger-looking than the person he's seen earlier on the security film, and, of course, this man has no beard, no tattoo. However, the scruffy jeans, sandals and bare shins are common to them both. Vince pauses the film again and looks long and hard into the image of the man's face, and a slow look of realisation creeps over his own face.

'Robert!' he shouts. 'Robert, come through here now!'
Robert appears in the doorway. 'What's the panic?'

'Look at this face. Look at this face and tell me you don't know who that guy is. Go on.'

Robert peers at the screen. He pulls off his glasses and rubs the lenses with his hanky before putting them back on and looking closer.

'Well,' he begins, 'if the body was a lot skinnier... but then the face is pretty thin, isn't it? It's a bit grainy too, but if you held a gun to my head, I'd say that young man is... but mind you, we ain't seen him for a good, long while, have we? Do you think it's really him?'

'I do,' says Vince, tapping at the face on the screen. 'That's Daniel McIntyre, or I'm a liar!'

Vince looks at his watch. It is 6.10 p.m. 'Has anyone seen Mr McIntyre today? He typically comes down around lunchtime, doesn't he?'

'Come to think of it, I haven't,' says Robert. He sticks his head through the back-office door and shouts, 'Benny, you seen Mr McIntyre from Flat 67 today?'

Benny scratches his head. 'No, boss. Not today. Last I saw of him was late last night, and he was a bit worse for wear, you know?'

'Ain't he always?" chips in Robert.

'I think one of us needs to knock on his door,' says Vince.

'Better if we ring upstairs and ask if he is OK,' says Robert. 'After all, he doesn't like being called on if he's a bit the worse for wear. You know what he can be like. That seems the best option to me. Then if we get no reply, we can let ourselves in and check what's what, without fear of having him come down on us like a ton of bricks.'

Benny's phone chimes on the desk. He stares at the screen, looking shocked.

'Fuck, have you heard what's happened in Oxford Circus? Some kind of terrorist attack. It's like 7/7 all over again – looks like loads more people are dead, though!'

'What?' Vince looks at Robert, incredulous. 'You think it was…?' The desk phone starts to ring.

'Good evening, Buckingham Court, Vincent speaking. How may I help?' His voice is shaky.

'Vince? Vince. Flat 67 here—'

Vince holds the receiver to his chest and whispers, 'Fuck me, Robert. You couldn't make this up. Sounds like someone's in a bit of a state!'

Chapter Thirteen
Then

Daniel lay on his bed, trying to blot out what he'd seen. He knew he hated Tom. It had started before Mum died. The reason had never been clear; it was just a growing, nasty feeling, like the cancer that had been growing inside her. The reason was never clear. Until now. The crack he'd taken earlier wasn't making things any better, so now he sucked on the pipe and watched the liquid bubble below the grey vapour. The smoke from the weed bong gripped his throat, and he felt the calm of its effects permeate through him accompanied by a sharp tingle from the crack cocaine in the base of his cranium. Still, what he'd seen banged against the windscreen of his mind. Bang. Bang. Bang. Was this why he was the way he was? Is this what had given him his nature? Or, was it that bastard – that fucking lorry driver – all those years ago?

That dust came into his brain again and again, and he knew he'd never been able to shake it off, not even now. He'd tried to shake it from his clothes, from his hair, from his brain. It had been a grey cloud, something that hung over him, a film that was impossible to scrub off. Not until now, anyway. Bastards. Bastards. Bastards ruled the world, and now the biggest bastard was his father. He wasn't going to rule his world any longer.

Tom had always been a bastard, really. He'd lied about

Mum and her illness. He'd kept all that from him, when he could have been preparing him, getting him ready, allowing him to spend more time with her. Worse than that, he'd kept things from Mum, more than kept things – he'd lied to her, treated her like dirt, taken her for a fool. Liar. He'd treated him – his own son – like some fucking stranger. Well, who really knew what a stranger Tom had been? Had Mum known? Was he a stranger to her? Too right he was! Tom was a strange apology for a man. Hateful bastard.

The liquid bubbled harder as he sucked in the smoke. His mind became ever clearer. The guy in the lorry – he couldn't have made him this way. No. It ran deeper than that. What a cunt. What a cunt. Cunt. Cunt. Cunt. Who, though? That stinking-arsed fucker in the lorry? Or the liar, the cheat, the demi-man who'd made him? It had to be Tom. The guy in the lorry was an unlucky aberration. His mistake. His bad. Tom was his blood, his flesh. Tom had made him this way. Worse than anything that cunt in the lorry had done. Bastard.

Where was the fucker anyway? Drunken cunt. Drunken cunt. Hateful bastard. Liar. Liar. Poor Mum. Poor cow. Poor fucking cow. Did she know? She couldn't. Couldn't possibly. She'd have thrown him out if she'd known, wouldn't she? No way would Mum have stood for that. She had been fooled by him just the same way as he had been. But what had *he* done to deserve this? This nature. This horrible, hateful nature he'd been given, which he lived with every fucking day. He hadn't asked for it. All he had ever wanted was to be normal. Who wanted to be a queer, poof, faggot? All came to the same thing though, didn't it, Tom? Well, didn't it? What made you that way, cunt? Cunt. Cunt! I didn't ask to be like that, did I? Did *your* dad do it *you?*

Was it you that killed Mum? Did she find out? Was that the last straw for her? The revelation that took away all the fight from her? Daniel had watched her give up, all from nowhere, no visible reason; he watched her throw in the cards and accept what was happening to her. She'd promised him time and again that she wasn't going to die. But then the light had gone out in her, and all of her strength and resolve was gone. All of a sudden. No warning. She'd found out, hadn't she? It was then that she couldn't face going on. There was nothing to fight for any more.

Not me? Not even Jenny?

But the bastard in the lorry park kept coming back, even morphed into Tom sometimes. Had Tom known that bastard? Cunt. Cunt. In any case, he wasn't like that because of the lorry driver. Tom had done it to him. Or maybe the lorry driver. Either way, it wasn't his fault. Tonight had changed everything. Everything. The answers hadn't been clear. Not until now. Until now. *It was you all along, Tom, wasn't it? Bastard. Cunt.*

Daniel couldn't taste the weed any longer; all that was coming through the pipe now was air. He squinted at the bowl and pulled it from his bong. It was full of ash, which he threw into a saucer that was already brimming with ashes, causing it to spill over onto the bed. There was enough water in the glass by his bed to top up the reservoir, and he'd still got plenty of the stuff he'd bought in the pub last night. His grinder had disappeared. *Fuck it. Why does the damn thing always go missing just when you fucking need it?* He raked his hands over the bedclothes, patted the pillows and checked around the floor. Then – head-slap moment – he patted the pockets in his shorts. Of course, he'd put it where he'd remember it. In his fucking pocket.

He ground the weed thoroughly and stuffed the contents into the bowl, throwing in a bit more acid for good measure, rechecked the reservoir that he'd filled moments before and spun the wheel on his lighter. When he got a flame to show, he lit the contents of the bowl and watched the chamber fill with smoke, feeling his anger dissipate with each swirl in the glass. Maybe this hit would help him forget the bastard for a while.

But his first deep inhalation brought the anger back. A chest full of vapour spread into his brain and agitated the synapses. Filthy images and messages permeated his thoughts again, and the blame spread through them like acid leaking from a battery. Corrosive, damaging, filling his thoughts with hatred again, making him twitch and spit out bleak words into the air. He threw his grinder at the wall and then his water glass. Fuck you, Tom! Fuck you. His phone glowed and buzzed beside him on the bed: DAD CALLING. Before the buzzing stopped, that too crashed against his bedroom wall.

A long inhalation, followed by another and another, had him standing upright. He lurched towards his chest of drawers and pulled the top drawer open. A pile of papers lay on top of the neatly stacked underwear and socks. Daniel grimaced as he thought of the cleaning lady placing things there, where his mother would have placed things in past times, but not as neatly. He snatched up the papers and looked at them closely – MORTGAGE AGREEMENT – Tom's name plastered all over the documentation as depositor, guarantor, co-signatory, etc. There was no escape from this fucker. He wanted to rip them all up and throw them out of his window. But he didn't. Fucker had him over a barrel, like always. Fucking control freak.

More long sucks on the bong. What day was it? It was any day. Every day was like this now. Even the days he stacked the shelves at Tesco. How else would he get through those days? The idiots, the losers, the bastards that he worked with and served. What were days anyway? The only day that mattered was the day he would walk out of this fucking place with his bags, without ever looking back. Fuck this place, fuck Tom, fuck the world! More inhalations, more pauses, more anger, more pauses, more pauses. Then stop. Head on the pillow. A semblance of sleep. Sleep? Something that wasn't being awake, not thinking. A thin trickle of thoughts sneaking through his head.

Then the door. Bang! Angry Tom was home. Drunk Tom. Nasty Tom. Well, let's show him some nastiness too. Yes, let's. Daniel looked out of his bedroom window. Tom's car was half on the lawn, almost at right angles to his own car. The fucker had been driving drunk again. Maybe next time he'll kill himself. As long as he doesn't kill or injure any innocent fucker in his wake. He opened his door and listened. A familiar clink of bottle against glass, then, on cue, 'Hallelujah' blaring through the speakers. If he never heard that fucking song again, it'd be a lifetime too soon. He stamped hard on the landing floor, knowing it was right above where Tom would be sitting. Nothing. 'Hallefuckinglujah' drowning out his pain as usual.

Daniel stamped downstairs, sure that nothing would stir his father, and went into Tom's study. He glared at the computer on the desk, which was displaying a screensaver of Tom's favourite album covers. A swipe of the mouse got rid of them, then a few taps into the password box got him in again. He was going to stuff those images into the bastard's mouth, one by one. He'd print them off. He'd turn them into a screensaver, one that would burn its meaning onto Tom's retinas forever. He'd let him know that he knew and that he blamed him for it. Tom would never forget this night. The night he lost his son forever. Jenny would know too. An email from Tom's account would do that trick. Then he'd have nobody. Nobody but the cheap shags he seemed to crave. His meaningless assignations. There would be no need to say he was working late when he wasn't. The world would be his putrid fucking oyster. Free of Mum, free of him, free of Jenny. He could do what he liked and live with the loss. Tom's dirty, drunken, cock-sucking mouth could chew on the filthy images and messages. He would make him choke on them. Make him eat his own shit.

The computer seemed to glare back at him. It challenged him to do his worst. He hovered the mouse cursor over the Finder icon and clicked DOCUMENTS> WORK> SPECIALISED> PROSPECTS> VERIFIED SPECS> REPEAT INGRESS> DOUBLE-CHECKED> PRIVATE> IMAGES> then there was a whole list of image files. Bingo! Thought you had it buried nice and deep, Tom, didn't you? This is exactly where he'd found it before. Didn't know what he'd been looking for then, but he knew he'd find something. And he did. Daniel clicked on the first image.

What appeared on the preview screen was not what he had seen last night. It was a photograph of Mum, smiling, leaning against a tree. She must have been nineteen or twenty in that picture; it was grainy, scanned from somewhere, sepia- tinted, almost. What was that doing there? It hadn't been there yesterday. He clicked on the next image: Jenny one side, Mum in the middle, him on the other, all smiling. The next, Tom and Mum. Next, the cats. Every image he clicked on revealed another idyllic family scene – all smiles, happiness, deep family joy in every possible circumstance. Had he dreamed it? Was the sordid pornography all imagined? He drilled down into other folders, searched the whole hard disk for images, but every single one he opened was either family snaps or professional photos of properties and building sites. What the fuck?

What about his internet history? That's where it had all started, the suspicion, the realisation, the proof he'd wanted so badly. He hadn't imagined that. He clicked the Google icon and then PREFERENCES, followed by HISTORY. A long list appeared: FACEBOOK, TWITTER, property site after property site, ANCESTRY.COM, YOUTUBE, VEVO, SPOTIFY, IPLAYER, BOOKING.COM. Innocent web searches abounded. No dogging sites, no gay sites, no porn searches, nothing. What the fuck was going on? He couldn't have changed all this since he looked. Tom had been at work all day, or fuck knows where, drinking, shagging, who knew? One thing Daniel knew: Tom was as computer unsavvy as a fucking retard. Another thing he knew: he hadn't imagined what he'd seen.

Time Machine backups! They would be there, wouldn't they? Tom wasn't going to get one over on him, that was for sure. He clicked on ENTER TIME MACHINE from the menu.

Everything on the screen withdrew to what looked like a sole, single Finder window. The scroll bar to the right showed TODAY and NOW in red. Where the fuck was yesterday, the day before, the week before, the month before, the fucking lifetime before? This couldn't be possible. What the fucking fuck? He had imagined it. Had he dreamed it? Did he need to lay off the weed? What the fucking fuck? He stood up, looked around the room. Was this a dream, maybe? The walls felt solid. The chair was real. His toes could feel thick carpet beneath them.

Daniel left Tom's study and stood for a few moments in the hall. 'Hallelujah' still blared from the living room. Did he want to go in there and have it out face to face with Tom? His guitar lay abandoned at the foot of the stairs. Had he brought it down with him? Was that his weapon of choice with his pathetic father again? He picked it up and pushed the living room door open. The music hit him like a wall.

Tom lay on the sofa, legs splayed in front of him, candles burning on the coffee table. He was hugging the wooden cat, the one he'd given Mum that final Christmas. A silver-framed photograph of Mum, Daniel and Jenny lay on his lap. His face looked wet with tears, but his eyes were shut, and he was snoring gently. Daniel turned the music off. The sudden silence had no effect on Tom. He lay peacefully, clutching the cat, soft light from the candles fondling his face in the otherwise dark room. Daniel felt his eyes welling. This wasn't right. He sat next to Tom and poked his chest, but got no response. Fucking drunk.

The deep, woody musk of Tom's aftershave reached him and reminded him of his childhood, of innocent days, of being whirled into the air with that smell in his nostrils, of laughing and begging for more. The scent dissipated his anger and he moved closer to his father. Before he could stop himself, he pushed the wooden cat from Tom's grasp and lifted his father's arm. Tom wriggled a little and called out Daniel's name in his sleep. Daniel took Tom's arm and draped it over his shoulders. He burrowed his face into Tom's chest and inhaled, trying to capture more lost innocence. He stayed there for half an hour or more, trying desperately to find lost love, almost begging to find it there. Nothing came. When he couldn't stop the sobs rising within him, he stood up, picked up his guitar and left Tom on the sofa, closing the door behind him.

Suddenly thirsty, he went to the kitchen and scowled when he saw the new computer box lying in the conservatory with Tom's old computer beside it. At least he wasn't going out of his mind. He'd teach that fucker a lesson, but maybe not now, not tonight. He'd wait until the deal was signed and there was no going back. You'll get yours, Tom.

Chapter Fourteen
Then

Tom heard a loud crunch. 'Fuck.'

He yanked the handbrake and pulled himself out of his seat, placing one hand on the open door to steady himself. A slight hiss fizzled from the front of the car, and he swayed a little as he went to investigate. The front grille of his Mercedes had a deep dent and was wedged against the large granite urn that contained the new cherry tree.

'At least your tree's OK, darling,' he muttered.

He looked up and saw Daniel's face staring back at him from his bedroom window. The rest of the house appeared to be in darkness. Tom waved to his son, smiling, but Daniel pulled his curtains closed.

'Charming!'

Tom walked unsteadily towards the front door, the car engine still running. He'd left the driver's door wide open, with the full beam of the xenon headlights washing the house in a ghostly blue light. He aimed his keys at the front door, but it gave way on him and he fell face down on the hallway carpet. Who left the fucking door ajar? The new carpet smell filled his nostrils, and the plush pile against his face made him glad the fitters had finished laying it. At least there'd be no bruises.

'The world's out to get me tonight,' he said through gritted teeth, reaching for the spindles of the banister. Rufus scampered towards him and rubbed himself against Tom, purring. Falling back to his knees, he ruffled the fur on the cat's neck and smiled.

'Hello, buddy. Where's Jasper?'

The cat scuttled to the kitchen, reacting to the sudden sound of strumming and banging from upstairs. A pungent stench of marijuana wafted through the house. Pulling himself up, he mumbled, 'Open a fucking window, will you?'

Almost in response, the strumming grew louder, and he could hear Daniel chanting something unintelligible above the tuneless strings. Tom felt his way into the kitchen, where he unscrewed the top from a bottle of wine and poured himself a large glass. He ambled to the living room, splashing drops of wine on his shirt as he went, and switched on the lights.

'Evening, Dad.'

Tom dropped his glass, spilling red wine over the new carpet. 'Hell, Jenny! What are you doing sitting there in the dark?'

'Did you drive in that state? Dad, you're starting to worry me...'

'Oh, no lectures, please,' said Tom, picking up his glass. 'I get enough of that from Danny. It's constant.'

Jenny rolled her eyes. 'You've left the car running with the lights on. And you'd better do something about that wine stain on the carpet. You won't be able to get it out if it dries, and the carpet's brand new.'

'Be a love and go and turn the car off, will you?' said Tom, feeling in his pockets for the keys. He threw them to her. 'And please tell your brother to open a window and shut that racket off.'

Jenny picked up the keys and said, 'It's been like that all evening. It's always the same when he smokes that stuff. And you know he's mixing it with speed now, don't you? When's he moving out, Dad? Can't come soon enough for me.'

Tom shrugged and slumped into his chair, feeling for the TV remote. Jenny sighed as the jangling music from some game show began to fight with the strumming from upstairs.

'I'll lock the car, then I'm going up to my room.'

Tom stared blankly at the screen, hardly aware that she was speaking. She slammed the door as she left. Tom heard that alright.

Tom awoke, still upright on the sofa, an empty bottle of wine by his side, spluttering, trying to make sense of what was before him: Daniel stood over him, his legs straddling Tom's. He leaned in towards Tom, strumming his guitar tunelessly, his knuckles hitting Tom's face intermittently. Tom lurched forward. The half-full wine glass beside him tipped over, splashing them both, and he banged his head on the guitar.

'Fucking drunk, useless cunt! Fucking drunk, useless cunt! Fucking drunk, useless cunt! Fucking drunk, useless cunt! Fucking drunk, useless cunt!'

Daniel chanted over the discordant rhythm and Tom felt his son's warm spit on his forehead, like fine spatters of blood from the raw words. The noise of the guitar was pounding in his ears, and the determined look of hatred in Daniel's eyes filled him with a panic he could hardly comprehend.

'Stop this!' he shouted, trying to push his son away.

'Fucking drunk, useless cunt!'

'Daniel, please! What's got into you?'

'Fucking drunk, LYING cunt!'

Tom felt the side of the guitar bang his head, and he fell to the floor. As he tried to pull himself up, Daniel pressed his foot onto his heaving chest, chanting and strumming the whole time.

'Daniel! What are you doing? Stop it now, or I'm calling the police.' It was Jenny, standing in the doorway.

Daniel smashed his guitar on the floor, close to his father's head, and spat. 'Out of my way!' He pushed past his sister, and Tom heard the front door slam.

Tom pulled himself up, using the arm of the chair. He stood up and faced his daughter, hardly able to look her in the eye, an unstoppable quiver in the corner of his mouth.

'What's got into him, Jenny?'

'He's been acting weird for days, Dad,' she said. She took his arm. 'C'mon, let's get you to bed. It's late.'

Tom pulled away. 'Jenny, I don't know what I've done wrong. I'm helping him to buy his flat. I've offered to help him furnish it too. I gave him your mother's car. I've done nothing but try to help him. Why does he hate me? What have I done wrong?'

'Dad... he doesn't... we don't... need anything like that.' Jenny was twisting her long dark hair between her fingers. Tom watched her eyes welling with tears. It felt as though Alison's deep-blue eyes were staring back at him, chastising him.

'It's *you* we need. We miss you, Dad. We hardly see you any more since Mum... you need to stop drinking so much.'

Tom reached for her hand and pulled her closer.

'Danny hasn't been coping well. He's been smoking weed constantly, and I told you he's using harder stuff too...' she

143

said, wiping her eyes with her sleeve.

'Jenny, I'm sorry.' Tom could feel his own eyes moistening and blinked hard. 'It's been hard for me, hard for all of us, I know.'

'Dad, between you and Daniel, I feel like I'm out on a limb. This new house feels empty, soulless. We should have stayed where we were.'

'I couldn't, love. I just couldn't. And anyway, we were committed to this place. This was your mum's dream house—'

'It was only a set of foundations and a floor plan when she saw it. It was never her home.'

'We chose everything in here together. Every tile in the bathrooms, every unit and appliance in the kitchen, every rug, everything. She's part of this place. Everything she loved is here with us now. Her pictures, her ornaments, her books.' Tom picked up the wooden cat and held it to his chest.

'There are five bedrooms, Dad. We rattle around here as it is. With Danny gone, it'll just be stupid for the two of us to stay here. Even Rufus and Jasper don't know what to do with themselves in this barn. And I'll be going to uni in September too…'

'We'll talk about it tomorrow, Jen. I need to straighten my head.'

Tom woke up fully clothed on his bed. His tongue felt like a lump of pumice in his mouth as he tried to moisten it with the scant saliva he was able to summon up. The water glass on the bedside table was empty, and he peered through the open curtains at the rain pattering against the window. As he dragged himself to his bathroom, he noticed the stains all over the front of his shirt. Had he been bleeding? The strong whiff of stale wine gave him his answer. He hauled off his jacket and pulled the shirt over his head, throwing both on the floor. Greedy gulps from the cold tap made his mouth feel almost human again. Then he took the rest of his clothes off and got into the shower.

Feeling a little better after his shower, Tom went to the kitchen and became very aware of the silence around him. No radio blare, no TV babble, no phone chatter. Peace. There was a scribbled note on the kitchen table, held down by a half-drunk cup of coffee that was long since cold. He picked it up:

Had to dash, dad. Late for college. No sign of Danny. I tried calling his mobile, but he didn't answer. I'll see you tonight. Don't drink any wine please! We need to talk properly.
Jenny x

Tom crumpled the note in his hand and tossed it into the bin, then turned the kettle on. The rain was coming down even harder now, battering the glass of the conservatory, making him feel as if it was driving its way into his skull. He made some tea and grabbed some painkillers from a bottle in the cupboard. Walking into the living room, he saw the wine stains on the carpet and the smashed guitar nearby. The Mercedes seemed to be glaring at him from the driveway, parked in a way that Tom felt was not of his doing, as the events of the previous evening began to bully their way back into his brain. What had got into Daniel?

The phone rang, interrupting his thoughts. It was his secretary wanting to know where he was. He looked at his watch: eleven thirty a.m.

'I've decided to work from home today,' he told her. 'Cancel any meetings for the rest of the day. Say I've been called away. I'll try to come in tomorrow.'

As he put down the phone, the front door clicked, and he heard footsteps pounding upstairs. He looked up at the ceiling as he heard movement coming from Daniel's room. Tom closed the living room door, picked up his book and pretended to read. His heart was hammering in his chest, and he couldn't stop himself glancing upwards every few minutes. Every so often, he got up and placed his hand on the door handle, sometimes twisting the knob, debating with himself whether to go upstairs and face his son or not. Each time, he returned to the sofa instead and picked up his book, staring at the pages, never reading a word.

Eventually, the noise above him stopped, and he could feel panic rising within him again. He went into the kitchen and made a pot of tea as noisily as he could. Daniel must know that he was at home. He would have seen the car in the driveway, wouldn't he? By the time the tea was ready, there was no sign of his son, so he took his cup into to the living room and closed the door again. He waited.

The sound of heavy footsteps on the staircase made him start. The living room door opened slowly, and Tom looked at Daniel standing in the doorway, staring at him impassively, a large rucksack on his back.

'Daniel, I—'

'I'm going away for a few weeks. I think we both need some space.'

'Where will you go?'

'Friends. It doesn't matter. Look, I just want to know that you'll still help with my mortgage and the legal stuff...'

'I said I would, didn't I?'

'Well... after last night...'

'That wasn't you, Daniel. That was drugs. I know it, and you know it. You have to stop with that stuff. It's changing you. I've been reading a lot about how long-term use of cannabis causes—'

'Fuck off, Dad! Try spending time researching the damage that booze does to your brain. The hurt and injury that booze does to your family. The mess you're making of your life and mine and Jenny's.'

'It's hardly comparable, is it? Prolonged heavy use of marijuana can cause psychosis, bipolar disorder...'

'It's theory. Nothing's proven. On the other hand, alcohol abuse and its effects are much more thoroughly researched and... it's much more addictive and harmful to the brain and other organs than anything I use.'

'Daniel, I don't drink every day, and I'm certainly not addicted to it. It's not a drug. The way you behave and the mood changes really make me think you might be bipolar...'

Daniel sighed and dropped his backpack to the floor.

'So you're a fucking psychiatrist now too? You fucking need to see one more than I do. Why don't you take a look in the mirror – other than to admire yourself? You're deluded. Ever since Mum died, you've been a fucking drunken wreck, and I can't even remember the last time I saw you completely sober. You're not even sober now. And to be honest, that's not all—'

'I've never been soberer, thank you. And my life has been

unbearable since your mum died. Can you not give me a break? I've said nothing about the constant reek of your bongs and God knows what else throughout the house. It smells like a drug den every time I come home. And what do you mean – that's not all?'

Daniel's face twisted into a sneer, and Tom began to wish he'd gone to work and avoided all this.

'Well, I know more about you than you think.'

What did Daniel know? What had his son found out? He'd always been careful, covered his tracks. If it was what he thought it was, the only person who did know – and who could justify him – was dead.

'Daniel—'

'Save it! You disgust me. The sooner you're out of my life, the better.'

'Daniel, what exactly have I done? If your mother…'

But he was gone. He'd snatched up his backpack and run for the front door. Tom ran to the open door and stood despondently, watching his son speeding off in Alison's car. Turning away from the driveway and the sight of his dented car, he closed the door and went straight to the kitchen, where he opened a bottle of wine. May as well live up to Daniel's expectations of him. Work wasn't going to happen today, anyhow. He sat on one of the bar stools, drank down a glass and refilled it at once. Picking up the framed photograph of his wife from the windowsill, he touched her smiling face.

'Alison, I wish you were here to tell him. I wish we had told him before you left us. He'll never believe me now. I'll be a liar and a cheat in his head forever. This isn't fair, darling. Apart from me, you're the only one who knows the truth. I miss you.'

Chapter Fifteen
Then

Speckles of dust danced in angled bars of sunshine. The light pushed its way through the panes of glass onto the twist of sheets at the end of the bed. Daniel squinted at them and scowled as the piles of cardboard boxes all around him came into focus. He kicked the sheets away and sat for a few minutes gazing through the window, wondering what to do next. The remains of a joint lay by the lighter he'd bought from the all night garage the night before. Weed spilled from the poorly rolled Rizla as he pressed it to his lips and spun the wheel on the lighter with his thumb. He wondered which box his bong might be in as he sucked in a long, crackling throatful of smoke.

Rubbing his eyes, he got up and shuffled through to the kitchen, scratching his naked behind, every bit as undressed as the windows in his third-storey flat. He pulled the fridge door open and took out the solitary half-full bottle of water from the otherwise empty space. Boxes littered the kitchen island, blocking his view into the small sitting room. The agent had described the flat to his father as an 'open-plan, living/diner'. He'd even said it was 'loft-style'. This had made Daniel laugh; what he saw was a small sitting room with a kitchen area stuck on one end as if it didn't belong there. At least there were two bedrooms and a reasonable sized bathroom with an actual bathtub.

This fêted 'Art Deco' block was, in fact, a post-war, grey concrete filing cabinet, five storeys high. Brutalist architecture at its finest. Daniel had considered placing a large letter 'D' on his front door so he could tell people he had been filed under 'disillusioned', but had quickly discarded that idea when he realised that everyone would think it was his first initial.

From his window, he gazed out at the rows of cars glinting in the sunshine and, beyond those, the grey blocks mimicking his. Daniel imagined the windows on every block as handles on the filing cabinet drawers and wondered what pulling the drawers out of each might reveal. He took a sharp step backwards when he saw his father's black Mercedes moving slowly through the rows, apparently looking for a place to park. He went back to his bedroom and closed the door. Picking up the tangle of jeans and T-shirt that lay crumpled on the floor, he dressed without checking which way round his top was. He lay down on his bed and listened.

Even though he was waiting for it, he started when the door buzzer sounded; the disproportionately loud vibrating drone, like a factory summons to work, seemed to make the silence that followed sharper. He waited. Again, it vibrated through his flat, and a third time. Then he heard the letterbox flap clatter open, followed by his father's slightly muffled voice calling through, 'Daniel, are you in there...? Daniel?' The buzzer sounded one final time, followed by the noise of something dropping through the letterbox. Daniel waited a few minutes before getting up and quietly opening his door.

He peered into the hallway, listening. He knew his father's tricks. An envelope was just visible on the bare floorboards behind the rows of boxes. A familiar growl from the fat Mercedes outside made him turn and walk to the window. He watched the car drive onto the road and move cautiously over the speed bumps before it turned onto the main road and disappeared. Only then did he retrieve the envelope, tearing it open and pulling out the card that was inside. On it was a picture of Jasper and Rufus staring up at the camera. At the top of the card, in yellow letters, were the words: HAPPY BIG 2-0 TO MY BRILLIANT SON. Daniel opened it and four crisp fifty-pound notes fell to the floor. He threw the card onto a pile of boxes, without reading the message written inside, and picked up the money.

The first few bars of 'The Scientist' crept into his consciousness from somewhere. He patted the pockets of his jeans and scanned the room. As the volume increased, he went to his bedroom and peered under the bed. His mobile phone was there, glowing through the gloom, partly visible behind an upturned shoe, next to a half-eaten slice of pizza. He stretched his arm underneath the bed and pulled it out, squinting at the number on the screen. A withheld number, so he rejected the call, suspecting it may be his father. A few seconds later, it rang again. Daniel pressed the answer key and quietly said, 'Yes?', his finger hovering over the end-call button.

The voice at the other end was faint, sounded foreign. 'Hello, can I speak to Doneel. Doneel Moc... intoor?'

'Who is this?' said Daniel.

'Hello, Doneel? My name is Waqar... I saw you are renting a room... I saw card in supermarket...'

God, he'd done that even before he'd completed on the flat. It had completely gone from his mind.

'Oh… right… Sorry. I'd forgotten all about that. I pinned that up there ages ago, and it completely slipped my—'

'The room… is still for rent? I need soon, you see?'

Daniel thought for a moment and looked around at the mess of packing cases everywhere.

'The place isn't quite ready,' he said.

'Please, Doneel. I'm desperate. I sleep on the floor. I'm good, clean man. I need very little. I am good person. I have good job, I work hard.'

Daniel liked the deep timbre of his voice, the accent, the way each 'r' was rolled and every consonant pronounced clearly. The voice conjured a picture of the man in his head: tall, young and dark, with curly black hair and an infectious grin.

'What did you say your name was? Vacker? I'll meet you, OK? Then we can see…'

'Yes, please. I meet you. You sell me the room? Where we can meet? Tomorrow, maybe?'

'You know the Cranemakers pub in London Road? It's near the town centre.'

'No, we meet Starbucks, yes?'

'Sure… if you prefer that,' said Daniel, wondering what might be wrong with the pub. Things would be easier with a proper drink, and he was flush, thanks to Tom. 'The one in Scotch Street? Shall we say Saturday, one o'clock?'

'Yes, good. Starbucks. Saturday. One o'clock. Thank you, Doneel. I see you Saturday. Bye.'

'Hang on, hang on,' said Daniel, 'tell me your number, Vacker. And maybe what you look like… How will I recognise you?'

The line was silent. Daniel threw the phone onto the crumpled bedclothes and looked around the room. Saturday would be here in no time. When had he put that card up? Strange that there was no interest for so long, then this out of the blue. Sighing, he pulled at the loose flap of the cardboard box closest to him. Clothes. At least the first box would be easy to empty.

Rain battered Daniel's bedroom window on Saturday morning, waking him before he was ready. This time, he couldn't blame the light because his new curtains, pulled tightly shut, were thick and black. There were no boxes anywhere on the floor. The bong he'd been craving so hard on his birthday now stood on the table next to his bed and had been put to good use for much of the previous night. He rubbed his eyes and checked in the drawer next to him to see if there was any weed left. Sighing at the empty pouch, he got up and pulled on his dressing gown.

'The Scientist' chimed from his pocket and he pulled out his phone. Tom's name shimmered on the screen. Daniel rejected the call and stuffed the phone back into his dressing gown pocket, making a mental note to change his father's ringtone to something different, maybe the dreaded 'Hallelujah'. That would be just right for the old cunt. If any tune would put him off answering, it'd be that one. He looked around the living area, now clear of all boxes, and smiled at the new feeling of space before him. The sparse furnishings – a scruffy futon, two kitchen chairs and the threadbare red rug that had been in his old bedroom at his father's house – made the room seem more expansive. Daniel carried a small table from the spare room and placed it in front of the futon. The picture of his mother on the mantelpiece caught his eye. He picked it up, went to his room and lay down with it. Holding it to his chest, he fell back to sleep.

Starbucks was full of people when Daniel got there at 12:48 p.m. He ordered an espresso and stood by the counter, scanning the crowd around him. None of the other customers appeared to be alone, so he sat down on a chair that had just been vacated, facing the doorway. Couples with kids pushed through the entry way, then a group of girls, followed by a traffic warden. Daniel glanced at the clock. Waqar was five minutes late and still no sign of him. Keeping a watch on the front door, he went back to the counter and ordered another coffee.

As he sipped the last drops from his second cup, Daniel looked at his phone – no missed calls – and finally got up, ready to leave. Just then, the door opened, and a dark-skinned man stood there looking around anxiously. He was tall and slim, with a mound of bushy black hair tangled on his head. His eyes were large and searching, scanning the room. Daniel smiled and got up. He felt his heart quicken as he approached the man. As their eyes met, Daniel found it hard to form any words. This had to be him, and he was way better than he had imagined. The man walked towards him, eyes quizzical.

'Vacker?' said Daniel.

A broad smile spread on the man's face, revealing crooked white teeth a little too large for his mouth.

'Doneel? Praise be! You waited. I apologise a hundred times. My boss—'

'Well, you're here now,' mumbled Daniel, taking his hand and noticing how long his fingers were and how clammy his grip was. He took a deep breath and tried to get the thoughts straight in his head.

'My name is WaqAr, Doneel,' said Waqar. 'W-A-Q-A-R'

A family nearby got up and made to leave. Daniel gestured to Waqar to follow him over there.

'And my name is Daniel pronounced Danyel OK? Not Doneel. What can I get you to drink?' said Daniel, throwing his jacket on one of the chairs. He felt his face flush and looked away, searching for his wallet, hoping Waqar wouldn't see.

'Ahh, sorry Daniel... No, please, I will...'

'Sit,' said Daniel. 'What'll it be?' He was already walking to the counter. The idea of having this man stay with him was almost thrilling. He'd have someone to talk to every day, someone to eat with, someone to laugh with. Maybe even... His flat would feel less empty. Waqar could help with the bills. He looked back.

'Thank you. Water, please. From tap.'

Daniel returned with their drinks and handed the water to Waqar, who smiled, looking nervously at him. They sat in silence for a moment, each taking stock of the other. Waqar pulled a piece of paper from inside his canvas bag and smoothed it on the table, pushing it towards Daniel.

'Here is recent bank statement,' he said. 'This gives you confidence to rent me the room, yes?'

Daniel glanced at the paper. He pushed it back to him. 'It's not just a question of money, Waqar,' he began, hardly knowing why he was saying it. 'If we decide to share my flat, I need to know that we are, well... compatible.'

He gulped, thinking what an idiot he was being. Offer him the room. Don't frighten him off.

'This word... com...? I do not know this word.'

'I mean that we need to get along, be friends. You see?'

'I want us to be great friends. I am so friendly. We get on like burning house, yes?'

Daniel laughed and felt glad that Waqar seemed oblivious to his awkwardness.

'I know my English is not yet perfect,' said Waqar. 'This I can improve. You can help me. We can talk all the time. I love to talk. I love to read too. I have lots of English language books.'

'Where are you from, Waqar?'

'Palmyra, but my parents from Pakistan. Me, my sister, my parents, travel here as refugee. Only I made it here.'

'Where are you parents and sister now?'

'Allah has them.'

Daniel looked into Waqar's eyes. There was sadness there now, his smile gone, and were there even tears? He took hold of both his hands and said, 'I'm sorry.' These brown eyes gave him a strong sense of his mother's gaze, of her presence almost.

Waqar pulled his hands away, but stood up and came to Daniel's side of the table. He put his arms around him and kissed him on both cheeks. Daniel's face started to burn again. He glanced nervously at the other people around him, but no one seemed to be paying any attention.

'You see? We are friends,' Waqar said.

'Yes,' said Daniel, blood throbbing in his cheeks. 'Let's go. I'll show you the flat. It's nothing special.'

Daniel swung back on his chair when he heard the front door click and watched Waqar pull off his parka. He glanced out the window; it was already dark and barely four p.m. He smiled as his friend folded his scarf into a neat rectangle, laying it on the hall table and placing his gloves and keys on top. Since spring, Waqar had a coming home ritual that changed with the seasons – light scarf and hat at first, sunglasses and cap in summer, and now this autumn/winter routine. Daniel loved watching these rituals change, and this was his favourite.

'Hello, Waqar. Good day?'

'Yes, my friend. Thank you. I bring for you some buns and bread that did not sell today.' Waqar held out a plastic carrier bag. Daniel took it and placed it in the kitchen.

'You look tired,' said Daniel.

'Four o'clock is early to start, yes? I get up when it is dark, I finish work, and it is dark. I forget what daylight is.' Waqar laughed as he spoke. 'Come sit with me on the sofa. I learn more English with you. What will you teach me today?'

Waqar draped his body on the futon with a careless grace. Daniel joined him, pushing his friend's legs a little, so he could sit down without disturbing him too much. Waqar brought his legs onto Daniel's and wiggled his toes against his thigh.

'Your English is nearly as good as mine. You practise all the time. You're even correcting my grammar sometimes. What can I teach you any more?'

Waqar laughed. 'But then I go to the mosque, and it all goes again. Everyone there wants to speak their own language.'

Daniel leant over and took his friend's hand, then cupped

it in both of his, rubbing.

'Those gloves don't do much good, do they? Your hands are still like ice.'

'It is freezing today. Wind feels like spikes. This is my first winter here. Very cold.'

'OK, I have an idea... go and get changed. I will fill a hot bath for you and get you warmed up.' Daniel looked for some reaction from his friend, but Waqar's face remained impassive. 'What's more, I'm cooking tonight, for a change. It's not fair that you cook for us all the time. I bought some chicken falafel for us, and I've made rice with saffron and onions. Oh, and I have some fresh dates for after.'

'Am I hearing right?' Waqar was cupping his ears and looking up to the ceiling for answers, smiling. This was something Daniel had often seen his mother do. Her face filled his brain. Was his mother somehow channelling herself through this lovely man? Had she brought Waqar to him?

Daniel pushed him, playfully. 'OK, if you're going to be like that—'

'No, no, no. I get ready now.' He jumped up from the futon and headed towards his room. 'You are so kind, my friend. Thank you.'

Daniel smiled and went to run a bath, pouring Radox under the flowing water. An aroma of spicy menthol began to permeate the steam, filling the room. Pulling his lighter from his pocket, he lit candles that he'd placed around the bath. He agitated the water with his hand, stirring up bubbles and checking the temperature. Turning off the light and the taps, he went to Waqar's door and knocked.

'All ready,' he said. 'Enjoy. Food will be on the table in

an hour or so, take your time.'

Waqar came into the hallway, a brightly coloured beach towel wrapped around his waist. Daniel looked at it and laughed. 'Way too cold for the beach today.'

'I know,' said Waqar, laughing, poking Daniel's stomach as he walked to the bathroom. 'This is all I had in my room, and you don't want me walking around in, how you say it? My birthday clothes.'

They both laughed as Waqar closed the door behind him.

Daniel went to the kitchen and turned on the oven, taking the falafel out of the fridge to reach room temperature. Then he filled up a jug of water and took it to his bedroom. He poured the water into his bong and lit the weed he had bought earlier that day. After a few minutes, he inhaled deeply from the bong and felt his inhibitions float away from him. When his deep drags finally dissipated the smoke in the pipe, he opened his bedroom window; Waqar wouldn't approve of him smoking weed. He returned, smiling, to the kitchen.

When the falafel was in the oven, he took off his shirt and pushed his iPod into the sound dock on the kitchen island. He scrolled down the screen and found the playlist he wanted, one he'd created after hearing the traditional Syrian music that Waqar often liked to play in his room. The music started to fill the flat, and he turned the volume up a little, kicking off his shoes. He stood there for a few minutes, rubbing his finger on his lip, staring into the distance, then he pulled off his jeans. Dressed only in underwear, he tapped on the bathroom door and gently pushed it open.

Waqar lay in the bath, bubbles up to his chest, his head back against the edge of the tiled surround, eyes closed. His thick black hair was wet and clinging to his face and head, glistening in the candlelight. Daniel gazed longingly at the curls of dark hair at the top of his chest rising just below his neck, moving softly in the water with each breath. He knelt down and whispered into Waqar's ear, 'You like this music, don't you?' As he did so, he placed his hand on Waqar's chest, feeling for his nipple, enjoying the coarse wet hair against his palm. The wave of joy that was gently washing over him disappeared abruptly as he felt Waqar's body tense and sit upright, his sleepy eyes now wide.

'Dani! What are you doing?'

'Nothing, Waqar. I just wanted to keep you company. Maybe rub your back... I could join you in there...'

'No! No, Dani! I don't want this.'

Daniel stood up and took a sudden step back. Waqar's astonished expression was all he could see; it was all he could focus on. It seemed amplified, frozen in the moment. A wave of nausea washed over him.

'I'm sorry,' he said, not waiting for any response. He rushed out, closing the door behind him.

When Waqar emerged from the bathroom, he had Daniel's dressing gown wrapped tightly around himself. Daniel sat on the futon, fully clothed, his head bowed.

'The food smells good,' said Waqar. 'I'm hungry.'

Daniel said nothing. He felt chastised, disapproved of. He couldn't look at this man who'd made him feel so like his real self. He hated that he had offended him. Felt as if he'd lost something of supreme importance. Since his mother, he'd had nobody who made him feel safe, warm and loved.

'Dani, my friend, let us have no bad feeling between us,

please. Let us eat. Then let us talk. We must talk, and you must understand me. OK?'

Daniel looked up at him and smiled weakly, a sense of hope returning. 'Sure,' he said.

They ate their meal, saying little. A question now and again about each other's day, about how early the darkness descended, about the rat that Waqar had seen at the bakery where he worked. Each subject would come with its own difficult silence at the end. Daniel typically would have explained any idioms that his friend was unfamiliar with, and compliment him when he used words and phrases that were used well, but not this evening. He found it hard to look Waqar in the eye.

Daniel took the dirty dishes to the kitchen and put them in the sink. He turned on the tap and concentrated on the stream of water splashing against the plates. His heart quickened when he felt Waqar's hand squeeze his shoulder from behind. He turned to face him, looked into his wide clear eyes. Their deep brown lashes reminded him of his mother's. Waqar's eyes had the same love and trust exuding from them. A soft smile widened across Waqar's mouth, revealing a glint of white teeth.

'Come, my brother. Sit with me. I have much to tell you. Turn off the music, please,' said Waqar, gesturing to the iPod.

Daniel got up and pulled it from the dock. He returned to the futon, sitting as far from his friend as the small space would allow.

'Come closer, Dani,' Waqar pulled at Daniel's arm. 'Nothing is changed between us. Know this please: I love you.'

Daniel heaved a great sigh, and he could feel the tightness across his chest loosen. He shuffled closer to Waqar and took a deep breath as he felt his friend's arm tentatively work its way around his shoulders. Daniel took hold of Waqar's free hand and squeezed it.

'My life was hard, Dani. My path was not straight, but I have known my true way for a long time. Now I know my destiny. I think we are the same. You haven't found the way that is yours yet. We are on the same journey, my brother, you just need to know it and understand it. I feel sure we are meant to lead each other towards a true path.'

Daniel felt Waqar pull him closer. He could feel the hot breath of his friend's words caress his cheek. He craved this closeness. He craved the sound of his soft, reassuring voice. The only thing in the room was Waqar. Everything else had melted away. This is where he wanted to be. Waqar placed Daniel's hand underneath the dressing gown, against his chest.

'Feel my heart, brother.'

Daniel felt the warmth of his skin, the rough, moist hair on his palm, the soft motion of him breathing. The euphoria he had felt earlier was slowly returning, but it felt different, deeper, more visceral.

Waqar spoke quietly. 'When I was a boy, I was lost. I did not know Allah. He had not shown Himself to me and I know now this was a test. In my country, men who sleep with men are no better than dogs. This is what my father told me when he found me with my friend, Mahdi; we were fifteen or so, only boys. He beat me.'

Waqar stood up and opened the dressing gown, revealing his back to Daniel. Deep-red scars, white at the edges, corrugated the skin on his back. Daniel winced when Waqar dropped the dressing gown to the floor, and he saw the same welts on his buttocks and legs. Waqar pulled the gown back on and sat close to Daniel once more.

'He almost killed Mahdi. I think he wanted to kill me too, but my mother stopped him. My father took me to the imam, and I stayed many months with him, going to the mosque six times a day. I missed my family, at first. I missed Mahdi. I missed the closeness I had shared with him. I missed his body. My flesh was weak, Dani, but the imam showed me my mind was strong. He guided me to the light. He taught me the law of Sharia so that I took it inside me. Everything my parents tried to teach me began to make sense. Allah came to me as I became a man. Allah protects the children who are lost.'

Waqar paused. He took Daniel's hands.

'Wait here,' he said.

Waqar went to his room and returned with a book. He held it out.

'This is the Qur'an. I give it to you. This will show you your path, Dani, just as it showed my path to me. Together, we will find yours.'

Chapter Sixteen
Then

'Your post, Mr McIntyre.' Moira placed a pile of mail, neatly bound with a red rubber band, on his desk. 'Shall I bring your coffee now?'

'No thanks, Moira.' Tom stared at his screen, hardly registering what was on there. As his secretary started heading towards the door, he became aware of a faint smell of Opium wafting back from her. Alison's scent. A flood of memories came on the back of it, and he stood up, trying to inhale its last traces. Her hand was on the handle.

'Just a second, Moira.'

Tom walked around his desk and beckoned towards the sofa by the window. 'Take a seat, will you?' he said.

Moira looked at him, a perplexed expression on her face. She moved tentatively back into the room.

'Have I done something wrong?' She sat down on the edge of one of the cushions, looking tense and uncomfortable.

Tom sat opposite her in one of the armchairs. He smiled at her, trying to look reassuring.

'No, it's nothing like that,' he said. 'The thing is... well, I'm going to be moving to London. Permanently. Soon. Early May, in fact.'

'What? Are you closing the office here? Am I losing my job?' Moira looked as if she might start crying.

'No. No, your job here is safe. I have a young man, Martin Hope. He'll be starting here the week after next. He'll manage things until I decide what I want to do in the long term. Whatever happens, Moira, you'll be looked after. I promise you that.'

The phone in the reception area began to ring. Moira got up, smiling weakly. 'I'd better—'

'Yes, go,' said Tom. 'Let's talk about it more over lunch.'

Tom sat down at his desk again and pulled the rubber band from the pile of letters. One envelope stood out from the others. It was green and had a white label pasted on top of another address. Sellotape secured the ragged flap on the back. The spidery scrawl on the label was unmistakably Daniel's. A visible unevenness made the envelope look bloated, and he squeezed it; there was something soft inside. He reached for his letter opener and sliced the top open. A strong smell of patchouli leaked out as he pulled out a folded piece of lined, hole-punched paper from inside.

There was something in the fold that had been causing the bumps in the envelope. Tom had heard nothing from his son since he'd helped him move into his flat. Daniel hadn't even thanked him for the birthday card he'd sent him. This could even be the envelope he'd used for the damn card. Maybe this was his thank you note, but seven months later? Probably not. He opened the page: a few words scribbled without any heed to the lines. Attached to the bottom-right corner was a small square of red satin and glued to that was a pink feather. Tom ran his finger along the edge of the feather, wondering what it meant. The message in blue biro was very simple:

NEED TO BE ALONE FOR A WHILE. HOPE YOU

UNDERSTAND. PEACE. DANIEL

Need to be alone? He'd been alone for close on a year. Zero contact for all that time. He threw the note and envelope into the waste paper bin, but immediately fished it out again. The postmark was smudged. A second-class stamp was stuck sideways on the edge. The first line simply said MCINTYRE, no initial, no first name, no title. What is going on with you, Daniel?

Tom picked up his phone and dialled Daniel's mobile. After a few rings, his voicemail message sounded:

'You want me; you ain't got me. Try later, loser.'

Yes, it was Daniel's voice. Tom wanted to think it sounded typical, but it didn't. It was like the Daniel of semi-recent times, his latest transformation. The ugly Daniel. The unforgiving Daniel. The judgemental Daniel. The dogmatic Daniel. *Give. Me. A. Break.*

He spoke, softening his voice as best he could. 'Hi, Daniel. It's Dad. Son, can we talk? I... got your note. Can we at least have a conversa... Can we put the bad times behind us? I have stuff I need to tell you. I hope you haven't gone yet. That's if you are going somewhere. You didn't say in your note. You know I love you, right? OK, I'm not making sense. I never know what to do with these bloody things. Look... Can we just... Can we just... Daniel, I want us to be...'

Tom looked at the phone as if somehow his son would come on the line and stop him rambling on. How could he end this? What else could he say?

'What I need to tell you... what I want to say to you... well, I'd rather tell you face to face. You know? I wish we could just talk like we used to. You remember how we could tell one another anything? After your mum died? I couldn't have done it, without you. You know that, don't you? OK, well, son. Call me back—'

The phone cut him off. No more time. He slammed the phone back on its cradle and dragged his jacket off the back of his chair, picking his car key up from the dish on his desk. Moira looked up at him expectantly as he walked through reception.

'Sorry, Moira.' He glanced back absently. 'Something's come up. Lunch tomorrow? OK?'

There were only a few cars in the car park. A quiet day. Tom stood in front of his vehicle, twiddling with his key. He looked out into the road, eyeing his way out, wondering if he should make the journey. He had to. That was that. A push of the key and he was in; then he was on the road. On the motorway. The M6 was quiet. There was nothing to think about, no one to overtake. None of the usual annoyances. He hardly knew how he'd got on there. There seemed to be no journey between where he was now and where he'd started.

As he turned on his indicator and pulled off at the junction that would lead him to his son's flat, he couldn't work out how he'd got there. It was as if something had transported him. Time had shrunk, somehow. Some strange autopilot had control of him. When he pulled up outside Daniel's block, every moment – from getting into his car to arriving there – was lost in some vacuum. It didn't matter. He had to see his son.

The building looked bleak. What had attracted Daniel to this monstrosity? This place didn't improve, however many times he came here. Art Deco? Who was fooling who? Close to the building, parked near the entrance, stood a small blue Vauxhall Astra – AL1 50N – Alison. One of the wheel trims was missing, and the nearside front wing had a substantial dent in it. Oh, Daniel, what would your mother think? On the back bumper was a bright new sticker: FREE PALESTINE – ISRAEL OUT.

The Palestinian flag adorned both sides of the boot. On the rear windscreen, which had a crack in it, was a black ribbon sticker with FUCK THE TROOPS emblazoned on it. Either side of that was an Afghanistan flag. Tom scowled. As he approached the main entrance, a woman was coming out, struggling with an infant in a pushchair. Tom held the door for her, grateful for the free entry into the building. Daniel would ignore any entryphone calls from him, he was sure of that.

The area around the lifts was already looking seedy. Flyers and pizza boxes were strewn around. One of the lifts was out of service, a scrawled note announcing the fact. Tom pressed the call button on the other one and waited. Two women got out when the doors opened and looked him up and down. 'He's a bit of alright,' one of them said as he got in.

He couldn't even manage a smile. When he arrived at the third floor, a rusty bike and a discarded fridge greeted him. Is this how things were, after only nine months? He pushed the bell on Daniel's door.

There was a sound of movement behind the door and then a muffled voice. 'Who's there?'

He didn't recognise the voice. Tom pushed the bell again. The door opened a fraction, and he could see a brown hand. He put his own hand on it and felt it pull away.

'Hello. I'm Tom,' he said.

The door opened a little wider, and a brown face appeared.

'Hello,' said the man. 'My name is Waqar. You must be... Are you Dani's father?'

'I am,' said Tom. 'Is Daniel at home?' Waqar opened the door fully, beaming.

'My word,' he said. 'I'm delighted to meet you, sir. You and Dani look so alike.'

'I'm sorry. Are you Daniel's friend? I don't think he'd thank you for saying that. Is he here?'

'Not now, he is... He will be back soon. Please, come in.'

Tom went inside. This man, Vacker was it? He was dressed only in a dressing gown. It was afternoon, for heaven's sake.

'Please. This way. Take a seat. I will come right back.'

Waqar beckoned towards the living room and disappeared into the spare room. Tom looked around his son's living space. The last time he'd been here was when the removal men had moved his things into the new flat. There was a sofa that he'd never seen and two armchairs that looked as if they'd come from a charity shop. On the wall, a large, framed poster that had a lurid orange background announced: AND ALLAH IS NOT UNAWARE OF WHAT YOU DO. A caricature of a mosque was adjacent to it. Tom sat down and waited.

Waqar reappeared, dressed in jeans and a T-shirt. He had on flip-flops and a multi-coloured, crocheted cap on his head. Tom recalled this cap was known as a *kufi* from an article he'd read recently as he took stock of the young man in front of him. This man was nearly as tall as he was and easily a foot taller than Daniel. Such a handsome face. What was he doing in Daniel's flat?

'Can I get you something to drink? Some tea, perhaps?' Waqar gazed inquisitively at him.

'Yes, thank you. Tea, please. When will Daniel be home?'

'Soon. Please, I will be back in a moment with the tea.'

Tom watched him turn the kettle on and take cups from a cupboard. He got up and joined Waqar in the kitchen area.

'Have you and Daniel been friends for long?'

'Only a few months, sir. Maybe six or seven? I rent a room here, you see? Please, sit down and be comfortable. I will bring tea to you.'

Waqar sang to himself as he prepared the drinks. Every time Tom looked over at him, he seemed to glance away. He looked around the room, feeling awkward and out of place. There were two small mats, close to one another and facing the window. At the end of the sofa, close to where he sat, was a blue ceramic hookah. A smell of apples mixed with tobacco hung in the room. It wasn't hard to guess its source. Tom wondered where Daniel might be. Did he even have a job? How had he gone from knowing everything about his son to knowing nothing? They'd been so close after Alison's death.

Waqar placed two cups of black tea on the table in front of the sofa and smiled at Tom. He went back to the kitchen and returned with a carton of milk and some sugar before sitting beside Tom – a little too closely. Tom could feel Waqar's thigh against his, and he shifted away from him. There was plenty of room on the sofa; maybe this failure to observe personal space was cultural. Waqar kicked off his flip-flops and placed his bare feet on the table beside Tom's cup. Tom tried not to roll his eyes.

Rufus appeared from behind a door and came running

towards Tom. He jumped up on his lap, purring loudly.

'Hello, buddy. Long time,' said Tom tickling his throat. 'Where's Jasper? Is he hiding somewhere?'

'Oh, I'm sorry, sir. The other cat… a van hit him. Only Rufi now. And Dani, he wants to get rid of him because he makes his asthma worse. He uses inhalers a lot now.'

Tom stiffened, causing Rufus to jump to the floor.

'Jasper's dead? That's awful. When did this happen? Why didn't Daniel tell me?'

'Before I came to live here. Dani said there used to be two cats.'

'And Rufus? What does he intend to do with him?'

'I think he wants you to take him back.'

Tom could hardly believe what he was hearing. How the hell was he going to transport Rufus to Central London? He pulled at his chin, trying to imagine a miserable Rufus stuck in a cat carrier for hours in his car. Just as he lifted his cup, he heard the front door open and put it back down again. Daniel's voice emanated from the hallway. Tom felt panic and looked away from Waqar.

'Waqar, Dad's car is in the car park. Has he been…?'

Daniel was in the living room now, and Tom could see the look of disdain on his face. He was wearing a *kufi*, the same as Waqar's.

Tom stood up, meeting Daniel's frown with a smile. 'Hello, son,' he said. 'It's been a while.'

'Didn't you get my note?' Daniel's voice was terse, accusatory.

'Yes, that's why I'm here. Well, that's not the only reason. Anyway, what's with the Muslim cap?'

'How did you like the imam, Dani?' asked Waqar. Daniel scowled at Waqar and turned back to his father.

'Didn't I say that I wanted time on my own? That I wanted space?'

'Not exactly. More of a Greta Garbo – "I want to be alone."'

Tom's attempt at humour missed its mark. Both Waqar and Daniel stared blankly at him.

'For fuck's sake! If I'd wanted to see you, I'd have come to you. Could I have made it any fucking clearer?'

Waqar stood up. 'Stop this, Dani. Sit down. I will bring you tea. Then let us talk.'

'OK, sorry,' said Tom, trying to recover the situation. 'I suppose I can extrapolate all of that from your short note, but there's something I needed to tell you. And you never pick up or return my calls, so I haven't a clue if you are getting my messages. That's why I'm here.'

Daniel's face seemed to soften. He sat down on the armchair that was furthest away from where his father had been sitting, pulling off his *kufi* and folding his arms tightly. Tom sat back down, and they both sat in silence until Waqar returned with Daniel's tea.

'OK, Mr McIntyre—'

'He's Tom,' said Daniel.

'Dani, why are you so aggressive?' Waqar flashed Daniel a warning look.

Daniel ignored him and addressed Tom instead. 'What is it that's so important that you ignored what I wrote and came here unannounced?'

Tom cleared his throat. Waqar's sympathetic expression

was almost a foil to Daniel's.

'I hadn't seen you since you moved. I came to visit on your birthday, and you ignored me. I've called your phone countless times and, out of the blue, I get this note from you. You attached a pink feather. The note was passive-aggressive. You know me well enough to know I'm going to react to something like that.'

'It's all I felt like writing.'

'But you felt like finding a pink feather and some cloth and sticking it on there. Was this an alternative message?'

'Read into it what you like.'

'I don't want to read anything into it, I want you to explain what you meant. That's partly why I'm here.'

'I didn't look for it specially. It was in my things. I don't know why I put it on there. Probably thought it'd cheer up the note. So what else are you here for?'

'Well, I wanted to tell you I was moving and to give you my new details. Also, I wouldn't mind knowing what it is that I've done to make you so damn angry towards me. We always had a good relationship…'

'Where are you moving to?'

'Alright, ignore the other thing! London.'

Tom passed him a business card. Daniel took it, glanced at it and threw it onto the coffee table.

'Fancy address,' he said.

'Dani and I are going to London in a number of weeks,' said Waqar. 'Maybe we can visit you.'

Daniel glared at Waqar.

'You and Daniel would be very welcome, Waqar,' said Tom. 'Why are you going to London?'

'Waqar has friends there.'

'Finsbury Park and Bermondsey,' said Waqar.

'I'll be in my new place, off and on, from the end of this month. You are both welcome to stay with me.'

'I told you, I want space, time on my own,' said Daniel.

'Dani, you can visit. It would be rude not to. Tom, Dani will see you in London, I promise.'

'Whatever,' said Daniel.

After an uncomfortable silence, Tom said, 'I understand that you want me to take Rufus.'

'Yeah, the doctor says my asthma is worse and that cat hair is no good for me.'

'You've been around cats since you were a kid, Daniel. They never affected your asthma before. And were you ever going to tell me about Jasper?'

'They affect me now. Things change… Jasper ran in front of a car. It was soon after I moved here. Things were bad between us.'

'I'll take Rufus, of course, but he isn't going to like being trapped in a cat carrier for hours, that's for sure.'

Tom stood up and extended his hand to Waqar.
'Nice to meet you,' he said. Then turning to Daniel, 'When you've had peace and time to think, I hope we can get back to normal again.'

'Normal? Yeah right. You know all about *normal* don't you Tom?' said Daniel, his arms tightly folded.

'Daniel, I only want you to be happy. That's all I've ever wanted.

Mum would hate us to be like this. You've all but cut your sister and me from your life. Can we please be a family again?'

'Mum would've hated a lot of things.'

'Oh, Daniel—'

'Just go, will you? The cat carrier is just there.'

Waqar had wrapped Rufus in a towel and was ushering him into the carrier, the cat miaowing in loud protest.

'Alright, have it your way. Hope to see you in London.' Tom picked up Rufus and headed for the front door, but paused before opening it. Nothing. He let himself out, closing the door behind him. He waited for a few minutes, listening, but all he could hear above the mournful miaowing of the cat was the muffled sound of arguing from inside.

Tom lifted the cat carrier from the back seat of his car. He noticed Daniel's envelope on the front passenger seat and reached in for it, stuffing it into his jacket pocket. When he let himself in through the front door, Jenny was standing in the hall, her face pink and radiant. She was grinning.

'What are you doing with Rufus? Is Danny-boy going on holiday or something?'

'Ahem! More to the point, what are you doing here?' said Tom.

'Oh, Dad, I have the best news!'

'Well, it better be, to bring you all the way back from uni in the middle of the week.'

She extended her left hand to him, fingers splayed to show an engagement ring sparkling in the light. She looked fit to burst. Tom braced himself.

'What do you think, Dad? Rashid asked me to marry him, and I said yes!'

'Jenny, you're only eighteen. Can't you wait a while?'

'Nearly nineteen, and I love him, Dad. Anyway, we're not getting married until we both finish uni… not until we both get jobs, too. We're being sensible.'

Tom took her in his arms and kissed her cheek.

'You're way too young to be committing to someone,' he said.

'Remind me how old you and Mum were when you both got together,' she said, gently poking his chest.

'OK, you win. But when Mum and I got engaged… well, those were different days. As long as you're happy, darling. I'll come over to Durham at the weekend and take you both out for a meal. Clearly, I should get to know Rashid a bit better.'

'That'd be great, Dad. Thanks. Rashid will love that.'

'And his parents? How have they taken the news?'

'Well, they don't know, Dad. They wanted him to do the whole arranged marriage thing. He's not talked to them since he started uni. It's what he wants. What we both want. I've never felt so happy.'

'And you think they'll come round?'

'Who knows? I hope so. I have met them, you know, before Rashid and I were going out. We got on fine. Anyway, we'll cross that bridge. Not today, though. Today, I want to bask in being newly engaged.'

'OK, love. Let's open some champagne. You'll stay the night, won't you?

'Of course. I have loads to tell you.'

After Jenny had gone to bed, he fished out Daniel's envelope from his jacket and put it on the desk in his study. It seemed to glare at him. Tom took a sip from his glass and refilled it. Not quite enough for a full glass, so he opened a bottle of red wine and sat down at his desk again. Rufus had followed him in from the kitchen and was now rubbing himself against his legs.

'Hello, buddy. How you liking the change of scene?'

Daniel's cat. Daniel's letter. Daniel. What was he going to do about Daniel? Alison had been dead for nearly five years and for almost half of that time, Daniel had been impossible. Had he been right to let him live on his own? Who was this Waqar? Tom stared longingly at a photograph of his wife on his desk, hoping for an answer, that she might come into his head and tell him what to do. All the clarity she'd always brought him was gone. Without her, how could he ever make Daniel understand who he was, deep down?

At least the wine stopped his mind racing – another long gulp, followed by another and an unsteady refill from the second bottle that was already half gone. Red droplets fell on the envelope, and he rubbed them off with his sleeve. He picked it up and pulled out the note, now crumpled, and spread it flat on the desk as best he could. The pink feather fluttered slightly on the paper. Tom stroked it, then pulled it from the piece of red satin. The smell of patchouli reminded him of his student days – those heady days of youth when life was easier. He twirled it between his thumb and finger.

'Somehow, you know, Daniel. Don't you?'

Chapter Seventeen
Then

All the furniture from the old house looked entirely out of place. This grand flat needed opulence, antiques, beautiful things. The plain magnolia walls needed Venetian plaster, and the parquet flooring cried out for Persian rugs. It would take time, but he knew it would be wonderful; this was the place he had always dreamed about, where he imagined himself living. The Queen Mother had dined in this very dining room, looking out at the view he was looking at now, sometime during the 1960s. Plush gardens with a scattering of palm trees, no less, green lawns shaded by mature trees and shrubs, and beyond, the Thames, the old City Hall and the London Eye. All this would have greeted her, apart from the London Eye.

Tom's old dining table looked almost comical in that illustrious space. Yes, he'd have to hire an interior designer, and soon. He couldn't possibly entertain anyone here while it looked as camped-in as it currently did. If the Queen Mother, God rest her soul, could see it now, she'd do an about-turn, remember a pressing engagement, do a runner. Not nearly grand enough for Her Majesty as things stood. Even so, you couldn't fault the view, or the location. London's epicentre. He was finally where he wanted to be. If only he could have shared this with Alison. But the deal had been done.

Even without the trappings, Tom couldn't stop himself

from wandering around the flat, lingering in every room and smiling. He had left the past behind, and this all represented positive change. Here, he could begin building a new life for himself. His new offices in Pall Mall were within easy walking distance; he couldn't ask for a better commute. And Moira was managing the other office very well with the help of the new chap. Next on the cards was a New York office, and from there, who knew? While this place had its makeover, he would spend most of the time scouting out locations stateside. Yes, life would be good again. Daniel would come round and be a good son again, eventually, and Jenny was doing well at university. He'd make everything peachy for them all.

Of course, all this had to be celebrated. Champagne was chilling. He took a glass from a cupboard in the kitchen and pulled one of the bottles of Dom Pérignon from the fridge, carrying both on a tray to the living-room. He admired the label before he uncorked it: 1998, such a good vintage and so lucky to get a case of it at such a fabulous price. It would be better to cellar it and let it increase in value, but wine futures were only for those who didn't want to enjoy the wine for themselves. Clearly not him. The cork came out with a soft sigh, just as it should, and he poured slowly, at an angle, thinking of the cretinous people who had no idea how to open or pour champagne properly.

As he sipped, it occurred to him that he had not tested out the music equipment since the removal men had left, so he powered it up and searched the menu. He had to hear what 'Hallelujah' sounded like with these new acoustics. And yes, it sounded great. Better than in the old place, but it would be better still when he got his audio-visual people in to integrate the systems. It was OK for now. Everything would be wonderful in time. He flicked through his music library, trying different songs for size, and before he knew it, the bottle of 1998 was empty. Better open another one – he was celebrating, after all. What would be the payback for this little bit of heaven? All debts settled, hopefully. Enjoy the spoils, Tom, while they last.

Back in the kitchen, another bottle opened, he heard the phone ring in the hallway. He left the champagne on the worktop and went to answer it, wondering who could have his new number.

'Hello? Tom McIntyre speaking.'

'Good afternoon, Mr McIntyre. Vincent on the front desk here. I have your son Daniel and his friend here to see you. Shall I send them up, sir?'

Tom paused for a second. His heart quickened. He took a deep breath. 'Yes, Vincent. Send them up, please.'

Putting down the phone, he picked up the bottle from the kitchen before returning to the living room and refilling his glass. It would take them a few minutes to get to his door. He drank the champagne back in one gulp and poured another. Again, he drank it back and was pouring a third when the bell tinkled on its coil in the hall. Tom put down his drink and went to answer the door.

As he opened the door, he saw Waqar grinning at him. Daniel stood a few feet behind, expressionless.

'Hello, Mr McIntyre,' said Waqar, extending his hand to Tom. Tom took his hand. 'Call me Tom,' he said. 'Come in, please.'

Daniel followed his friend. 'Hello, Tom,' he said,

brushing past his father. 'And you can call me Dad,' said Tom.

Daniel shrugged. He and Waqar stopped halfway along the hall, and Daniel turned to his father. 'This must have cost you a bomb,' he said, dispassionately.

'I did downsize,' said Tom.

'Your new flat is charming,' said Waqar. 'Will you show us around, please?'

'Of course, but first, come through to the living room. Let me get you both something to drink. How about a glass of champagne? I just opened one to celebrate moving here.'

Tom ushered them to the living room and noticed Daniel eyeing the two champagne bottles on the table. Tom felt his cheeks colour as he picked up the empty bottle.

'Could I please have a glass of water?' said Waqar.

Daniel was looking out through the French windows. 'I'll try some of your expensive champagne.'

'Won't you have a glass of champagne to christen the new place, Waqar?'

'I don't drink alcohol, Tom. We can toast you with water. You don't want champagne, do you, Dani?' Waqar was smiling. 'May we sit down?'

'Yes, please do. I'll be right back.'

'Water for me too, Tom,' said Daniel.

Tom heard his music stop as he threw the empty Dom Pérignon bottle into the recycling bin. Had Daniel switched it off, or had it stopped of its own accord? Returning with two glasses of water, he noticed two backpacks in the hallway. Had he told them they could stay, all those weeks ago? Yes, he probably had. Or maybe they had other plans. Why had Daniel acquiesced to this Waqar? If he'd taken a drink, he might be less touchy. This was going to be a long afternoon. The sound of murmured conversation stopped as soon as he entered the room.

'There you are, lads,' said Tom, handing them each a glass of water. He topped up his champagne. 'How was your journey? I forgot you were coming. To be honest, I don't even remember you saying you *were* coming. Did you drive or come by train?'

'We hitchhiked,' said Daniel.

'Yes, and Dani refused to get in any of the lorries that offered us lifts, so it took us a long time,' said Waqar, glancing accusingly at his friend.

'You should have driven, Daniel. There's plenty of residents' parking here, so it's easy. Think about that for next time.'

'I sold the car. Anyway, who knows if there will be a next time? I don't care for London that much.'

'Your mum's car? Oh, no! Why? If you needed the money, I could have helped out. I hope you got a good price for it. And surely you will want to come to London to see me occasionally.'

'My car,' said Daniel, firmly. 'She gave it to me before she died.'

'Sorry,' said Tom. 'I just think of it as hers. I know it was yours to do with as you like. How long are you planning to stay in London?'

'Three or four days,' said Waqar. 'I have some friends here I want to visit. We are hoping we can stay here with you, Tom, like you said we could.'

'Of course, but I only have one spare room. Don't worry,

though. There's a hotel attached to this building – you probably noticed it when you arrived – I can easily get a room for one of you there.'

'That won't be necessary,' said Daniel. 'Waqar and I are happy to share a room.'

Waqar nodded his assent.

'There is only one bed,' said Tom. Was this what he wanted? Was Daniel…?

'It is fine, Tom. Where I am from, I am used to sleeping on the floor on a mat. I have a mat with me.' Waqar smiled earnestly at him.

'If you're sure,' said Tom. 'I can easily pop out and get a camp bed for one of you.'

'There is no need to go to that trouble. We will be perfectly comfortable. I feel sure,' said Waqar.

'Alright, let me show you round the place. I only moved in a week ago, so it's all a bit makeshift. It'll be a lot better the next time you come to visit.' Tom picked up his glass and waited for them to follow.

Daniel was leaning on the desk, laughing. Vincent was telling him one of his stories, no doubt. Tom emerged from the lift and approached them, and Daniel stood upright, his expression hardening. Robert grinned from his chair behind Vincent.

'Good afternoon, Vincent, Robert,' said Tom. 'Any packages for me?'

'None as yet, Mr McIntyre,' said Robert. 'We'll be sure to bring up any that arrive.'

Tom turned to Daniel. 'Where's Waqar?'

'He's visiting some friends in Bermondsey,' said Daniel.

'Didn't you want to join them?' said Tom.

'Not really. They're all Pakistani friends, and they like to gabble on in Urdu. I don't want to feel like a spare part.'

'You can come and hang out with me at my new office, if you like. Maybe grab some lunch beforehand?'

'Nah, it's OK. I got stuff I want to do. I'll see you when you get home.' He was already walking towards the lift. 'See ya, Vince, Rob.'

Tom watched him disappear into the lift, said his goodbyes to the porters and headed out into the street. What could he do to get Daniel back onside? Why was this Waqar going off on his own every day? He was up to something. Three days they said they would be staying, and it was already five. The spare room was beginning to smell like a dosshouse. He couldn't even have a quiet drink without getting the evil eye from one of them. And he was sure he could smell weed – or at least weed being covered up with incense. Only when Waqar was out, of course. He probably felt the same about weed as he did about alcohol. Waqar the boss of Daniel and Daniel the boss of me. Quite a comedy. His mobile rang in his pocket; it was Jenny.

'Hello, love, how are you? How's uni?'

'I'm alright, Dad. Are you around tomorrow?'

'Yes, why?'

'Oh, just I have to come to London for the day. I have an interview for a summer internship that sounds hopeful. Planning to get the train in the morning then head back here early evening. Want to take me to lunch?'

'Sure, I'd love to. What's the internship, and where?'

'Brokerage firm in the City. Booths. You know it?'

'Yes, good firm. But what about teaching? I thought you had your heart set on that.'

'Always best to keep my options open, and the pay's better for what my qualifications will be.'

'Can't fault that logic. Voraciousness versus vocation. You're a greed monger just like me,' Tom laughed.

'Cheeky!'

'Oh, by the way, your brother's here, visiting. Shall I invite him along?'

'Danny? In London? God, what dragged him away from Carlisle? I haven't seen him for ages. Is he still stacking shelves for Tesco?'

'He's here with a friend. Waqar – he seems to be the reason he's come. As far as I know, he's on the dole. He's not very communicative, as you know.'

'Yeah, invite the weirdo along. It'll be good to see him, I suppose.'

'Maybe I'll buy lunch in and then he'll have no choice over whether to join us or not. You might get to meet the mysterious Waqar too, if he's not off out on one of his secret missions.'

'I can't wait. See you tomorrow, Dad. Have to dash. Bye.'

And she was gone. Tom would have to call in at Fortnum's on the way home and get some nice things for tomorrow's lunch. Best keep Daniel in the dark until the last minute, so he wouldn't be able to make any excuse to avoid his sister. Daniel had grown as far apart from her as from him. Maybe he and Jenny together could break through his shell.

Waqar came into the kitchen and stood watching Tom placing

canapés onto his best china.

'That looks nice, Tom,' he said.

'Thanks, Waqar. I'm preparing lunch. I hope you and Daniel will join me. Jenny, Daniel's sister, is coming to visit.'

'Lovely. Yes, I am staying here today with Dani. I have completed all my mosque visits. Tomorrow, we will head back to Carlisle. I would like to meet Jenny. I am glad of this chance before we leave.'

'Where is Daniel? I haven't seen him so far this morning. Is he still asleep?'

'No, he is downstairs chatting to the doormen. He likes the one, Vince, I think his name is. They have been keeping each other company while I have been busy in Bermondsey and Finsbury Park.'

'What sort of things have you been doing there that you can't do in the mosque in Carlisle?'

'Oh, there have been some very influential imams who have travelled there this week to teach. I wanted very much to learn from them. I have enjoyed the experience very much. These clerics come only to the big London mosques. I did not want to miss the chance to hear them speak.'

Good little Muslim, aren't you, Waqar? What ideas are they filling your head with? He recalled the *kufi* he'd seen Daniel wearing back at his flat in Carlisle. At least Daniel seemed to be steering clear of wherever it was that Waqar was going. Hopefully, he would keep his distance from all that fucking misguided claptrap.

'Nice. I'm glad it's been a useful visit for you. Will you help me take the food to the dining room? Jenny will be here soon.'

They were hardly out of the kitchen when the doorbell rang. Tom set the plates on the table and went to answer it. Jenny stood there smiling, with Rashid by her side and Daniel a few steps behind.

'Look who I bumped into downstairs,' she said, looking back at her brother, who was looking as deadpan as ever.

Tom grinned. 'Hello, you two. I had no idea I was going to see you today, Rashid! Come in, future son-in-law. Was it a pleasant surprise to see your sister, Daniel?'

'It was a surprise,' he replied. 'You could have told me she was coming. I might have smartened myself up.'

'You look fine, silly,' said Jenny. 'Doesn't he, Rashid?'

'Yeah,' said Rashid. 'And shorter than me, so all good. Great to see you again, Tom. Yeah, I wanted to see your new pad, so I tagged along. Not much doing at uni at the moment, so I was glad to have something interesting to do.'

Waqar stood at the end of the hall, waiting for them. He nodded at Jenny, introducing himself. Rashid approached Waqar and offered his hand.

Waqar took his hand and said, '*Adaab, mere Dost. Khuda sada tumhare saath rahe. Waise bhi tumhare naam ka matlab sacha yaqeen hai, aap ko ye sacha pata hoga?*'

Rashid looked confused. 'Sorry, matey. I only speak English.'

'Ah, sorry,' said Waqar. 'I just asked if you knew that your name meant "Of the true faith" in Arabic. I thought maybe you spoke Urdu, like me.'

They all laughed. Tom ushered them all to the table. 'Let's eat,' he said.

'Looks lovely,' said Jenny, sitting at the table. 'Sit by me,

Danny. We have a lot to catch up on.'

Daniel ignored her and took a seat next to Waqar. Daniel appeared to be more interested in Rashid than in his sister. He was smiling and chatting to him in a way that reminded Tom of how he was with Vince. Perhaps he was like that with Waqar – at least when they didn't know he was around, listening. Why were strangers more worthy of Daniel's good side than his father or his sister? The more time spent with his son, the more confused and confounded he felt. Daniel would be gone by this time tomorrow, and he would be no further forward, on no better terms with him than he had been. It would have been better if Waqar had not come, if he had been allowed to spend time with his son alone. But he couldn't stop thinking that, had Waqar not wanted to come to London, he would never have seen Daniel at all. And would that have been so bad? At least this way, he got to see he was alright. The alternative was worry, of course.

Daniel stood behind Waqar at the front door. Both had their backpacks on. 'Goodbye, Tom. Thank you so much for your hospitality. Perhaps we will meet again sometime,' said Waqar. He extended his arms to Tom and pulled him in for a cursory hug.

Tom patted Waqar's back and skirted around him to Daniel. 'Bye, son,' he said, arms stretched out to embrace him.

Daniel stiffened, keeping his arms firmly at his sides. 'Bye,' he said, tersely. He pulled the door open and was gone.

Waqar still stood there, looking at Tom sympathetically. Tom turned his back on him and walked towards the dining room. He heard the front door click shut before he got there.

Chapter Eighteen
Then

A soft breeze wafted a bitter green smell of bracken towards Daniel as he stirred from his dozing. He sat up, admiring the shimmering water of the lake below. Waqar lay on the grass beside him, eyes closed, the faintest of smiles on his lips. This caused Daniel to smile too. *What are you dreaming of, my friend?* Daniel wanted to reach out and touch his face. Instead, he lay back down again and gazed up into the cloudless blue sky. A perfect heaven above them. Here, for the first time, it felt as if there was no one else in the world but the two of them. Was eternity giving him a clue?

It had taken two hours to trek to this spot high on the fellside, and he thought of Waqar calling a cheerful 'hello' to every hillwalker that they had encountered, wishing them well as they passed. It was impossible not to like Waqar. Daniel had seen this from the first time they met. He still yearned for his touch and wished again that they could be together in the way he often imagined; he wanted to announce to the world that they belonged to each other. Fresh hillside air filled his lungs and left him, like a sigh, and he edged his body closer to his sleeping friend.

Waqar would be gone soon; he had told him that his path was clear, and he was determined to follow it. Daniel would have to follow his own path soon enough. As long as it brought him back to Waqar, he would be happy. Pakistan was such a long way away. So hard to imagine, especially on this breezy green hillside – a distant sun, baking sand, fierce heat, strange smells and foreign, warbling calls to prayer; how would all this feel? How would he cope in a land so far away, so different to here? He lifted up his skinny arm and stared at the pale skin with its covering of thin dark hairs. Waqar's skin was dark – prepared for that climate. Maybe he should go to the tanning salon in town.

Daniel stood up and spread his arms out, imagining they were wings and that he could fly into the sky so he might admire his friend from above. Then he could swoop down, pick him up and have him cling to his neck as he soared down to the lake, skimming the water with bare feet. He wanted to show Waqar his own inner power and convince him to stay here in England and follow a different path. His path. A happy road where the world's troubles were not theirs to solve. Where his God, their God, did not disapprove of their love. But Waqar's words could always overpower his. Waqar's ideas were always clear and well-formed, always rich with truth and conviction. Why did they ever have to be apart?

For a second, he thought he felt Waqar's eyes on him and immediately felt ridiculous, but when he turned around, his friend was still asleep on the grass, his face a picture of peace. Daniel sat down beside him and rested his hand on Waqar's thigh. His friend remained still, and Daniel leant in towards him, bringing his face close to Waqar's so that his cheek almost touched the black beard that had grown thick on his dark skin. He could feel Waqar's warm breath against his lips and wanted to press his mouth against his. Daniel's hand was now between

Waqar's open legs, but when he felt his friend stir, he withdrew it as if from a flame. Daniel pulled himself away and stared up at the sky again.

'Hello, Dani. Have I been asleep?' Waqar turned to face him.

'Yeah, you were out for the count. I nearly put a mirror to your mouth.'

'Mirror? Why?'

'That's how you check if someone is breathing.'

'You are funny, Dani.' Waqar was rubbing his eyes. 'Was I asleep long? I was dreaming of heaven. Allah was holding me. It was beautiful.'

'What did Allah look like in your dream?'

'More of a feeling... a presence. I could feel Him holding me. We can't truly know how He looks until we are there with Him. We will meet Him together. We will understand Him together. I knew it was Him because I felt... euphoria... it flooded over me. He told me that we are following the pure path, the path to greatness, to glory, to love.'

'I wish I was that sure... this is a huge step for me.'

Waqar's expression hardened as he got up on his knees and leant over Daniel.

'We've been over this a hundred times, Dani. You are sure – then you are not sure. What more can I tell you? There is nothing for us in this world. Allah has chosen us. We have agreed to do his work. This is the only way we can be together through eternity. You want us to be brothers in heaven, don't you?'

Daniel gazed into Waqar's earnest eyes, looked longingly at his thick curly hair, framed by a perfect blue sky. Nothing for us in this world? Wasn't this enough? He propped himself up a little and brought his face level with his friend's.

'I want to spend forever with you – you know that. I believe Allah wants us to be together, and this is his plan for us. These are such big steps he wants me – us to take. Can we not be together here... now... properly? Just until we start our journey?'

'Properly? What is not proper about this? Our journey has already begun, Dani. It started the moment we became friends. The moment we became brothers. We are approaching the most fantastic part of our road. There are only a few weeks left now—'

'A few weeks for you. Six months for me! Why can't I travel to Karachi with you? Why do we have to go separately? I've never travelled so far on my own.'

'I told you, Dani. I need to prepare the ground for you. I need to make sure that you are certain about this. I need to assure the leaders there that you are ready and that you are committed to our cause. They don't accept strangers at face value. They know about you from the emails I have sent, but they need to hear it from my mouth, they need to feel my sincerity.'

Waqar paused and looked at Daniel squarely, waiting for a response. Daniel rocked from side to side, nodding. Would he ever hear from Waqar again? Maybe this was his way of escaping him.

'You have to buy the tickets soon. I need to arrive there on the tenth of June. This is what I have agreed with our sponsors. You must come, six months later, then I will know enough to be your sponsor. And I have to take the money with me. Have you fixed that?'

'Yes, I can transfer it to your bank account whenever you want.'

'No, Dani. Cash. Remember? I need to take cash.'

'OK. We'd better head back. It'll be getting dark in an hour or so.'

There was only one small bag of clothes, with a tattered copy of the Qur'an on top. The room looked bare; random beads of Blu Tack gave clues to where the posters had once been. His bookcase – once full of English, geography and religious philosophy books – stood empty. Waqar sat on top of the bare mattress, arms clutching his legs and his head resting on his knees. He seemed to be concentrating on the bulging black binbags at the end of the bed.

'What's in the rubbish bags?' asked Daniel.

'Blankets, books, things. You'll take them to the charity shop?'

'Are you keeping nothing? What about the presents I gave you? Your watch? The gold chain? The DVDs, the music?'

'None of that stuff is necessary, Dani. You know that. We can't take it with us, can we?'

Daniel turned away and left the room. He heard Waqar move off the bed to follow him. For once, he wanted to be on his own. Facing this separation felt like too much. It even masked the dread of the journey that had been haunting him all these months, the fear of the camp in Pakistan. Waqar was his world, and now Waqar's world was his. A speeding train was pulling his friend away, leaving a blur of their life behind. Waqar had brought all these joys to his life, only to take the most important part of it away.

'What's wrong, Dani?'

He felt Waqar behind him, his arms wrapping around his chest, and his anxiety seemed to disappear at once. He placed his hands on Waqar's and squeezed them before turning to face him.

'Waqar, I love you, and I want us to be one, always. You know how I feel about you, and I can hardly bear to be apart from you, even for those months – time that you say will pass quickly, but will seem like a lifetime to me. Can we please travel together? I'm afraid to go to Pakistan without you.'

Daniel's eyes were pooling with tears. Waqar placed his hands on Daniel's shoulders and pulled him closer.

'Be brave, brother,' he said. 'I will be in Pakistan making things right for you. I will be there when you step off the plane and for every step of the way after that. Allah will give you courage and keep me in your heart. See it as a test. I will be with you always, through God. It is Allah who holds us together and Allah who will bless us when we join Him in *Jannah*.'

Waqar wiped tears from Daniel's eyes and gently kissed his mouth. When Daniel tried to respond, he pulled away from him.

'That is all Allah will allow,' said Waqar. 'We are brothers here together. In *Jannah*, who knows?'

'OK, Waqar. If you want me to wait, I'll wait. But why will Allah allow us to be together in *Jannah*? He doesn't allow it here, does he? Here, we are no better than dogs in the eyes of Islam. You said so yourself.'

'In paradise, we will not be judged, brother. There we will

have whatever rewards we desire for the great deeds we will do here on earth. Paradise will be whatever we want it to be. Eternal happiness. No more tears, brother. This world's rules are there simply to test us.'

'You're so sure. I trust you, Waqar, you know I do. There's no one in the world I trust more.'

'I am glad, Dani. This last night here, I will sleep in your bed, with you. I will hold you until morning. This will let you know how things will be in *Jannah*. It is for this reason that Allah showed us this road we must take. Come, brother. Let's eat.'

The clock by the bed glowed: 3.12 a.m. Waqar was snoring gently beside him, his arm draped around Daniel's waist. Daniel had seen every minute pass since they had lain down together shortly after midnight. Time was moving slowly, but strangely fast too. Each moment dragged, but every hour brought him closer to separation, and this made the night move quickly. This arm, this closeness, would be a distant memory the next time he lay down on his bed. This nearness would be gone. The thought of this closeness being his through eternity was the only thing that kept him from going out of his mind.

Ten minutes passed, and he put his hand on Waqar's, enjoying Waqar's warm breath on his neck, the mumblings he uttered through sleep. Foreign words, words that were in his friend's brain, but meant nothing to him. Waqar was at peace, surely discussing his journey with Allah. Would Allah help him in the same way? Of course, he would. His other hand drifted to Waqar's stomach, bare, covered in soft hair, swelling with each breath. His hand quivered against the warm skin. He reached further, felt the band of his underwear. He pressed his fingers against the bulge of the cloth lower down, wishing to feel a response even close to the one he was experiencing at that moment.

He turned to face Waqar and drew close to his face, so that their noses touched. He kissed him gently, pleased that he didn't pull away from him. His soft breathing almost sounded like pleasure. Daniel pressed his body against him and began to cry. All this meant nothing if there was no loving response. If only Waqar had woken him up and touched him in this way, everything would be perfect. He turned over again and looked at the clock: 3:47 a.m. He pulled Waqar's limp arm and placed it around his waist, closing his eyes, hoping for sleep.

Terminal Five felt like one of those faceless shopping centres multiplied by ten. A warehouse of people dodging one another with their luggage trolleys. False exclamations of 'excuse me' and 'I'm sorry'. It was as alien to Daniel as all his imaginings of Pakistan had been. He hated this place. It represented separation, distance, departure. The day had come. That dreaded day when he would say goodbye. His mother filled his brain. That goodbye had been the most wrenching one he'd known, and here it was again. Why was life like this? Waqar was right. Daniel almost knew he would never hold him again. Not the way he had last night. Not the way he wanted. Waqar was right.

At least they didn't need a trolley. Waqar's bag was nothing to speak of. A holdall. 'Carry-on baggage,' the girl at the desk had said. A few clothes? He'd no idea what was in there, but Waqar clung to it as if it was his life. The check-in girl had asked if there was anything in it that was against regulations. He couldn't remember what the regulations were, but Waqar had said, 'No.' So what did it matter, anyway? What was in there couldn't be part of their final journey here in this world. He knew that much. He knew they'd agreed their paths would join at the same point and that they'd be together forever within hours of fulfilling their purpose. Waqar had been clear about that. But Tom. He'd have to deal with him. Tom wasn't for now, however. Waqar would be gone soon. Focus on that.

'Let's have some tea before I go through the security checks,' said Waqar. He pointed to a Costa, crowded with people. They'd first met at Starbucks.

So much time had passed since then. Daniel nodded, trying to remember their first meeting. How did they come so far in such a short time? Was falling in love this easy? It wasn't easy, though. It was fucking hard, and he didn't even know if it made him happy. All he knew was, he couldn't fight it. He didn't want to fight it. All he wanted was to be with Waqar, no matter what. Waqar pushed ahead and placed his bag on a spare seat at a table for two. The man sitting there eyed him suspiciously. Waqar turned on his best beaming smile.

'Sir, would you mind sitting at the bar? I am saying goodbye to my dearest friend and we would like to sit together, here.'

The man scowled at them, but got up anyway and let Daniel sit. 'Wait here,' said Waqar. 'I'll get some tea.'

Ordinary people sat around at the tables, close to where Daniel was sitting. Holidaymakers, families, businesspeople. The place reeked of disappointment. Yet smiles were everywhere, railing against reality. Did anyone feel like he did? Maybe this was a dream, and he was still embracing Waqar in bed. Please let it be a dream. His lungs were constricting; his heart was pushing through his chest. This moment was killing him inside. Was he to sit here and drink tea? Don't leave me, Waqar! Please, don't let me stay here on my own.

Waqar returned with a tray that held a pot of tea, two cups and cellophane-wrapped biscuits. He was smiling. It was that same smile, that first smile, the winning smile he first saw him give. Daniel felt a sense of the first day they met course through him. He had to stop himself thinking this was the last time he'd see this smile. How could it possibly be the last time? He would see this smile now, then and forever. Shut up, Danny. Your mind is fooling you, stupid. Waqar had said it would and that he must fight it.

Waqar sat down and rubbed his foot against Daniel's. 'Not long now,' he said.

'And not long until we see each other again,' said Daniel.

Waqar lowered his voice, almost to a whisper, 'That's right. When we see each other again, the sun will be shining. Our future will be clear. Our journey's end will be close. Paradise beckons, my brother.'

'Every moment will be like an eternity until I see you again.'

'Those moments are worthless, Dani. We have forever together. What can compare to that?'

Forever? Really? What made Waqar so sure? He wanted it to be true, he wanted to be sure. But Waqar was intent on doing this and nothing he could do or say would stop him. Surely he had some fears, some doubts? His own fears and doubts were as many as the stars. Maybe when they were both in the camp, Waqar might change and decide against this whole mad plan. The only thing Daniel was sure of was that life without Waqar would not be worth living. He would have to take the leap. Maybe this eternity would be theirs. No point saying this to Waqar. Faith, Daniel. You must have faith.

'I just want it to be over. I don't want to think about what we have to do. I don't honestly want to do whatever it is I have to do. I know I have to do it to be clean and to have our life in *Jannah*. You must be frightened too. Are you not scared, Waqar?'

'No, brother. I am not afraid. I do not want you to fear this either. Take courage from our love, our friendship, our brotherhood. Know that I would never harm you, never leave you, never ask you to do anything that wasn't right, that wasn't the best thing for us both. I leave you today for a purpose. Our shared purpose. I'm not afraid. I have you. I have you for always, as you have me.'

They both looked at the departures board that was adjacent to where they were sitting. BA Flight 125 to Doha showed it was ready for boarding.

'That's my flight. I still have to go through security,' said Waqar.

'Yes, but we have five minutes or so. The security gates are just there, and the departure gate is close.'

'I can't miss my flight. Come on, Dani. If there's a queue at security, I might miss it. Let's go.'

Waqar stood up and picked up his bag. Daniel looked up at him, admiring his tall stature, his curly black hair falling over his dark features. He stood up and faced him.

'Let's walk to security together,' he said.

The entry way was up ahead. There were already crowds of people queuing at it. Not all for Waqar's flight, Daniel knew, but they'd be waiting for one of the many flights on the other side, and Waqar would have to queue along with them.

'You'd better go,' he said.

'In a moment,' said Waqar. 'Let us spend these last seconds together.' He dropped his bag on the ground and pulled Daniel towards him, whispering, 'I love you. Know that.'

'You are my world,' said Daniel, also in hushed tones. 'Life will be impossible until I see you again.'

'Be strong. I'll be with you. Allah will be watching you, keeping you safe for me. Six months is nothing, brother. Paradise is waiting for us.'

Waqar picked up his bag. Daniel saw his eyes were wet with tears and watched him rub them with his free hand.

Daniel put his arms around him and kissed his face with force, again and again.

'Stop it,' said Waqar. 'People are watching.'

He pulled away and walked towards the security gate. Daniel stood watching him, aching to follow. Waqar walked through the gate, without looking back.

Chapter Nineteen
Then

The call to prayer began to push its way into his consciousness before the first weak fingers of light touched the rough cloth that covered him. Even after so many days, he still wasn't used to the acrid smell of sweat and food-tinged gases that made their way into his nostrils from the sleeping bodies lying on mats that were scattered around the room like a disassembled patchwork blanket. Sleep had evaded him for many hours, and he glanced over at Waqar, who was just beginning to stir. He closed his eyes quickly and turned to face the wall.

'Wake up, my brother. We must pray. Today is a momentous day for you, Dani.'

Daniel groaned and turned over again to face Waqar, scrunching his eyes, hoping to give the impression that he had just awoken. Waqar was grinning at him as he scratched his thick black hair. It was hard to get used to him with the long beard and the much longer hair. He'd said it was the look of the prophet, and it was his way of respecting God. Daniel's stomach was churning, and he could feel a band of panic tighten in his chest. None of this felt right, and Waqar seemed different. There was a detachment to him that didn't make sense after six months apart.

'This day has come so fast, Waqar,' he said. 'I don't think I'm ready yet…'

Waqar laughed, stretching over to take Daniel's hand. 'No one feels ready the first time, dear brother. Allah will guide you. Allah will help me guide you. Together, we will make you ready. When this day is over and you wake tomorrow to pray anew, you will feel different. You will *be* different, Dani. *Allahu Akbar*.'

Words, just words. It was as if he was reeling them off a rehearsed script. Ever since arriving in Pakistan, he'd craved some closeness from his friend, a sign that he still felt the same about him. His feelings for Waqar had grown like bamboo in a rainforest; he couldn't stop himself craving his company. Now he was here, he mostly wanted them to be alone together. Waqar stood up and pulled Daniel's arm. The other men in the room were also stirring, and one opened the door, allowing the smell of something rotten to leak into the already rancid space.

'Come, we must go to the well and wash,' said Waqar.

They both picked up their prayer mats and headed outside into the softly rising light. The well thronged with men anxious to cleanse themselves in preparation for the first worship of the day. The sky, pulled apart by sinewy clouds, was beginning to turn a pale orange. Daniel gazed at it for a few seconds, wishing he could push back the sun and keep this day from dawning. There was almost a sense of safety in the dark. Here light always brought a vicious brutality with it.

After prayer, Daniel and Waqar went to one of the tables outside and joined the other men for breakfast. Mustard leaves and cornbread lay in piles on large tin plates, and everyone clustered around them, snatching as much as they could. Waqar split his portion in two and passed half to Daniel.

'Come, Dani, you must eat,' he said. 'Today will be hotter

than yesterday, or the day before, and you must be strong. We will go soon, and this will be our only food for many hours. Drink plenty of the water too.'

Daniel pushed it away, only taking a gulp from his cup of water. 'I'm not hungry. I'll be fine.'

'Eat!' Waqar's eyes hardened as he thrust the food back at his friend. 'Or I'll make you.'

Waqar's eyes fixed on him in a cruel stare; there was violence in them that Daniel had never seen before. Daniel forced some bread and leaves into his mouth and chewed quickly, swallowing them down with some more water. He tried to fight off an inexorable push of nausea that was spiralling up from his gut, but was unable to stop himself. He jumped up and ran over to a nearby bush where he vomited noisily, retching and gasping with each new spasm from his stomach.

Waqar came running after him. 'You make me feel ashamed, my brother. Why do you do this?'

Daniel turned towards him. 'Waqar, you think I can help it? That I can stop myself throwing up when everything in my gut says I must? I feel sick to the bottom of my soul. I've been vomiting since I got off the plane.'

'You display your weakness like a badge. I brought you here. I vouched for you. I have spent the last six months convincing them that you are a good jihadi. You are making me into a fool. The others will gossip to the commanders about this.'

Daniel pushed his hands against his head. No one had seen him, apart from Waqar. Why was he being such a cunt to him? Plenty of others had thrown up, and no one had even turned to look in their direction. This place was filthy; there were bound to be stomach bugs and the like. Back off, Waqar.

But he forced a smile. 'I'm sorry. I'll make you proud,' he said. 'We are joined forever. I'll never forget the promise we made to each other. Together we are one.'

Daniel wondered if his eyes betrayed him the way that Waqar's did. Waqar pulled Daniel close to him and kissed both his cheeks, gazing earnestly into his eyes. For the first time, Daniel felt he saw something of the man he'd held in the departures lounge at Heathrow all those months ago. Daniel felt his anger wane as he lost himself in that familiar velvety-brown stare. The closeness of his body caused a throbbing in Daniel's groin; he wanted to pull him nearer and hold him, even if just for a moment. There had been nothing but coldness and remoteness since he'd arrived in this awful place. 'Waqar, I lo—'

Waqar stopped him, pushing his long fingers against Daniel's lips. 'I know,' he said. 'Come. We must go.'

The road from the encampment was makeshift and rocky. Daniel looked back at the armed men guarding the gates as the canvas topped open-backed truck he was in rumbled away from their stony faces. As they drove further away, he saw the camp gates open again and a small jeep appear, which followed them, remaining several thousand metres behind.

'The infidel is in that vehicle,' said Waqar. 'I saw them put him in it before we left the camp.'

'I know.' Daniel kept his eyes fixed on the jeep, afraid to look at his friend. He felt sure the cruelty had returned to his eyes, and he didn't want to remind himself that it even existed.

It was for his own good, he knew that. There was no room for love in this awful place. He had to find strength from somewhere, and fast.

The mountains receded into a cloudless unforgiving sky, and in the near distance, heat vapours skewed the harsh brown landscape, making the day seem even more surreal. The fetid smell of stale sweat and flatulence, increasing with each hot kilometre, no longer assaulted Daniel's nostrils; it was finally becoming part of the dark fabric of his new life here. He looked back into the crowded dimness of the truck and noticed, for the first time, two of the men clutching something long and thin, wrapped in burlap. Daniel quickly turned away from it and focused on the dusty road stretching far behind him.

Around midday, when only an edge of the shimmering sun was visible in the sky from the back of the truck, they ground to a halt, and a few seconds later the jeep following them stopped too. The driver of the truck jumped out of his cab with his prayer mat and everyone jumped from the back clutching theirs. Daniel was glad to escape the cramped sticky bleakness of the truck. They all knelt, facing east, and recited the *Zuhr* prayer. When they were finished, the driver shouted something in Urdu. Daniel knew enough by now to know that this was telling them they could have something to drink. One of the men pulled a large plastic canister of water from the back and everyone clustered around it. Daniel joined them, eager to quench his thirst. The water was thick and warm. The only thing in its favour was that it was wet. No wonder he felt sick half the time. Some of the men were splashing it over their faces, before being snarled at and told it was for drinking only.

'We are about an hour's drive from the place now,' said

Waqar. 'This day will be in your past soon, and you will look upon it as one that brought you closer to God, Dani. You will be overjoyed and never fear a task like this ever again.'

Daniel nodded. Waqar's smile was soft, sincere, almost comforting, and he tried his best to return it, desperately hoping that Waqar couldn't see the fear that was eating up his guts. His water cup quivered in his hand, so he grasped it with his other hand, trying to steady it. The jeep had stopped some distance further back. No occupants were visible. They must be at the rear of the vehicle, drinking their own water. That was as much as he wanted to think about them. He would see them up close soon enough. By then, his fear would be complete, consuming every part of him; he would have to find some way to control it. Whatever fear he felt would be nothing to the abject terror felt by the man in the jumpsuit, tied up in the back of the jeep. What was his fear in comparison to that? That poor bastard was in an unimaginable hell right now. And it would only get worse with each mile they travelled. When the driver called to them all to get back on the truck, he took a deep breath and tried his best to fight back the bile rising in his throat. Throwing up now would be noticed and would get Waqar angry again. He jumped back into the foul-smelling truck.

'Not long now,' said Waqar. 'Another hour, two at most. I remember this road when I too had this task to fulfil. You will prove to me and to the commander that my trust in you is warranted. I have complete faith in you, Dani.'

Sand blew up into Daniel's eyes as he jumped down from the truck. There were several large dunes up ahead, and the sun beat with an unforgiving ferocity above. Waqar pulled two large rolls of canvas from the driver's cabin and called to Daniel to help him unroll them. One was black and the other was white. There were poles attached to each, and when they were fully unravelled, Waqar forced his pole into the hot sand at an angle. The flag wafted gently in the soft breeze. He told Daniel to do the same with the pole he was holding, to form a cross with them. There were large calligraphic Arabic words printed upon the canvasses, with an image of two crossed scimitars beneath the script. Each flag was like a negative image of the other.

'What do they say?' asked Daniel.

'This is the shahada,' he replied. 'It says that "There is no god but God. Mohammed is the messenger of God."'

A few metres away, one of the other men positioned a camera on a tripod, facing the flags. As he did so, the commander, dressed all in black, called over to the jeep, which was now just a short distance away and had its engine still running. The noise of the engine stopped. One man got out of the back seat and pulled another man – dressed in an orange jumpsuit – from the same seat. He fell face down onto the sand. Daniel could see his hands tied behind his back, and there was the knot of a blindfold on the back of his head. Another man jumped from the vehicle, and each took one of the bound man's arms. They dragged him, protesting, to the flags and forced him to kneel down in front of them, facing the camera. By now, he was sobbing, mumbling something unintelligible.

The commander approached the kneeling man and removed his blindfold, throwing it on the ground beside him. Another man untied his hands.

'Please, please, don't do this. I am here in this country to help your people. I'm a doctor.'

The commander slapped his face and forced a card into his trembling hands. 'Face the camera and read this,' he said in heavily accented English.

'I, I, I need my eyeglasses to read it…'

Daniel could tell that this man was American, maybe from New York. His accent sounded like those he'd heard on American shows he'd watched with Tom, long ago, when his mother was alive. The man looked tall and distinguished, and his dark-brown hair was flecked through with grey. His face was covered in small cuts and both his eyes were black and blue. The commander shouted something in Urdu at the men who had dragged the American from the vehicle. One of them ran over to it and retrieved a pair of glasses from the back seat. He handed them to the commander.

Now the man began reading from the card. 'I call on my friends, family and loved ones…' He stopped and began to sob again.

The man in black struck him a second time and poked the card. 'Read!' Daniel stood with Waqar nearby and watched as the man read from the card, faltering often and crying at points. The commander, now wearing a black cloth over his face, leaving only his eyes exposed, stood beside the kneeling man. Every time the American hesitated or cried, he would strike him and make him start again. The trembling man spoke unconvincingly about American atrocities in Syria and Afghanistan and stated how his government should take responsibility for his death. When he finally managed to read the entire speech with no mistakes, Waqar gave Daniel a black cloth to put around himself.

'Cover everything, even your eyes,' he said. 'You will be able to see through the cloth. And try to disguise your voice like I told you.'

Daniel remembered well what Waqar had told him and the many weeks of preparing him for this awful task. He had wielded the sword and taken the heads off so many stuffed resemblances of kneeling people. They reminded him of the guys that would be put on fires on Bonfire Night. 'When the time comes, you will be able to do this with your eyes closed,' Waqar had told him.

With trembling hands, Daniel wrapped the cloth around himself and wound the end of it several times around his mouth, nose and eyes. Waqar took him by the arm and led him over to the kneeling man who was now crying again. The commander moved out of the camera's range, and Waqar withdrew a long, straight sword from the burlap wrapping. He laid it on the ground, went over to the man and replaced the blindfold over his eyes, tying it tightly at the back. Then he returned to Daniel and picked up the sword again.

'It is time, my brother. Allah expects this of you.' Waqar held out the sword to Daniel. 'This will be no different to all the practices we did.'

With trembling hands, Daniel took hold of it and walked over to the American. He could see and smell that he had emptied his bowels in the orange jumpsuit. He was sobbing and pleading, 'Don't do this, please. Please, I have a wife and two sons. Please don't let them see this.'

Daniel lifted the sword, closing his eyes against the sight in front of him. Chanting the words that Waqar had made him learn and repeat over and over, he swung it as hard as he could and heard the sickening crunch of metal on bone. There were no more words from the man. Just a hot, metallic-smelling silence that seemed to persist until a resounding chorus of '*Allahu Akbar*' rang out from the assembled men around him. He kept his eyes closed. It was different – nothing like he'd imagined.

Chapter Twenty
Today, Friday

Tom shifts a little and calls out Daniel's name in his sleep. Daniel pulls the dagger away from his father's neck and feels bile rise in his throat.

'You'll never let go, will you? I wish you'd never met Mum. Never put me on this earth. I wish I never knew you, you worthless cunt.'

Daniel stands up and goes to Tom's bathroom, leaving the dagger on the bed. He turns the tap on full in the marble sink and sticks his face under the rushing cold water. *C'mon, if you can't face this, how the fuck're you going to do the big stuff, later?* He returns to his father's bedroom. Rufus looks content, still settled on Tom's heaving chest. Maybe he thinks the snoring is how humans purr. Daniel slaps his father's face lightly a few times. Tom is comatose. Daniel can do what he likes, and he won't know a thing. Why the fuck should he be allowed to go into oblivion, knowing none of it? Feeling nothing? One thing is for sure: he'll not be seeing Tom in *Jannah*; Tom will get the filthy purgatorial eternity he deserves. But he isn't going to make it easy for him. Slicing his throat is going to be way too kind an exit for this pointless piece of shit. Let him suffer a bit longer. Let him see everything that he made possible. Let him witness the aftermath of what is to come. Let him crucify himself with doubt and self-recrimination.

But what to do? Tom can't see the news, thinking that his beloved son has left without leaving a token of his hatred. Rufus adjusts himself into a circle on Tom's chest. Shame for the poor cat to be left on his own and, even worse, for him to be a comfort to Tom after the fact. Daniel strokes the cat and whispers, '*Inaa lillaahi wa innaa ilayhi raaji'oon.* In English, Rufus, this means: "To Allah, we belong and to Him is our return." We'll meet again in paradise, Rufus. Waqar and I will look after you there. He waits for us there.'

Rufus purrs now. Is he enjoying his words and his touch? Daniel stands up and returns to Tom's bathroom. He picks up a large towel and goes back. Man and cat still lie together, eyes closed. He places the towel over Rufus, surprised he doesn't stir. With a quick motion, he scoops the cat up in the towel and wraps it tightly around. Rufus begins to struggle, but makes no sound. This was always Tom's method of getting the cats into their transporter basket to go to the vets, so Rufus probably thinks this is what is happening. Daniel picks up the dagger and plunges it into the cat's neck. Blood gushes over the hilt and the struggling stops. He places the bloody bundle back on his father's chest and pulls the towel away.

Tom doesn't move when he turns the cat on its back and slices it from the neck, down its belly to its tail. Warm blood gushes all over Tom, seeping into his underpants and the sheets. Daniel turns the carcass over and splays it over Tom's chest – the head and wide lifeless eyes pointing towards his neck. Each of Rufus's legs dangle over Tom's ribs, blood and entrails leaking down his abdomen. Daniel gazes at the bloody mess for a few minutes. He remembers the American bleeding on the sand. Red satin, red walls, bloody knees, stained sheets, red sputum. The movement of Tom's heaving chest gives a strange animation to Rufus's carcass.

But this isn't enough. One final detail will help make this even more horrific for his deserving father. He lifts the cat's head up and hacks it off with the bloody dagger, sawing at the sinews and bones. The eyes are wide and green and already clouded over. As he places the head on the pillow next to Tom's, he thinks of the American again; his neck cut was clean, straight, precise. Poor Rufus's looks ragged and untidy, like a head pulled off a stuffed animal. The thought quickly passes, and he pulls open the mouth, making sure the dead eyes face his father.

Laying the dagger on the pillow, Daniel feels for the ring in his ear and removes it, along with the chain linking it to his nose. He digs deep into his pocket and takes out a gold locket, which he prises open with his thumbnail. Inside, two tiny black and white photographs show his mother's face on one side and a young Tom on the other. Another dying gift from his mother, its chain long lost. There's a feline tooth-mark on its surface: a bite from Rufus the kitten, attacking the dangling menace it represented. His mum's sweet voice comes back to him as he remembers her telling him how it happened. Banishing any further memories, he threads the chain he's taken from his nose through the loop, leaving the locket open, and drapes it over Rufus's head. This will be a clear enough parting message for his father. *Won't it, Tom?*

There will be no doubt what he means by this. *But Rufus. Poor Rufus. You don't deserve this, do you? You didn't deserve to die this way, yet another casualty of this wasted man's pointless life. Somehow it is right. Everything destroyed, everything ruined, everything tainted that Tom had ever touched. I'm sorry, Rufus. You had to die for this. My death will make it right, I promise.* He takes one final look at Tom's face. This will be the last time he will ever see him. No regrets. At least none for Tom. Rufus will see his purpose and thank him. Won't he?

Daniel picks up the dagger again, takes the key from the lock and leaves, closing the bedroom door behind him. The first light of morning is pushing its way into the hallway through the French windows. Traffic noise is slowly building momentum on Embankment. The world is awakening, and Daniel feels his stomach tighten. He turns the key in the lock and twists the door handle to make sure it is secured. Then he pulls out the key and throws it on the carpet.

Soft light bathes the hallway, giving the flat an ethereal aura. Outside, the sound of traffic seems distant, almost like an echo of itself. Daniel feels he is looking in on himself, that he is part of a movie that has already played. He knows how this film will end; he has played the dénouement in his brain a thousand times. It is as if he has already experienced it, felt it, lived it, over and over again. The problem is the sequel: what will happen afterwards? Waqar had been clear about this, but everything had been easier to imagine and believe when Waqar was in his world. *Come to me now, Waqar.* Whatever happens, he will know no more loss, no more sadness. If it is nothingness he faces, it will be better than this. Waqar comes to him. His love fills his brain and he knows his doubts are stupid and futile.

In the study, the silence is pervasive; even the growing

rush of traffic on Embankment cannot penetrate this space. The rows of books seem to close in on him, accuse him; they reek of Tom. Had he even read any of them? Rare first editions, signed by long-dead writers. Spending his final hours among this opulence isn't what he has imagined. Everything has taken on a life of its own. It is was as though Waqar had said, 'Destiny will drive everything. Follow it, let it happen.' Tom had never figured in Daniel's own imagined destiny. Waqar would say that that is the nature of destiny; he must let it lead him as it had led Waqar. *What happens when we reach our destiny? Does the afterlife not contain destinies of its own?*

There are more questions than answers and only one person capable of providing him with those answers. But Waqar was already where he wanted to be. Waqar, first as always: first to the training in Pakistan, to his mission in Paris and now to *Jannah*. His destiny had found him and taken him to his own peaceful, joyful place. Not long now, for Daniel. These questions wouldn't even need to be answered then. All his questions would be nothing when he was with his brother again. His brother? His lover? There, would it change? Waqar had hinted at it. If only he had been more persistent, tied him down, been sure. Better to not be sure, not be disappointed. The note in the box had spoken of his love. Love and lover are not the same things, although, the two are inseparable. In *Jannah*, he'd be happy, whatever happened. That was the nature of paradise. He'd be happy for the first time. *Thank you, Waqar.*

Daniel lies on the bed and pulls out his phone, swiping with his thumb until he reaches his saved videos. *Hello, Waqar! Speak to me.* He presses on the most recent thumbnail; this face is like a drug to him. Those eyes! Waqar smiles back at him. Daniel presses 'play'.

'Hello, my Dani. Here, I say goodbye. Today, I answer my calling. My only regret, for you know I have always told you that regrets are futile, is that I will not be there to help you through your journey. See my clothes? I am a warrior. My fight will take me to heaven, and there I will wait for you, my brother... my...' Waqar's voice drops to a whisper. 'My love.'

Daniel pauses the video. 'My love.' He keeps saying it over and over again. His eyes fill with tears.

'I do this for you, Waqar.' He presses 'play' again:

'... what seemed like a lifetime away, is now. Can you believe it? I am ready, Dani. Truly ready. I have dreamed of this day as you will dream of yours. Ours. These next weeks, months, however long it takes, will seem like nothing to you. For me, it will be an instant. I will not wait for you, for time will be meaningless. There is no time, no space, no waiting in paradise. Look into my eyes, Dani.'

Waqar's eyes now fill the screen. Daniel brings his phone closer to his face, closer to Waqar's, trying to imagine that he is right there in the room beside him. More than anything, he wants him to be there, by his side. All this would be so easy then. The video rolls on:

'I do this for you, for us, for the world. You have helped convince me of this, and this is my last chance to convince you. The world ends today, for me. Don't let me down, my love.'

'My love.' Again, it rings through his brain. 'My love.' He continually rewinds the video, listening to Waqar say it over and over again, pausing it each time to stare into his eyes on the screen. Is there any love in his eyes? All Daniel can discern is fear. Where was Waqar, when he recorded this video? The banner of the eagle hangs behind him and beads of sweat trickle down his face. Paris? Far away from his birthplace in Syria. Paris, where Waqar's destiny was to begin. Maybe he'd recorded this before he travelled there. But no, he must have been there because he'd said that the world ended on that day, for him.

It was Paris for Waqar, London for Daniel. Daniel had wanted them to do whatever they must do, together. The camp leaders had other ideas. Waqar had put up no protest and Daniel didn't have the language skills to make a case. They would have ridiculed them if he'd even asked. Waqar had played down their friendship when they were together in the camp. Daniel lets the video run again.

'You must have courage, Dani. It is the only way that we will see each other again. When you play this message, I will already be with Allah. I will be floating on a cloud of bliss. Paradise will only be better with you there. When your time comes, join me. Know that everything you do is for this purpose. I will be there to welcome you, just like I waited for you in the camp.'

Waqar's eyes look away from the screen, and a dark voice utters something in Urdu, off camera.

'I must go now, Dani. Be strong. Think of me until *your* time comes.'

The video shrinks back to a thumbnail, and Daniel lets his phone drop on the bed beside him. He reaches for the remote control at the side of the bed and points it at the TV, flicking through channels, looking for something mindless to keep him from thinking. He finds a documentary on one of the cable channels called *Fighting Terror: A Global Threat*. It is halfway through and is showing footage of 9/11, demonising the men who had flown the planes into the World Trade Center. The murder of Lee Rigby is described as 'an atrocity'. Daniel wonders what will be said about him when his deed is done. He remembers the terrible things they had said about Waqar, after he died, words like 'sociopath', 'misogynist', 'terrorist'. No one knows the people who fight for their cause, they only see the acts and vilify them for those acts. Waqar had made such an impact, changed the world. He'd brought Islam to the streets of Paris, shown the world that Islam is everywhere. Six months ago now. The prime minister's voice overlays the next piece of film, repeating what was said in Parliament: 'This was an evil act of terrorism and hatred, and we, as a nation, utterly condemn it. More recently, the attacks in Florida and Germany make it clear that we must defeat the poisonous ideology of *Daesh* both online and on our streets.'

Daniel flicks the TV off. *You can try, Prime Minister.* He recalls Waqar's words. The words he had left the world to listen to: 'Islam is bigger than any half-cooked philosophy of the West. Islam is the solution, not the problem.' Of the 'poisonous ideology' that the prime minster called their faith, Waqar would respond in the way that he would knock down all such lies. He would say that Islam is a revolutionary doctrine and has systems that will overthrow governments. *Yes, Waqar. Governments like yours, Prime Minister. Everything in this pathetic world will change. Islam will quash all your pathetic religions. Waqar and I will laugh at you from heaven.*

There will be no sleep for Daniel. His last hours on earth will be spent awake. Sleep would only take him into the terror of dreams, and dreams are the source of many of his doubts. The room takes on an eerie silence again, and he clicks on Waqar's video. Would Waqar look the same when he sees him again? Waqar's voice, his eyes, his face, comfort him. Waqar will keep him company during these last few hours. Waqar will be with him, after all, when he departs this life. He clicks on the video and watches it again and again until his eyelids begin to droop, and the unwanted, dreaded sleep finally comes to him.

Chapter Twenty-One
Then

'No!'

'It has to be like this, Dani. I'm sorry.'

'No, Waqar. You promised we would do this together. I can't do this on my own. All the way to this you told me I wouldn't have to do anything without you. And you first? I can't face this world without you. I hate it here.'

'It was never my decision. You could see that from the moment you arrived in the camp. All of this is bigger than us. If you see nothing else, you must see that.'

'I can't live without you, Waqar. It's the truth. I can't do it. I can't face any of it if you're not with me.'

Daniel fell to his knees, sobbing. Waqar slapped his face and pulled at his tunic.

'Get up, you fool! Someone might see us.'

Daniel looked up at him. Waqar's eyes were hard and looked away, skimming the distance, fearful. Waqar didn't give a toss about him. He'd fooled him. Got him here under false pretences. What a fucking nightmare this was. One thing after another. One thing after afuckingnother. It was endless, unstoppable. Why had he ever come here? It was love. It was belief. It was love.

'I can't do this. I'm going back.'

Daniel stood up. Waqar's attitude had completely sobered

him up. He looked him square in the eyes and said, 'I'm done, Waqar. I'm going home. Do what you like. Kill yourself, if you want. This isn't my fight.'

Waqar slapped him again. And again. And again. Daniel could feel blood in his mouth. He could feel pain. He felt desire. The bruises started to make themselves known. But he felt love. Above all, through the pain, through the hurt, he felt love.

'Have we spent all this time, all these months, these years, for nothing? Have I taught you nothing? Has this all been a waste of time? You know our purpose. You know why we are here. Dani, it was never about one thing except the end. *Jannah*. Paradise. Our destiny. Paradise never meant one thing. How we get there never was prescribed.'

Waqar pulled him towards him, his eyes scanning the air as he did so. His hands touched Daniel's neck, moved to his back, rubbed his muscles. Daniel felt his body tighten, felt his desire stir. He suppressed his need. Stopped himself pulling Waqar closer. It was torture. Worse than anything he could imagine. A suppression of want, of desire, of love, of lust. His mouth was dry, but his mind imagined it wet, imagined pressing his lips against Waqar's. This whole place was dry; it was devoid of everything but purpose. It screamed a misery that had nothing but ugliness. This place was a chrysalis that would bring forth no butterflies. All it would produce was destiny. There lay the beauty.

'Talk to me, Dani. Tell me what you feel.'

Waqar pulled him into the shade. Looked to his left. Looked to his right. Pulled him into the hut. Looked around. Listened. He pressed his body against him. Daniel smelled his sweat. Smelled desire. Smelled sex. He could feel Waqar's desire against him, wanted it. Craved it. But not now, not here.

'No,' he said, again. 'No, Waqar.' Waqar pressed his mouth on Daniel's.

'Quiet,' he said.

'No.' Daniel could hardly believe his resolve.

Waqar let him go. Stood back. His eyes were wide, wounded, looking him up and down, almost as if he was a stranger.

'But...'

'Waqar, I love you. I'll do anything for you. You don't have to persuade me. At least, not this way.'

No response. Could a silence this cold, so distant, be possible in this heat? Could it? Why now? Why, after all this time, did Waqar lay this on him? Had he not tried, made his feelings known and suffered the rejection? Been pushed back and told it was wrong? Been left clutching at air? He pulled him back. Pulled him closer. Pushed the coldness away.

Waqar held him again. 'Dani, I want you to know what this means to me. You see? This is the only way we can be together. My religion... our religion doesn't allow it. In paradise, it will be different. There, it won't matter. Here, I can show you a little of it, show you what it might be like.'

'No.' Daniel felt as if someone else was speaking his words. His body was screaming 'yes'. 'No, Waqar. We talked, and we talked and we talked. You were clear. Not here. Not now. Allah would not allow it here. You were clear about that. You couldn't have been clearer. We have agreed on this. But the commands, what we must do—'

'Dani, we can do it now. I must convince you. I must

remove your doubts.'

'No.'

'But you want to go home. You don't trust your destiny. Here, they will kill you if you choose to leave. That way, our destinies will never meet. We'll be spilt for eternity. I can't let that happen. We are to be together in heaven.That can never happen if we fail to fulfil our destinies. Please, Dani, trust me. We must do this, and we must do this alone. Show them no doubt. Please, show them no doubt. Please, even if you decide not to follow me, please don't let them know. In *Jannah*, I cannot be at peace if I have no prospect of you joining me there. I will disappear if I know you will not be mine for eternity.'

Daniel stood back. How could he deal with this? Was this simply a way to convince him to do everything Waqar wanted him to do? No. He'd felt his desire. It was real desire. Physical. Unmistakable. Viscerally real. That reaction couldn't be false. In these last years of trying, wanting, craving... this was real. Real. REAL. He had felt it. For the first time. Now he knew this was genuine. Hadn't he always? Yes. Of course. It was Waqar, it was true, it was Waqar's desire for him. What must be, must be. *Thank you, Waqar. Thank you.*

'Waqar, I am yours. You are mine. I'm sorry for being so weak. Here, now... it's but a moment. You have told me this often. So often, I can't even believe I had doubts.'

Waqar looked at him in a way that he never had before. He saw real pride in his eyes. Waqar was proud of him. Daniel continued.

'You will go, and although it will seem like I will be a long time here on my own, it will be over in an instant. And I will be with you again. The time will be nothing against the eternity we will spend together. Again, I'm sorry I doubted you.'

Waqar smiled and stood close enough that Daniel could feel his breath. 'Thank you, Dani. For me it is Paris. For you, we don't know yet. But six months, a year, two years? It will be nothing. It will be longer for you than for me. But even for you, it will be short. When your mission becomes clear, that will be your route to paradise and back to me.' Daniel kissed Waqar's cheek, and for once, he didn't flinch.

'We are meant to be together,' Waqar continued. 'This has always been the case – what Allah wants for us. Today, I wanted only to show you what we will have forever. If not that, something better.'

Waqar put his hand on Daniel's crotch. Daniel felt the blood rush and pump. His heart quickened and his resolve weakened. But the door opened, and three men came in, chattering unintelligibly. One of them addressed Waqar in Urdu, and he stood up, laughing. Daniel forced himself to smile too. What had the stranger said? He would never know. Others would come now, and he would forget to ask Waqar what the joke had been. Daniel couldn't help imagining that he was the butt of some primitive, xenophobic joke directed at him. Why had he not kept pushing himself? Why was he not as fluent in Urdu as Waqar was in English? Waqar had tried to convince him, spent hours teaching him back in England, but with the Qur'an and everything else, it was hard. He'd try harder. Here, especially, it was so difficult to feel part of everything. He could work out a lot of it, but mostly it was like pushing his way through a treacly darkness.

'C'mon, Dani. Let's eat.' Waqar spoke to him in Urdu. He could understand that much, and he knew Waqar was trying to make him seem better than he was.

The sun burned the sky red. No blue could push its way through the heat, and the horizon shimmered as it boiled in the unrelenting intensity of the sun's rays. Black shapes of men with targets painted on their heads and chest seemed to move against the continually moving backdrop, making them look like a mirage. Daniel, flanked by other men, pointed his rifle at the head of the target in his line of sight. The other men – boys, really – took the same stance and waited for the command to shoot.

Daniel tried his best to get the target's head in focus through his sight. When the guttural order came, he pulled his trigger and felt the stock crash into his clavicle. The explosive chaos of the other rifles firing made him flinch, and his ears felt punched and filled with wire wool.

All day, it had been aim, fire, reload, repeat. Daniel's head throbbed with the echoing thrash of gunfire and the dehydration. Only twice had they been allowed to put down their weapons and have some water. He felt he had shed half his body weight in sweat and fully expected to see a pool of it at his feet. All he saw was bone-dry sand and the shuffling feet of his companions. Waqar was off doing something else, but he didn't know what, or where. More and more often, he wouldn't see Waqar for days, and when he did, he was too exhausted to tell him much. And to be honest, Daniel was too exhausted to ask him. None of this was making sense. He longed for home, green fields and normality.

The sun was behind them when the captain told them to hand in the rifles and go back to the camp for the evening. That didn't mean rest for Daniel or any of the others training for their destinies there. It meant a short break for some food and then hours in a stuffy room watching hours and hours of videos showing Western atrocities against Muslims, just in case there were any lingering doubts about the cause of, and the need for, jihad. Before evening prayers, there would be lectures and talks about the nature of their training, with a constant reminder of the rewards they could expect for their labours.

At night, Daniel always searched for Waqar. He felt safer when he could sleep near him, even within sight of him. But Waqar did not always return at night, and those were the times that he slept in short fitful bursts. This night, after three nights of being away, Waqar was in the sleeping hut, sitting alone on his mat. Daniel almost ran to him.

'I've missed you,' said Daniel, sitting down on the mat beside his friend. Waqar looked tired and sad.

'The days have been long,' he said. 'I've thought about you a lot, Dani.'

'Why are they making me learn how to shoot, Waqar? When they interviewed me all those times, I told them time and again that I wanted to be a suicide bomber — like you said you wanted to be, like you told me to say. I don't want to fight in a war, like a soldier.'

'We have to learn everything, Dani. I already knew how to shoot. That is why I am not doing that with you. You need to know everything that may help you succeed in your task. You won't have to make the bomb that you will use when your time comes. More than likely, that won't be your job. But you will have to learn how to do it so that, if whoever is supporting your mission gets captured or killed, you don't have to abandon the task that is yours. We must all be multi-skilled for this war that we have all agreed to wage.'

'Why was I made to kill that American?'

'Because you needed to prove that you are capable of taking life. If you had shirked from that task, then you would have been useless to the jihad. Not only are you being trained here, but you are also answering the tests, showing you are capable. It is important that you follow every instruction to the letter, Dani. You are being watched, even when you think you are not.'

'OK. What is it that you've been doing these last few days?'

'My time is near. I have been going over every detail of my mission. I will leave here on Friday. We must say goodbye soon.'

Daniel felt his heart pounding in his chest. His throat tightened, and his eyes started to well with tears. Waqar took his hand.

'Stop, Dani. Control yourself. You knew this was coming. Don't let anyone see your weakness.'

'It's so soon,' Daniel said, rubbing his eyes. 'I thought we had many more weeks, months even. I hate being here on my own. I don't know how I'll cope when you are gone.'

'Dani, you'll cope. You'll cope because you know it's the only way to make sure that we will be together. That will help you continue here. It will help you complete the task – whatever it might be – that is given to you.'

Others started coming into the room, and Daniel moved to

the mat next to Waqar's. When the lights went out, he lay looking over at his friend's shape. As the hours ticked by, he kept his eyes on Waqar, wishing he could join him on his mat and hold him until morning. Occasionally, he whispered his name in the hope that he might still be awake, or have awakened, but Waqar never responded. It was hard to believe that he could fall asleep so readily when he knew what lay ahead of him in such a short time. Maybe he was pretending to be asleep as he had done so often himself.

Thursday started with the usual call to prayer. Daniel had been awake for many hours and was waiting for the familiar tinny warble from the speakers that could be heard echoing from places far away from where he lay. The coldness in the hut had been bitter overnight. Daniel had wanted to roll closer to Waqar and hold him for warmth, if nothing else. It felt even colder as Daniel and Waqar walked together, carrying their prayer mats. On the way, one of the camp elders approached Waqar and spoke to him in hushed tones, in Urdu, looking at Daniel often during the conversation. A growing unease tightened in Daniel's stomach as he tried to make sense of the words without success.

When the man had gone, they were almost at the makeshift mosque, and Daniel pulled Waqar's sleeve.

'Was that about me?'

'We must go in and pray, Dani. I will tell you after we are finished. Don't worry.'

Waqar pulled the door open and ushered in Daniel. The place had the smell of thick, bitter sweat. This was no different than any other day, but the smell seemed more cloying and oppressive, in spite of the chill, and the prayers seemed to take much longer. The room seemed more claustrophobic. Everyone had already washed at the well, but nothing could take away this smell. The smell he kept telling himself he had become used to.

When they were kneeling, Daniel could hardly concentrate on the words of the *Fajr* and ached for it to stop so he could find out what Waqar had heard about him. Waqar was engrossed in the worship, oblivious to Daniel's attempts to make eye contact. One day left and so little time. This whole thing was like being on a runaway train, with no prospect of getting off even just to catch his breath. What would the next weeks, months, or however long he had left be like? On his own. Alone. No one to talk to.

The prayers took no longer than any other day, but had seemed to extend into hours in Daniel's mind. His knees ached, his head ached. His back felt as if it had been permanently buckled. As they left the mosque, Daniel moved close to Waqar.

'Tell me, please.'

'The commander wants to see us after you have finished instruction for the day,' said Waqar. 'I'll meet you outside the hut when you are finished. I have no training today, as you know.'

'What does he want? Why does he want to see us together? What—?'

'Don't worry, Dani. It will be nothing bad. I guess he will want to tell you what your mission will be. He knows you are not fluent in our language, and his English is not perfect either. I am most likely to be there to help you both understand.'

'Maybe he wants us to work together. Maybe I can come to Paris with you.' Daniel started to feel excited, hopeful again.

'No, my friend. That will not happen. I leave tomorrow. There would be no time for you to learn the mission. It has taken me weeks.'

'But you can explain everything to me on the journey. There is time. And you won't be doing it the second you arrive there, will you?'

'No, Dani. Stop hoping for that. It won't happen. Of this, I am sure.'

The few seconds of hope were gone almost before they had a chance to form fully, evaporating into the unforgiving air. Daniel felt the familiar blackness reclaiming him, and his shoulders dropped along with his spirits.

'I wish I could escape the training today,' he said, eyes fixed on Waqar's. 'Then we could spend this last whole day together. The very last day that we will spend together on this earth.'

'These days don't matter. This is part of your test, and you will bear it because you know what it will bring. You cannot measure time on earth against eternity. That is what we will have.'

August, the second Friday of the month. Daniel's day of destiny. Now it was fixed. In eight months, on the anniversary of the bombing of some mosque in Afghanistan where the imam and his son had been killed. That had been a Friday too. Daniel would carry out his mission in London. He was to let the British feel the pain of their misdeeds abroad. Best of all, he was to travel back to the UK in a few weeks and lay low until the time came. At least he wouldn't be stuck in this circle of hell for all that time without Waqar. Just a few more training days and he would travel to Turkey, then to Greece. From there, he would travel by road and rail back to Britain. Now he couldn't wait for his life to be over so that eternity could begin.

'I will not see you tomorrow,' said Waqar. 'I start my journey before dawn, and I will not sleep in the hut tonight. We must say goodbye soon, my love.'

Daniel felt an echo of warmth course through him. He couldn't even respond. 'My love.' Had Waqar said that? The sadness his friend's departure would have provoked had been rubbed out by those two words. Daniel could feel a smile blossoming into a grin on his face.

'What makes you smile so?' asked Waqar.

'In four-and-a-half years, I have never heard you say those words. You have made me so happy, Waqar. Today we will part, but I have never felt happier. Thank you, *my love*.'

Waqar laughed. 'Did I never? I'm sorry. I felt you knew it, and it did not need to be said out loud. Better to be late than never. Yes?'

'We can tell each other every day in *Jannah*. Once, here in this terrible world, will be enough for me, Waqar. You said it once, and that will keep me alive until my time comes. I will smile every time I think of this moment.'

'I will give you more reason, in that case, and I say it again, my love. And I will say it again when we say goodbye.'

Waqar looked all around himself and pulled Daniel's arm until they were out of sight behind the sleeping hut. Everyone else had gone in to eat the evening meal. He pulled Daniel close to him and pressed his body against his, kissing him hard on the mouth, pushing his tongue inside. Daniel gripped Waqar's neck and pushed his groin against his. This awful day had become incredible, and this moment was as close to heaven as he had ever been. He could feel the strength and purpose this intimate truth had given him. It had all happened in an instant, but in moments, truths are revealed. Waqar was his and nothing could change that now. Waqar was his and an eternity of love would be theirs.

Daniel lay awake, not because he was miserable or terrified, but because he was playing back that last conversation, that amazing kiss with Waqar, in his mind, again and again. He closed his eyes tight, trying to remember every detail, every smell, every nuance. As he was reliving the kiss in his mind, he felt warm lips on his. Then a whisper.

'I leave now, Dani. Goodbye, my love, until soon.'

And he was gone, like a shadow blending into the others, disappearing. 'Goodbye, my love. Goodbye, Waqar.'

Chapter Twenty-Two
Today, Friday

Tom is awakened by a chime from Big Ben. How many have there been? He hears three more tolls of the bell breaking through the hum of traffic on Embankment. He tries to open his eyes, but meets some resistance as they screw up in protest at the sour dryness in his mouth. What? What time is it? The peal of the bells has made the pounding in his head triple in intensity. Four o'clock? Jesus. He yawns deeply, forcing his dry tongue from the roof of his mouth and, as he stretches himself, he slowly becomes aware of a cold, thick wetness on his bare chest and a tight stinging sensation across his throat.

Tentatively, he brings his hands to his upper body and feels a mass of matted fur where his chest hair should be. What the fuck? Now his eyes snap open, and he sits upright and watches a bloody pile of fur and entrails slide off his torso and onto the bed.

'What?' His scream is hoarse and broken. His arms stiffen, and his hands tighten into claws. 'No!'

Tom pushes the congealed mess from his body and throws himself onto the floor, vomiting acidic pink foam in spasms onto the carpet. Retching again and again, unable to prevent the last traces of moisture forcing its way up from his near-empty stomach, he wonders if this is real. The pounding in his head feels real enough, and the burning in his throat is far from dreamlike. There is no way to make sense of what is happening to him as he grabs his glass of water from the bedside table and gulps it all down. An intense metallic stench of stale blood and warm meat hangs in the air. He draws himself upright, only to confront himself with more of what he does not want to see; on the pillow next to his, a pair of dead green eyes stare back from a severed head.

'Oh, no. No. Please, no. Rufus!'

Tom forces back another dry retch pushing its way up his gullet and presses his blood-soaked hands to his eyes. He refuses to see the bloody sight again. His legs begin to buckle and, lurching for the bedroom door, he falls hard against it, grabbing for the handle. The handle turns, but the door stays closed, so he stands up and twists the knob, pulling as hard as he can. The door is stuck. Did he lock it? He begins to remember turning the key as he went to bed. There is no sign of the key on the floor. Where can it be? He pulls again, kicks the door and begins punching it with all the strength he can summon. Someone has locked the door from the other side. They did this to Rufus then locked him in. Why? Now the memory of Daniel enters his throbbing brain again.

'Daniel! Daniel. Why?'

Tom looks down at his chest and sees the streaks of blood again. Daniel, why have you done this? Why have you locked me in here? Why are you punishing me like this? What have I ever done? He skirts around the end of the bed, staring away from the mess all over it, and pulls at the handle of the French windows. They open effortlessly, and Tom rushes onto the balcony.

Children run around in front of their parents, enjoying the

last few minutes of evening sunshine, while impatient joggers rush past them. Traffic honks and motorcyclists coax their way around cars that are bumpering against one another on Embankment. Save me from this, please! Horns blare and the day is typical in every way; this is Friday; this is Central London.

Tom screams, 'Help me! For fuck's sake, help me! *Please!*' He doesn't know why. The world below is oblivious to him, and he can shout and scream as much as he likes without a soul paying him any heed. Maybe the French windows to the dining room or living room are open; he rushes to each and pushes them hard. They are locked tight. There is no trace of his son in either room. Peering through the dining room windows into the dark hallway, he can see the wooden cat lying on its side. Why, Daniel?

He walks back to the open bedroom window, his shoulders hunched, tears streaming through the dried blood on his cheeks. Help me. Will somebody please help me? What have I done? The phone! He rushes inside, trying his utmost to block out everything else in the room and grabs the handset from its cradle, jabbing frantically at the buttons. Fucking contacts list, where are you? He finds it, scrolls down to PORTERS' DESK and pushes the call button hard. After a few rings, it answers.

'Good evening, Buckingham Court, Vincent speaking. How may I help?'

'Vince? Vince? Flat 67 here. Tom McInt—'

Tom can't prevent himself from bursting into tears. He can hear muffled talk on the other end of the line.

'Good evening, Mr McIntyre. How are you, si—?'

Tom's voice is thick with tears and snot. 'Vince, get up

here now! Use the spare key for the front door. Let yourself in. I'm locked in the bedroom and something… Look, just come, will you?'

'How's that, sir? How have you managed th—'

'Shut the fuck up, Vince, and get up here NOW!'

Tom waits, facing the door, unable to look back inside the room. After a few minutes, he hears noise from outside the bedroom door and then Vince's voice calling.

'I'm here, sir. Gimme a second. I'll have you out in a jiffy.'

'I've no idea where the bedroom door key is, Vince. Can you force the door?'

'It's here on the floor, Mr McIntyre. Don't worry.'

Tom hears the key being put into the lock. There's a click, and the door opens slowly.

Vince looks him up and down, clearly trying to hide his disgust. The smell of stale blood and vomit is pervasive. Tom can only stand there, arms hanging limply at his side. It feels surreal to be standing there in his underwear with Vince gaping at him. Vince is looking past him at the bed. He looks horrified.

'What on earth's been going on, sir?' he says.

Tom feels reality grip him again and he grabs Vince's lapels. 'Vince, Vince. Have you seen my son?'

'Young Danny, sir? Erm… not to speak to, as such. Has he been here, in your flat?'

'I think it was him who locked me in and did this to Rufus.'

He pushes past Vince and runs towards the study. He puts his hand on the doorknob and pauses, turning to look round at Vince who is right behind him.

'Oh, God. Vince, what am I going to find?'

'I really don't think he's in there, sir. I'll take a look, if you like.'

Tom stands aside, and Vince pushes the heavy door open and goes inside. The light is still on. Tom can see the backpack in the corner and the dirty mound of silk on the bed. There's a picture of Alison on the bed too. Vince comes back into the hallway and says, 'He's not here, sir.'

Tom lets out a loud sigh of relief. 'Thank God.'

'Let's get you cleaned up, Mr McIntyre. Then I think you better come downstairs with me. I'd like you to look at something on the CCTV.'

It is a strange experience for Tom, being on the opposite side of the porters' desk, wearing his dressing gown and seeing the vast foyer of his building from the porters' viewpoint. Vince and Robert are busily winding back the video feed on the CCTV system.

'Come and look, Mr McIntyre, please,' says Vince.

Tom walks to the corner where the screen is and stands behind Vince, squinting at the grainy image coming into view.

'Do you recognise this fellow, sir?' asks Vince.

The time on the display shows 04:03. Tom watches the dark-bearded figure looking all around himself. He is carrying a backpack, and he quickly disappears into the stairwell adjacent to the porters' desk.

'That's Daniel,' Tom says, flatly.

'Bloody hell, sir! I wouldn't've recognised him in a million years. That tattoo! He was a proper clean-cut young man last time we saw him, wasn't he, Robert? We did think we recognised him on the later footage, though. We'll show you that in a second. The thing is, he ain't got no tattoo later on.'

'He was unrecognisable to me too, Vince. Took me completely by surprise las—'

Vince doesn't allow Tom to finish. 'You better have a seat, sir. You're not gonna like what I have to tell you…'

Vince replays the other fragments of CCTV footage that he has, showing Daniel returning from King's Cross, then the cleaned-up larger-looking version of him leaving the building via the hotel corridor at 16:58.

'We reported this man – well, actually, we thought it was two men – to the police earlier. Robert thought that he was up to no good, sir.'

Tom blinks at Vince and looks back at the paused image of Daniel on the screen.

'Explain, please, Vince.'

Robert casts a worried glance at Vince and looks away from them both, before disappearing into the staff kitchen to the side of the desk. Vince begins explaining what he has seen and heard in the gardens. Tom wants to cover his ears and block out everything Vince is saying.

'What the fuck? Is he alive? Have the police found him? For fuck's sake, is Daniel anything to do with this?' Tom fires the questions as they come to him.

'I've no idea. The last I heard was that they were going to search the area and get the transport police informed to look out for him. There's been an explosion at Oxford Street Tube, though…'

Tom loses all his professional pretence and drops to his normal register. 'Fuck, fuck, fuck! Vince, I'd better go back upstairs and call. Fuck, I can't face going back anywhere near my bedroom. I can hardly face going back in my flat. Can you please get somebody to go and clear up that mess? I'll fucking die if I have to go back in there.'

'Best to let the coppers have a look first. Call them as soon as you get upstairs. I can call from here if you'd rather. Whatever, just steer clear of there until they get here.'

'I'll call them,' says Tom.

He bounds up the three flights of stairs to his flat. The front door is still slightly ajar, and he feels a pang of fear as he pushes it open. As he closes it behind him, he starts to cry again. Help me, Alison, please. Tell me what to do here. Alison always helps him, in some way, through his worst times, but nothing can feel as bad as this feels tonight – except for losing her, of course.

'I'm blocking you out, aren't I? God, I wish I could turn my brain off.' The phone begins to ring, and Tom rushes to pick it up.

'Daniel?'

'Hello. Is this Thomas McIntyre?' The voice is female. It sounds soft and sympathetic.

'Yes. Yes, who's this?' Tom can feel his heart pounding.

'Oh, hello, Mr McIntyre. My name is Veronica Willis. I want to talk to you about Daniel—'

'Veronica who? Why are you calling?'

'I'm calling from the news desk at the *Evening Standard.* I want to… well, the news coming from—'

'What the fuck do you want? I'm going through fucking hell here.'

Tom hangs up. He goes into the kitchen and pours himself

a glass of water. His head is still thumping, and he can't face calling the police yet. As he heads back to the living room, the phone rings again.

'Yes, who is this?' Tom shouts.

'Hello, Mr McIntyre. This is James Aitken from News International. Can I talk to you about—?'

'What the fuck?' Tom slams the receiver down and clenches his head in his hands. What the hell is going on? Again, the phone rings, and he pulls the wire from the socket. The ringing continues in the study and the bedroom, so he runs to the study and pulls the cable from that phone. As he nears his bedroom, he pauses for a second and slams the door shut instead. The muffled ringing continues as he staggers back to the living room. Where's the fucking remote? He turns on the news and sinks into the sofa. At the bottom of the screen, a red banner announces:

Breaking news. Oxford circus underground evacuated after terrorist incident. 38 dead. Nearly 100 believed injured, 27 critical.

'God! What on earth has happened? This isn't you, Daniel. It can't be you.'

Tom watches the grim scene above the banner; smoke is billowing from the tube entrance, and people are running out of it. Police cars and ambulances are everywhere around the station, their emergency lights flashing and uniformed men and women running around. Tom stares at the screen in horror. Not Daniel. No. Please!

He stands up and walks closer to the screen, searching for some sign of his son. Tears blur his vision as he listens to the commentary. He hangs his head, defeated, disbelieving. The doorbell rings, and he ignores it, along with the incessant, muffled ring of the phone in his bedroom. But Vince and Robert wouldn't allow any reporters to come upstairs before checking with him first, would they?

Tom answers the door and is greeted by a uniformed police inspector, who stares at him with serious, piercing eyes. A young looking policewoman stands by his side, carrying a portfolio.

'Hello...' Tom hadn't expected anyone other than Vince to be there.

'Mr McIntyre?' asks the inspector.

'Yes. Yes, how can I help you?'

'I am Inspector Arthur Walker,' he says, showing his warrant card. 'This is Sergeant Gemma Ingram. Can we come in?'

'Yes. Of course... come in,' says Tom.

Tom shows them into the living room, and Inspector Walker points at the TV and says, 'I see you're aware of what's been going on this evening, sir.'

Tom nods, trying to stop himself shaking.

'Sit down, please, Mr McIntyre. We need to ask you some questions.'

'Yes, of course, Inspector,' replies Tom. 'Please take a seat. Can I offer you both something to drink?'

Both of them decline with a shake of their heads and sit down. Inspector Walker indicates that Tom should sit opposite them.

Opening her portfolio, Sergeant Ingram lays some photographs on the table in front of Tom. Two of the pictures show an image of Daniel: no tattoo, short hair. Much as Tom remembers him before he saw him last night. They look as if they've come from CCTV footage in a shopping centre somewhere. A third shows Daniel with a criminal record number in front of his image. His hair is slightly longer. The fourth photograph is closest to him and shows Daniel as Tom had most recently seen him on the video footage downstairs. This picture is grainy and shows his son in the ticket hall of a tube station.

'Are these pictures of your son, Daniel Thomas McIntyre?' she asks.

'What's he been involved in?' Tom begins to feel evasive, that he might be under suspicion.

'Is this your son?' asks Inspector Walker.

'Yes.'

'When did you last see him, sir?'

'Last night,' says Tom. 'Well, the early hours of this morning, I suppose. He turned up out of the blue. I hadn't seen him in nearly three years. It was a shock, to be honest.'

'Did he stay here overnight, Mr McIntyre?' asks Sergeant Ingram.

'Yes. Yes, he did. I was just about to call you when... I think he did something terrible here last night...'

'Why do you say that?' Sergeant Ingram pauses and begins scribbling into her notebook.

Tom stands up and starts walking towards the hallway.

'I think it may be easier to show you. Follow me please,' he says.

Both officers follow Tom to his bedroom and watch him fling the door open before standing to one side.

'This is what he did to my cat. He placed the body on top

242

of me as I slept, and he put the severed head on the pillow next to me. Then he locked me in my room. I had to call the desk to come and free me.'

Neither police officer enters the bedroom.

Sergeant Ingram speaks into the radio clipped to her lapel: 'Get a SOCO team to Buckingham Court, ASAP. Flat 67. Inform CID that we need a D.I. here too.' Then she turns to Tom. 'Where did your son sleep last night?'

Tom points towards the study.

'Have you been in there since you last saw him?' she asks.

'No,' says Tom. 'But Vince, one of the porters, popped his head in to see if he was there. I was worried that he might have done something to himself...'

'Good,' replies Inspector Walker. 'We will have to cordon off that room as well as your bedroom.'

'Why?' asks Tom. 'What else do you think Daniel may have done? Where will I sleep tonight?'

'You've seen the news,' he says coldly. 'We think your son is responsible for that.'

'The Scenes of Crime Officer will be here soon, Mr McIntyre. I don't expect they will need to keep the areas off-limits once they finish. Tomorrow, we'd like you to come into the station. Can we say two thirty? We will need to interview you formally about past and present dealings with your son and any of his associates,' says Sergeant Ingram.

Tom nods. Fuck, I've allowed all this to happen, haven't I? All that money I threw at Daniel, his flat, the allowance I paid monthly to him. They're going to say I financed him to do this, aren't they? Fuck, fuck, fuck. I just keep having to pay the price. There is no end to this. Let it stop, please!

She continues, 'We have a car downstairs waiting for you. My colleagues will need to take you to identify your son.'

'Identify him? You have him in custody, don't you?' Tom looks at them both, confused.

The TV now shows Daniel's YouTube video. Tom inhales deeply. 'Turn up the volume,' says Inspector Walker. 'This is your son's suicide video – he uploaded it before he went into the underground system. He blew up a train and himself. We need you to identify his... remains.'

Chapter Twenty Three
Then

Carlisle was grey, wet and windy. A month since he'd said goodbye to Waqar. Three weeks since the news reports from Paris, when that strange 'terrorist' face appeared on TV screens all around the world. It wasn't Waqar's face. Even Daniel didn't recognise those photographs, those blurry images from CCTV footage showing that bearded, long-haired, evil-looking man. It wasn't Waqar's face as he wanted to remember it, at least. That face was the face he had seen once or twice in the camp. A cruel face, lacking in any emotion. One that looked as if it had never loved. A face that could never love or be loved. Even the name they printed underneath was not his: MOHAMMED WUAQIR LAKHEMI. That's why it wasn't Waqar. Not the name, not the picture. That was a photograph of an ugly chrysalis that had since metamorphosed into a heavenly spirit. One that illuminated many sunrises and cast warm peach shadows on sunsets all over the earth. Knowing this would keep him alive until it was his turn to change himself, to metamorphose, change completely and join his love in *Jannah*.

The journey from Pakistan had been grim; first, it was Mumbai and from there, Ankara. Ankara, what a nightmare. Three days of being preyed upon by the dirty, hairy, fat Turk who was responsible for his ongoing passage. 'You want massage? I give you very good massage. No cost to you, my friend. You enjoy a lot. I take care of every stress inside you and outside you. You feel great, you love it. I touch you everywhere.' No refusal. Refusal was like a curse to this deodorant-deprived gorilla. He had to let him do it, and the filthy outcome was against all belief. Three dire days in Turkey, followed by a flight to Athens, and from there it was land-based travel all the way to France. France was like heaven, almost like being home again. Here, he felt he shared the final steps taken by his love. He had walked the streets where Waqar must have taken his last, fateful journey.

Home was here, for now. This grey, concrete filing cabinet he had occupied so long ago. Back in his flat. Back to normality. But Waqar wasn't here. For three years, he had loved here, lived here, discovered feelings. Back here, he still had feelings that he never felt capable of, even when Waqar was here. But Waqar had made these feelings possible. Real. Palpable. Without Waqar, he could never have believed any of this was possible. *Thank you, Waqar, for showing me this road, this path to truth.* This journey would end soon, and he would see his love again. Now was the time to prepare himself, make his truth real. Start wrapping himself in the layers of his chrysalis. He would stain the sky with his sacrifice. He would colour the world with the beauty of his transformation, his passage to God.

There were things to be done first. First, he had to take on the layer of change, show the world that Daniel was gone, that he had taken up the mantle. The change had begun, the ugliness before the beauty. Few would understand his journey, his metamorphosis, his sacrifice. In time he would be recognised as Waqar was already recognised. His path was unwitnessed, unwritten, still to be revealed. Waqar had proved this, shown Daniel his true path. His destiny was written, proven. Real. But first, he had things to do.

Tom's house, the house that once had been home to him too, hadn't changed since he walked out the door for the last time. Mum's cherry tree was full, vivid, healthy. The driveway was populated with different cars; the grass seemed greener, more coiffured, than when he lived there. Daniel walked around the fence, peered over the top. Children lived there now; there was a tricycle like the one he used to have, a Wendy house like Jenny had played in, that he had smoked weed in, where she had dropped her pants for him. He had reciprocated, never knowing that this physical mystery would be forever strange to him. This was a world away. A lifetime away. A complete separation of family away. All gone to him. All of it gone, unimportant. Finished. Had he ever lived there? It was a different person who had. Not him. Goodbye, Cherry Lane.

Another cherry tree. Mum's grave. This one was bigger, even though it was planted later. Maybe the sapling had been bigger. Tom would say it was her way of telling us she's fine. That being dead for her is all blossom and branches, sunshine and breeze. Maybe she had already met Waqar in heaven. Waqar had said that he would find her and that he would wait with her. Mum would love Waqar as much as he did. All Waqar's anger would have disappeared in heaven; he would be just like he was all those times they spent together here. *Keep Waqar safe for me, Mum.* He put his arms around the trunk and pressed his face into the bark, felt the striations pushing into his skin. The echo of them remained when he let go, and he touched his cheek, feeling the indentations left there. It was time to start the process.

All the natural beauty of the woodland graveyard changed into regimented paths and rows of sad headstones as he walked through the archway into the main cemetery. Light rain began to fall; was Mum letting him know she was sad? *Don't be sad, Mum, we'll be together again soon. Be happy about that.* Growing old, being successful, spending time in the world, didn't make any difference to anything. What he would do, young as he was, would make a lasting difference, and he would be rewarded for it, just as Waqar had his reward now. In response, the rain stopped, and patches of blue pushed the grey clouds apart. He was sure he could see a rainbow. *Thank you, Mum. Thank you, Waqar.*

It took him less than half an hour to walk from the cemetery to the small back street near the castle. The name of the tattoo parlour made him smile. The sign, in gothic script, said: IMMORTAL ETCHINGS – TATTOO, PIERCING AND BARBERSHOP. A man in his thirties – tall, stocky and with long, greasy, brown hair – greeted him. He wore jeans and a leather waistcoat with nothing underneath. Tattoos covered his arms, his chest, his hands, his neck and his face. His body was a riot of colour, shape and form. Quite a picture.

'Hello, mate. I'm Jeff. What can I do for you?'

'Hi, I'm Lakky. I want a tattoo on my face, and I'd like my nose and ear pierced.'

'Lakky? What's that short for then? Or is it a nickname? Have you got any other tattoos, mate? A face tattoo is a big step to take if you're not absolutely sure about it. Why not try a small tattoo on your arm or chest, just to see how you feel about it?'

Daniel looked Jeff up and down.

'As sure as you were when you plastered yourself with ink,' he replied. 'And it's short for Lakhemi. My mother had a bit of a thing for the Middle East.'

'This has been a labour of love since I was fifteen,' said Jeff, pulling his waistcoat open, revealing dragons, daggers and naked women on his sides. 'And I started small. Once you have a tattoo, it's something you commit to for life. There's no going back.'

'I'm sure. I'm happy to accept this is a choice I make for the rest of my life. Now, will you do it for me? I want a snake with its fangs piercing my nose, and its body and tail twisting down my face and neck onto my chest. I want a piercing in my nose, where the fang will be, and I want a chain running from my nose to my right ear.'

'Wow, mate! As cool as that sounds, it will completely change the way you look – for, like, ever. And it won't be cheap neither. And you're talking maybe six or seven sessions to do something as major as that.'

'I want to change the way I look. It's the reason I'm here. This year, I change forever. For good. I have the time and the money. Are you able to do that for me?'

'As long as you're sure, mate.' Jeff was already pulling out some folders from a shelf near the counter. 'When do you want to start? I'll need a two hundred quid deposit. Cash.'

'Today. I'll just need to go to the cashpoint. Can you start today?'

'I'm free now for a couple of hours. Get the cash and then we can look at some designs.'

The only trace that showed that Waqar had ever lived there was a pewter trinket box that he'd given Daniel a few months after he became his lodger: his mother's trinket box: one she'd brought from Pakistan and given to him in Syria. It was the only thing belonging to Waqar's family that had survived the journey to England. And Waqar was the only member of that family to make it to Britain alive. It sat on top of the bookcase where all Waqar's textbooks and English courses had once been. Daniel picked the box up and ran his fingers over the snake engraved into the top, its fangs bared and a forked tongue extended. Waqar had said the snake would protect the contents of the box and that Daniel could keep precious things in there with no fear. Daniel opened the lid and was surprised to see a small folded piece of paper inside. He pulled it out and laid the box back on the bookcase.

Sitting on the chair that Waqar always preferred to sit on when he studied, Daniel unfolded the piece of paper. It was pale grey vellum, marked with a fountain pen in precise strokes of black ink. The Urdu characters begged to be read:

بلَّ:
کِجّ
تـب رلِیاذ
ھ
کِپ

Daniel knew enough by now to be able to understand what the words said, and tears formed in his eyes. He said them out loud.

'*Jab tak, ye mahabbat hai. Mai appka hi banke rahunga.*'

Waqar must have written this before they left for the airport for the final journey to Pakistan. The words simply said: UNTIL SOON, MY LOVE. I WILL ALWAYS BE YOURS, W. X. As Daniel kissed the words, a tear fell on the ink, causing the end of the message to bleed into a black cloud on the paper. For Daniel, this showed that his love was in the clouds. Another message from Waqar.

'Yes, soon, my love,' said Daniel, blowing on the ink, willing it to settle, pleading with the words to reappear.

He placed the paper on the windowsill to dry and went to the bathroom to examine his tattoo in the mirror, hoping to distract himself. The outline of the snake was complete, and the edges were raised on his skin like a glistening line of ink, bleeding from its edges. Tomorrow, Jeff would add the finishing touches, along with his piercings, and Daniel's chrysalis would have begun to form. His hair was already growing longer and tomorrow he would start letting his beard grow too. By the time he got to London, there wouldn't be a CCTV camera anywhere that would recognise any pictures of him that might have fallen into the hands of the security services.

Although Waqar wouldn't approve, he had bought some weed as well as a couple of sugar cubes of acid for good measure on his way home from the tattoo parlour. Now he retreated to his bedroom, stripped down to his boxer shorts, and set up the bong. Lying on his bed, he swallowed back one of the sugar cubes. The first rush of smoke he sucked into his lungs stung, and he coughed harsh barking hacks, but the soft euphoria of the drugs coursing through his brain came quickly, after so long without it, and brought a rare feeling of happiness. He put on some music that he and Waqar used to listen to together and lay back, sucking in the smoke, letting the happiness waft over and through him.

The light was beginning to fade by the time he stuffed the last of his mixture into the bong. Was it all gone already? He'd better make this final lot last a bit longer. As he lit the bong he popped the last acid cube into his mouth. The high began to take hold, carrying him outside his body. Sucking in some more of the weed, his hand fell to his crotch, and he rubbed his cock through the material of his underwear. As the blood started to pump and the vessels filled, he pushed the band of his boxers down and wriggled out of them, lying naked in the twilight, only the candle he was using to light the bong giving any added light to his skinny, exposed physique. Daniel stroked his shaft and fondled his balls with his other hand. The music transported him and gave rhythm to his hand movements and the fingers of euphoria enveloped him.

From nowhere, he came to him, a shadow at first, then more distinct, standing tall and unclothed, at the end of the bed. Bathed in the soft flickering light, his beloved Waqar stood, naked, smiling, erect.

'I am here, my love,' he said. 'The music, and your love, brought me here.'

'Come closer, my lost one,' said Daniel. 'Let me make love to you. Let me show my soul to you.'

Waqar came closer. His body was perfect, unblemished. Gone were the weals and the scars left by his father. His face was soft and shaven as it had been when they had first met. His hair was curly and full, shorter than in the camp. Thick bushy hair covered his chest, forming swirls around the dimpled flesh of his nipples. Waqar's cock pressed against the hairs of his stomach, quivering gently, oozing a strand of dark wetness from its tip.

'We need to get you ready,' said Waqar, his head now lowering over Daniel's erection. Waqar swished saliva around in his mouth and slowly let it trickle over Daniel's cock. He licked his lips and said, 'I want to moisten you, make you glisten, feel you inside me.'

Waqar was now squatting over Daniel, lowering himself closer to his penis. 'Wait,' said Daniel, pushing Waqar's stomach gently. 'Let me get it ready for you, make it smooth and slick.'

He reached for the lubricant he kept on his bedside table, squeezing the tube and allowing it to trickle over his cock, mingling with Waqar's spit. Waqar squatted lower and moaned as Daniel entered him. Daniel writhed – the wet heat made him feel ecstatic, beautiful, unimaginably fantastic. This moment was never meant to happen here, not here, not on earth. But this was something else, it felt ethereal, heavenly. Had he completed his task and already forgotten it? Was his destiny complete and he was now in *Jannah*? Daniel thrust against Waqar's resistant flesh, and his movements became faster, almost febrile. A fervour possessed him as if God was inside him, driving his ecstasy. Daniel threw back his head and arched his spine, thrusting and pounding.

But then a different sensation gripped him. A shimmering wall of red separated him from the beauty and the ecstasy. Pain.

Extreme pain in his cock and his hands. What had changed? Why was this incredible joy dissipating, disappearing? His eyes snapped open. Waqar was covered in dark red oil, engine oil. He remembered its smell. Daniel's hands dripped the same red-black filth. And Waqar's too, but these weren't Waqar's hands! No, these were older, coarser hands; they had cuts and old, untreated warts. Hands that he recognised from a time long past. Daniel looked up and now saw the driver from the lorry park, from all those years ago. His wet, scabrous lips stretched in a hideous grin, showing his yellow tobacco-stained teeth. He writhed on top of him, barking, 'Fuck me, you little bastard. Your cunt of a father will never know.'

'No!' shouted Daniel, his voice hoarse, hardly audible. Could he even be heard?

'No! Daniel, no!' replied another voice, louder, clearer. A familiar stern voice from the past. It wasn't the bark of the lorry driver. The voice wasn't sweet and soothing like Waqar's. Just as the hands had been unmistakable, the voice, too, was one that could belong to only one man. He looked up again and saw his father, Tom, naked and on top of him, where Waqar had been. Tom's legs, covered in thick grey fur, were dripping syrupy dark liquid onto the hooves that replaced his feet.

'Waqar, where are you?' Daniel's voice was feeble. An inaudible scream that reached no one. Even Daniel struggled to hear it as it gurgled noiselessly in a bubble in his throat. The curtain of red had devoured the vision of his love.

He pushed the aberration from him and stared at his own hands, now also covered in the thick liquid. His flaccid genitals were murky with the same filthy oil. He jumped up and turned on the light. The room was empty, only he was there, his pale skinny body reflected in the mirror on the wall. His hands were bleeding, and there were lacerations on his stomach, pubic area, penis and testicles. On the sheets, he could see particles of glass, and the bowl from his bong was shattered and splintered on the pillow and side table. Pieces of it still pierced his palms.

He took what was left of the bong and threw it at the wall. Waqar had shown him, made him see that the only escape from these horrors would be through God.

He stood under the shower and watched the blood swirl in the water and disappear into the drain along with the horror of what he had experienced. A sense of incredible cleansing coursed through him, subsuming any pain. Soon he would go to London. Waqar was calling him.

Chapter Twenty-Four
Today, Friday

The police car stops at the lights. Traffic is heavy on Horseferry Road. Life trudges on as normal for the rest of the world. It feels as if he is still reeling through the nightmare. This can't possibly be happening. Will he ever wake up from this? How much longer?

The policewoman seems to read his mind. 'Nearly there, Mr McIntyre,' she says.

Tom can see a row of police 'no parking' cones on the kerbside up ahead.

As the car draws level with them, the driver stops and jumps out. He moves a few of the cones to one side, drives the car into the space he's created and opens Tom's door. The policewoman gets out of the passenger side and stands by the open door, smiling benignly at him.

'Follow me,' she says.

Tom stays put. 'I don't want to do this.'

'We need a positive identification, Mr McIntyre. We'll make it quick, I promise. Everything is ready for you. It will be very quick – in and out.'

She offers her hand to him, and he shakes his head, but puts one leg out of the vehicle. He feels unsteady as he pushes himself upwards and out of his seat. People are walking back and forth on the pavement, paying no heed to him, probably intent on getting home, keen to see their loved ones, to relax, do normal things. How he wishes that was him, that he was one of those anonymous commuters who would read about this on their journey home and be shocked by it all, without being touched by it. He has the marks of it, has been tainted by it, eternally destroyed by it. This day, today, Friday will never leave him. It will slowly strangle him until...

Now he is out of the car. He looks around. Should he try running away? The policewoman beckons him over to the slotted metal gates. It reminds him of a prison cell. Is Daniel – what is left of him – in there, behind bars? After he walks through those gates, he will be in a prison of sorts. A prison of knowing, of being exposed to something that can never be unseen, never be forgotten. Once he walks through those barriers, there will be no going back for him, no return to normality. Normality? What is normality? Everyone has an idea of what it is, what it might be... until it changes, until normality isn't anything any fucking more.

'I can't do it. Take me home, please.'

'I know this will be awful for you. You have to be brave. We need you to do this, for your sake, if nothing else. You have to be sure that we haven't got this wrong.' Her voice is soft, her eyes narrowed, grave.

Maybe they had got it wrong. Please let it be a mistake. Let this be a mistake. But he'd seen the video that Daniel had made – on the news – or at least he'd seen the glimpses of it that they'd shown, slapped up against scenes of smoke, fire, bleeding people fleeing from the tube station. That had been like watching a dead version of his son. His eyes had been lifeless, passionless. His speech had been monotone, completely without emotion. Daniel couldn't have done something like that, whatever his words said. It had to be some internet hoax he'd got himself mixed up in. What had Daniel to do with terrorism? He was such a gentle boy. What could have happened to make him like this? It had to have been Waqar. All those trips to the mosque, the prayer mats, the *kufis*. He had wielded some power over Daniel, hadn't he? Daniel had told him Waqar was dead. Car accident. Was this one of his lies? Had Waqar been with him in the tube station?

The policewoman holds the gate open, an AUTHORISED PERSONNEL ONLY sign visible above her head. Tom follows the male police officer through the gate and hears it clunk shut behind him. A thick-looking, grey wooden door lies ahead of them. The policewoman mumbles something into the intercom at the side of it, and Tom hears a dull click from the door as it pops open. He hesitates again as she holds the door open for him, her eyes looking him up and down as if he's some pathetic lost soul. The other officer leans against a wall, pulling a pack of cigarettes from his pocket.

'I'll wait for you here, Julie,' he says, lighting up.

Julie. So there's a human being under that uniform. She might have introduced herself. The bastards that came to his flat were telling him who they were before he even had a chance to open his door fully. Julie? PC, sergeant, inspector, what? Maybe she's married. Too young for kids, probably. She can't be any older than Daniel. Probably a junior. A lesbian maybe? Lots of women in the police were, he'd heard. She seems too soft for that. Too feminine. God, he'd never met any of Daniel's girlfriends. He never would now, would he? There would never be any kids from Daniel. Tom had always hoped for a little girl, wondered if he would see some of Alison in a granddaughter, get a little bit of her back in his life. No hope of that. Daniel had all Alison's features and mannerisms, didn't he? Jenny was more him. No grandchildren from her either, if he knew his kids at all.

'C'mon, Mr McIntyre,' she says. 'The sooner we do this, the sooner it'll be over.'

Tom steps inside and the door clicks shut behind him. Cream-coloured walls meet a glossy, grey-painted floor, and a faint chemical smell reaches him. There is nothing about this place that makes him want to take a step further in. A small sign points towards the lifts. He follows Julie, who has come to a stop by the lift doors, pressing the 'down' button. There is no indication of what floor the lift is on, and they stand in awkward silence, waiting. After a few minutes, Julie presses the call button again.

'Shall we take the stairs?' asks Tom, now desperate to have this over with.

'We have to take the lift,' she says. 'Doors to the stairs are only released for emergencies. Security, you know.'

Tom nods, but he doesn't know. He knows fuck-all about these government mazes. These places wouldn't exist without their stupid rules and regulations and red tape. 'Maximise the misery' is probably the mantra of every government department. He closes his eyes and sucks in deep breaths. If only he could have a drink, something to take the edge off this. Bilious liquid still bubbles in his throat, burns his gullet. Only another drink could get rid of that. Every image he manages to banish from his brain quickly returns with added detail or different ugliness. He throws his head into his hands and presses his thumbs against his eyes to stop himself from screaming. Finally, a muffled, almost rubbery ding comes from the lift and the doors draw slowly open.

Julie takes his arm and leads him inside. She presses the '-2' button that has a small sign beside it that says: THE IAIN WEST FORENSIC SUITE. The lift doors close as slowly as they had opened. There is no sense of movement, up or down. Tom feels trapped in some endless purgatory. Julie seems to sense his thoughts again.

'Sorry, it's always like this,' she says, 'I'm sure the buttons get pressed a hundred times for every floor because people think nothing is happening.'

Tom forces a mirthless smile to his face and immediately chastises himself for even responding; he is here to identify his son. Focus on that. Show some decorum. He closes his eyes again, willing the lift to stop and the doors to open, then, just as forcefully, yearning for them to stay closed. Being trapped in a tunnel that is going to be filled with rushing water at any second is how it feels. When he opens his eyes, Julie is pressing the button again and again.

When the lift doors finally open, a grey corridor stretches before them, with the same glossy painted floor. Rows of dark wooden doors stand like sentries along the length of it. A heavy smell of chemical cleaner hangs in the air, and anti- bacterial lotion dispensers number almost as many as the doors. Tom shudders.

'Follow me,' says Julie.

She leads him down the corridor and opens one of the dark doors near the end. The room is small, rectangular, claustrophobic. Air with the same chemical taint whooshes through vents at either side of a long narrow window that has brown curtains pulled tightly closed, with a cord to one side. A number of seating rows semi-circled around it would turn it into a perfect mini theatre. A Punch and Judy show, maybe. Let him be Judy, let him be clubbed on the head until he bleeds and drops. There is a table with four chairs round it. Julie pulls out one facing the window and tells Tom to sit. He wonders whether she will say, 'The performance is about to begin.'

'I'd prefer to stand,' he says.

'It may be a few minutes,' she says. 'I have to find the pathologist so that we can go ahead with the identification. Sit down, please. Would you like something to drink? Tea, coffee, water, maybe?'

'Hardly.'

Tom sits down in the offered chair and folds his arms tightly. He fixes his stare on the covered window.

'OK,' says Julie. 'I'll be back shortly.'

She leaves the room, closing the door behind her. Tom feels panic rising in his gut. He stands up again and paces back and forth. The walls are blank. Nothing to focus on but the table and the window. And the door. Oh, how he wants to open that door and run and keep on running. He takes hold of the handle, but lets go of it immediately. She's probably locked him in, anyway. He sits down again, stands up, sits down, stands up. Paces the room. Walks around the table. Sits down again.

The only noise comes from the air vents and the adulterated air pushing through them. Occasionally, the air flow causes the curtains to flutter slightly, making Tom think something is finally happening. But nothing would happen while he is here in the room, alone. This much, he knows. Standing up again, he goes over to the window. Should he? His fingers reach for the cord as if somehow they are acting independently of him. Is Daniel behind these curtains? He pulls on the cord and the curtains part a few centimetres in the centre of the window, revealing the glass. Tom stops pulling and moves tentatively towards the opening. Can he bring himself to look through?

There is some chance it isn't him, that they have it wrong. The police get things wrong all the time, don't they? He pulls at the curtain closest to him and forces himself to look. All there is to see are the same two curtains closed on the other side of the glass. Tom heaves a huge gulp of air into his lungs; he's hardly aware that he's been holding his breath. He quickly goes back to the cords and pulls the curtains closed again. God knows what Julie thinks of him, but if she sees he's been taking matters into his own hands, she'll think less of him than she already does. Worse than that – the whole fucking thing – what would the neighbours think, the porters, what would the fucking world think? It isn't just his behaviour here, it's everything. Everything he knows, everything he holds good is disintegrating. He sinks heavily into the chair again and folds his arms.

If only he hadn't been so drunk last night, if only he had been able to sit down with Daniel and talk to him properly. Maybe he could have talked him out of whatever it was he was thinking. They hadn't spoken for so long. Oh, Daniel, there would never be another chance, would there? Why had he come to him last night, if not to talk? Had he wanted him to tell him not to do this? Had being drunk made Daniel angry again and stopped him even trying to ask for help? Might he have been able to stop him? Might he have been able to get his son to rationalise the anger he felt against the world? *Don't be fucking stupid, Tom. You couldn't even get him to stop being angry at you!*

The door clicks open again, and Julie comes in with a much older man who is wearing a white lab coat. He is bald, apart from an unkempt mound of grey hair that perches above his ears, straggling down his neck. Large black-framed glasses seem to sit uncomfortably on his bulbous nose. He carries a brown cardboard file under his arm. The man extends his hand to Tom.

'I'm Peter Scott, Mr McIntyre, one of the forensic pathologists here.'

Tom shakes his hand and nods, remaining seated. Peter Scott sits down next to him, and Julie takes one of the chairs at the end of the table. They sit in uncomfortable silence until, eventually, the pathologist clears his throat.

'This identification is going to be a little difficult, I'm afraid.' Tom looks at him, then at Julie who is studiously avoiding his gaze.

'Can we just get this over with, please?' Tom says.

'The thing is… we don't have… well, you understand the circumstances…' Peter Scott seems to be struggling for words.

'We were only able to recover parts of the body,' says Julie.

'I've arranged the most identifiable parts on a table,' says Peter.

'Oh, God.' Tom feels a wave of nausea rising in his throat. 'I don't think I can do this. I really don't.'

'Try to be strong, Mr McIntyre. We'll make it as quick as possible, and I'll be right here by your side. Alright?' Julie has moved around the table and now places her hand on his shoulder.

Peter stands up and starts towards the door. 'Alright, let's get this over with. PC Hepburn, will you open the curtains on this side, please?'

He leaves, closing the door behind him. Julie squeezes Tom's arm, then goes to the window and pulls on the cord, drawing the curtains fully back. The drapes on the other side of the glass remain closed. Tom feels his hands shaking and clenches them together to his chest. His whole body shivers in response as he stands up and walks over to the window. A wraith-like reflection of his frightened face stares back at him from the glass, but quickly disappears as the curtains slowly begin to open on the other side.

The room beyond the glass is vast and bathed in a harsh neon light that gives a surreal tint to the scene that faces Tom. It is like looking into some three-dimensional foreign film with no subtitles. Peter Scott stands behind the glass in front of a metal gurney that has a yellowish linen cloth covering it. Beyond that are other gurneys with the shapes of bodies under similar coverings. Peter is wearing a headset with a small microphone protruding from it. He taps on it.

'Can you hear me?' he asks.

Tom nods and Julie tells Peter that he is loud and clear.

'That's good,' says Peter. 'So I will begin. Mr McIntyre, in a moment I will uncover parts of the body that have identifying features. Please simply say "yes", or just nod, if you believe that this may be your son, Daniel.'

Tom tries to concentrate on not falling apart. His whole body shakes out of control, and he feels more nauseous than he can ever remember. He holds his breath as the pathologist lifts the cloth. Underneath are five small piles, individually covered in smaller pieces of material, each with illegible labels and marks upon them. Almost like a museum curator unwrapping a precious work of art, Peter lifts the covering from the first pile, his back obscuring whatever he is revealing. As Peter stands to one side and faces Tom again, Tom gasps and puts his hand to his mouth.

'Do you recognise this ring?' asks Peter.

Tom looks at the fragments of the hand on the table. Is it Daniel's right hand? Yes. He knows it. Only the little finger, the finger next to it, and a small part of the wrist are visible. On the pinkie is a gold wedding ring that has a thin band of platinum around the top and bottom. It looks as if it is fused into the skin, a permanent part of the dead flesh. Tom looks at his own left hand, at his wedding finger, at the ring upon it: a twenty- four-carat gold wedding band with platinum edges. It had been on his bedside table, even though he never took it off. His wedding finger felt raw and rough. Had Daniel pulled it off him last night? He and Alison had chosen them together. Daniel had begged to have his mother's after she died and had worn it on his little finger ever since. Tom's eyes fill with tears as he twists his wedding ring around on his finger.

'Yes,' he says.

'Thank you,' says Peter, covering the hand up again and moving to the next mound, which he uncovers just as carefully as he had the first. Standing back and facing Tom again, he says, 'And this?'

It takes Tom a few seconds to recognise what he is looking at. It is a face. Part of a face. Only a cheek, a corner of the mouth, a small section of the nose, an ear and a little bit of the head, visible as far as the temple. All the rest obscured by the labelled cloth. Any doubts that Tom is harbouring fly from his brain as his eyes take stock of the snake tattoo on the cheek. He falls to his knees, sobbing and shaking.

'Daniel, Daniel,' he cries.

Julie closes the curtains again and helps Tom back to his feet. She leads him to the chair and makes him sit down again. After some time, she says, 'You're sure that those are the remains of your son, Daniel Thomas McIntyre?'

'Yes. That was Daniel,' says Tom through sobbing gasps. 'At least, that was how he looked when I saw him last night. That's not how he used to look. He was such a sweet boy.'

'We can't take responsibility for what kids do as adults,' says Julie. 'Please, don't blame yourself for what has happened.'

After a few minutes, Tom stands up, wiping his eyes. 'Can we go now, please?' he says.

'I just need you to sign this sheet, formally identifying your son. Then we can go. Is there someone you can stay with tonight? Or can I call someone for you who can come and stay with you, look after you?'

'No,' says Tom as firmly as he can. 'I want to be on my own. I have a lot to think about. There are twenty-four-hour staff in my building. I can call on them if I need them.'

Buckingham Court seems unusually quiet when the police car drops him at the front door. It feels as if the world is paying its respects, somehow. Tom pushes his way through the revolving doors and sees Vince rushing towards him from the desk.

'Hello, Mr McIntyre. I'm so sorry, sir. Can I—'

'I'm all right, Vince. No fuss, please. I'll go up now,' says Tom.

'Your flat is all cleaned up, sir, you can—'

Tom brushes past Vince and takes the stairs two at a time, glad to leave the world behind him. When he gets to his front door, he stands for a few minutes, his key in his hand. Normally, Rufus would be behind the door miaowing plaintively for him, begging him to pet and stroke him. The silence brings all the horror of waking up flooding back into his brain. He takes a deep breath and turns the key in the lock.

The flat smells of disinfectant and reminds him of the putrid smell in the mortuary. The deep-red of the walls, glistening in the lamplight from the gardens, is redolent of the congealed blood he'd found all over himself when he'd woken up. He goes straight to the kitchen and opens a bottle of wine, then another, then another. One thing is for sure – he is going to wipe this day out of his brain. Grabbing a glass, he takes all the bottles to the living room and turns on 'Hallelujah'. He presses the continuous repeat button and pours himself a large drink.

The chords start to play as he swallows back the first glass, quickly followed by another. Anything to stop himself thinking, even though he knows nothing will keep the ugly thoughts from invading his brain. 'Hallelujah' has always made him think of Alison; it had been their song, one they'd listened to together more than any other. It also makes him sad and despondent, but that doesn't enter his mind. Now it makes him think of the doorbell ringing and seeing his much-changed son standing there in front of him. Once or twice, he thinks he hears it ring again, through his tears and the music. Each time, he tries to raise himself from where he sits to answer the door, but immediately forgets what has made him stand up. Filling his glass again, he slumps back into the sofa, begging the music to empty his head of thoughts.

There is no point to this anymore. He's been punished for wanting success and having it has brought him nothing. Maybe he'd made a subliminal deal with the devil, and now he is getting what he deserves. Maybe if he hadn't wished so hard for it, Alison would still be here, Daniel would still be here. Life would be worth something then, wouldn't it? All this wealth, all these fine things – was having all this worth losing the most important people in his life? If only it were possible to go back to the start. Undo the deal. Accept what is important and worthwhile. Live.

It would be easier not to have all this wealth. Better to have nothing, but not know it was nothing, than to have everything, but know that it means nothing. Better to have no future than a future full of regret, misery and guilt. Who will even notice if he ceases to exist? What is death anyway? An infinite, dreamless sleep. No regrets, no sadness, no pain, no guilt. For millennia, before he was ever born, he had been dead, hadn't he? Not being born is no different to being dead, surely? Millennia of sweet nothingness. What joy is there in this fucking life? All it seems to provide is misery and hopelessness. Who the fuck came up with the idea of hope? Nothing left to hope for, nothing that could make any difference, in any case. Everything worth living for has been stripped away, forever.

Tom tries to pour another glass of wine, but the bottle is empty. He pushes it away and tries the next bottle, but that only has a dribble of wine left in it. The third one is full, at least for now, and he fills up his glass. 'Hallelujah' still fills the room, Jeff Buckley's voice capturing Tom's mood perfectly. Broken. Cold. Dead. He turns the volume up until it will go no louder. How old was Jeff Buckley when he died? Was he even as old as Daniel? Are you gone, Daniel? Forever? No more? What for? Why? Should I not be the one to go first? Is that not the correct order of things? At least Jeff Buckley left something meaningful behind. Something that would make the world remember him. Who will remember you, Daniel? The real Daniel, not the one who came last night. Only me, and for how long?

The room begins to sway and bend, and when Tom stands up, he falls onto the coffee table, sending the remainder of the wine spreading all over it like a pool of inky blood. He has made up his mind now. Various options creep into his brain: jump in front of a train? No, too selfish. Too much like Daniel had done, anyway. Hang himself? Well, he wasn't sure of the mechanics of that, and he'd heard awful stories of failed attempts where the poor fools had been left paralysed or with terrible mental afflictions. Shoot himself? Yes, that would be ideal, if only he had a gun. He could always go and brandish a knife or something at one of the robotic gun carriers outside the Ministry of Defence. That would be too messy and public. The McIntyres don't need any more bad publicity, do they? And God knows, they would see that as another terrorist attack, wouldn't they? It has been pretty much clear all along what method he would use. He had planned it years before. Pills. It would have to be pills, and he has plenty of those. He's been imagining them putting him to sleep since he arrived back home.

Deep in a drawer in his dressing room, he has hidden all the unused drugs from Alison's final weeks. He searches for the brown boxes, the ones that contain the potent morphine-based painkillers that had ceased to work for her in those last, awful days. He'd been told to flush them down the toilet, at least he thinks that was what he was told. Maybe he was meant to take them back to the pharmacy. In any case, he always knew that one day he might find a use for them. And here they are, ALISON MCINTYRE — FOR ACUTE PAIN ONLY typed on the label. These will do it. His pain is acute. Does pain get any worse than this? Maybe for you, darling. God only knows the pain you endured. You don't mind me doing this, do you? If only you could talk now, my darling.

By way of the kitchen, he picks up a new bottle of wine and a fresh wine glass. He is sure he's broken the other one. But let's face it, this is going to be my last, anyway. The living-room is in darkness, apart from the sulphurous glow of the lamps in the gardens outside. He throws the boxes of pills on the sofa and sinks into the cushion next to them, still clinging onto the wine bottle and glass. With the glass clenched between his thighs, he unscrews the top from the wine and pours unsteadily, splashing red onto his trousers and the sofa cushions.

This is it. No more sorrow. He picks up Alison's pill boxes and presses out eight capsules from the first foil sheet. Without another thought, he stuffs them into his mouth and takes a long glug of wine. Peace will soon be his. Another mouthful of wine washes down another eight capsules, and he reaches for the second box.

'Hallelujah' still plays on repeat, but now something breaks into it, something quieter, but still something that muddies the melody. What is it? Then he sees the glow of his phone at the corner of the sofa. And there is Jenny's face. Jenny!

He reaches for his phone but can't quite get hold of it. It still rings; he reaches again. His vision is beginning to blur. He is starting to feel sick. Still, he reaches. He needs to say goodbye. He has to say sorry. He needs to throw up these pills and stop. Finally, he feels the phone in his grasp, but it isn't ringing any more. Where is the call button? Focus! And it starts to ring again, and there is her face again. Jenny. Tom somehow manages to press the answer key and swings the phone to his ear. His mouth won't work correctly, the words, clear in his head, won't come. He struggles to speak, breathing heavily into the mouthpiece. He feels he is gaping like a fish.

'Dad?'

'...hull! Hel J J J...'

'Hi, Dad? Dad, is that you?'

'Schjennnny, schmee.'

'Dad? Are you OK? Turn the music down, please. I can hardly hear you.'

Tom reaches for the remote control, what he thinks is the remote. What he finds in his grasp is a box of Alison's pills.

'...joo schtill there?'

'Dad, what's wrong? You're worrying me.'

Tom feels his brain closing down. No more words will come. His grip loosens on the phone. It falls to the floor as his body lurches forward and his head hits the coffee table with a crash.

Chapter Twenty-Five
Today, Friday

'Bloody hell!' Vince puts the phone down and opens the key cabinet above the desk, scrabbling for the key he wants. 'Benny, more trouble in 67. I'm going upstairs to check. Look after reception, OK?'

He doesn't wait for a reply as he pushes past his colleague and out of the reception area and starts bounding up the staircase. Gasping for breath, he thrusts the key at the lock on Tom's front door and pushes it open. Music is blaring all through the flat.

'What a fucking racket,' mumbles Vince, then, at the top of his voice, 'Mr McIntyre? Mr McIntyre, are you there, sir?'

He most probably can't hear him above the din. That'll be why he isn't answering. Vince makes his way tentatively into the dining room, switching lights on as he goes, and peers from there into the living room. He can see Tom's feet, one shoe on one, the other with his sock half pulled off, at the end of the coffee table. Vince ventures into the living room and immediately stiffens when he sees blood oozing from a wound on Tom's head. His face is in a pool of vomit.

'Fucking hell,' he says, pulling his mobile from his pocket and dialling emergency services. 'Ambulance, please!' At the same time, he kneels down and takes Tom's wrist, feeling for a pulse.

As soon as he finishes giving the relevant information to the operator, he radios down to Benny. 'Get yourself up here, pronto,' he says.

'But there's nobody to—'

'Now, Benny!'

Vince throws his phone to the floor and holds his breath as he feels for Tom's pulse again.

'Thank fuck,' he murmurs.

Vince wipes the vomit from Tom's face and pushes his fingers into his gaping mouth, clearing as much as possible from there, fighting an impulse to throw up himself. He yanks off Tom's remaining shoe and tries to pull him clear of the coffee table by the ankles. It is no use – Tom may as well be welded to the floor. As Vince pushes the heavy table clear of Tom's head, Benny appears in the room.

'Thank fucking hell,' says Vince, ignoring the shocked expression on Benny's face. 'Take his shoulders and help me lift him over there.' Vince indicates a clear space beyond the sofa. 'I need to get him into the recovery position, or we may lose him before the ambulance gets here. He still has a faint pulse. Last thing I want to do is give him the kiss of life. God forbid he throws up again when we move him.'

The two of them wrestle Tom's body to the open area, and Vince arranges his arms and legs into the recovery position before clearing the rest of the vomit from his mouth. He can feel bile rising in his throat again as he notices blood in the foul-smelling sick. Vince takes Tom's pulse again.

'It's still there,' he says to Benny. 'But it's very faint. Go back downstairs, and look out for that ambulance. Bring them straight here when they arrive. And throw me the remote that's on the floor over there. I can't stand listening to another note of this fucking song.'

Vince lightly slaps Tom's face.

'Mr McIntyre, wakey, wakey. C'mon, sir, you need…'

There is no response. Vince spies the boxes of pills on the sofa and the floor. He collects the empty foils together – evidence of how many Tom has potentially swallowed – and stacks the boxes neatly. He looks at his watch and checks Tom's pulse again. It is still very feeble.

'C'mon, you bloody ambulance. Where the fuck are you?'

He opens the French windows to let in some fresh air and take away the sour stench that is clinging to his nostrils. Every few minutes, he checks that Tom is still breathing and radios Benny almost as often to see if there is any sign of the ambulance. After fifteen minutes, he hears the sound of voices in the hallway and heaves a huge sigh when Benny appears, followed by two burly paramedics.

'Thank fuck for that,' he says.

Chapter Twenty-Six
A Future

Tom will awake to white walls, tubes and the unmistakable aroma of hospital. There will be no one else in the room. An easy chair will stand unoccupied in a corner, a table adjacent to it, and a few anaemic pieces of art on the wall will look as if they'd be happier anywhere else than here. A sense of hurried activity will rush back and forth beyond the closed door, and a faint noise of phone and medical chatter will be somewhere distant. He will inhale deeply and will groan at the burning sensation in his throat and chest. Didn't I die? Is this some new version of purgatory? Fuck, am I still stuck in the same fucking nightmare?

He will feel to his left then his right, searching for the call button. It will be there on his right. He will take it in his hand and hover his finger over the button. Bleak thoughts will come. Will he want to know? Maybe if he presses it, it will plummet him back into the nightmare he had so desperately fought to escape. Maybe this *is* purgatory, and he *will* go straight back to the start. Experience it all again. His finger will move away from the button then move back over it again. This will be real. Purgatory doesn't smell of anything. Does it? He will press.

He will feel tubes in his nose, and he will see more tubes running from a cannula in his right hand, which leads to a drip at the side of his bed. As he puts his left hand to his face, to feel for the tubes in his nose, he will touch the hard plastic of the oxygen mask that covers both his mouth and nose. A machine next to his bed will whirr and click, with an occasional beep that seems to spur a spike in the graph that will constantly refresh on the screen, creating a pixelated mountain range. The door will open, and a tall young man in green scrubs will enter, looking harassed.

'So you're back with us, Tom,' he will say, approaching the bed. He will touch Tom's hand as a cursory introduction. 'I'm Amos. What's the problem?'

Amos will study the screen by Tom's bed as he speaks.

'I just woke up. Where am I? How did I get here? Am I alive?' Tom will ask.

Amos will laugh. 'Yes, you're very much alive, lovey. It was a close-run thing, mind you. Did you think you were in heaven? This place is St Thomas's Hospital, Acute Admissions Ward. You were in a terrible state.'

'My head is aching,' Tom will say.

'Yes, that was quite a knock you gave yourself. Mind you, the turban suits you. Let me check your chart and see what you've had so far. We don't want to go giving you an overdose now, do we?'

'Ha, ha – very funny,' Tom will say, no vestige of mirth in his tone.

'Sorry, deary,' Amos will say, picking up the chart from the end of Tom's bed. 'Just trying to lighten the mood. By the way, your daughter is here – downstairs in the waiting room. She's been here all night.'

'Jenny?' Tom will ask, a rush of memories and guilt pounding his throbbing head. 'What time is it? How long have

I been here?'

'It's just after seven. Saturday evening. Do you want me to have her brought in to see you, or would you like a bit longer to come to? I can give you some more pain relief – you're well within the window for another dose.'

'Thanks, doctor. I'd like to see her. Maybe let me have some painkillers and give them ten minutes to work first.'

Amos will laugh again, and as he breezes out of the room, will say, 'I'm just a lowly nurse. But thanks for the compliment. I'll be right back with your pills.'

A soft hand on his cheek will wake him up. The same hand will squeeze his arm, the one without any tubes running from it.

'Dad, it's me.'

Tom's vision will be blurred, and he will blink repeatedly, screwing up his eyes from time to time to try and clear away the aquarium he will feel he is looking through.

'Jenny, love,' he will say. 'Was I asleep? I was waiting for you to come.'

'Yes, Dad. You were sleeping like a baby, but not for long. I didn't want to disturb you, but it's getting late, and I need to get home.'

'What time is it?'

'It's nearly eleven. I've been here since late last night. Rashid is worried about me so I want to get back.'

'I'm sorry, love. I've been such a fool. I should never have put you through this. Identifying Danny yesterday just pushed me over the edge. I just couldn't get my brain around it.'

'Dad, I'm very sorry about Danny. I had no idea when I called you. It's been all over the news, constantly. Rashid and

I only got back from holiday a few hours before, and I called to tell you something important.'

'I'm glad you did. The nurse said that you called the desk at my building after you spoke to me. It was young Vince who got me help. What an idiot I was. I'm so ashamed.'

'Don't beat yourself up, Dad. You're here now, alive and with us. That's what matters. And I'm going to tell you something that is going to hopefully take some of the pain away.'

Tom will look deeply into her eyes, willing his daughter to tell him this good news. Jenny will stand up and move away from the side of the bed so that he can see her better, and begin stroking her abdomen. Her dress will be thin cotton, a bright-blue summer one, and it will hug clear signs of a bump on her slender figure.

She will beam at him and say, 'You're going to be a grandad.'

Tom will look up to the ceiling and experience a small shard of pure joy coursing through him. All the bleakness and misery that has pervaded these last hours will not exactly disappear, but this happiness will at least make it bearable. He will pull off his oxygen mask.

'Thank you!' he will say, grinning so hard that his jaw will hurt.

'I'm over the twenty-week mark. I'm due at the end of December. It's a girl, Dad.'

'My God. A girl? You've given me the most incredible gift. And if she comes on the first of January, that'll be the anniversary of…'

'I know. It's the first thing I thought when the doctor told me the due date.'

Tom will feel his eyes welling up, and he will fight the urge to burst into tears. The tears will come in any case, but for once – for once in the longest time – there will be happiness behind them. Jenny will lean over and put her arms around him.

'You'll name her Alison, won't you? You have to call her after your mum, given when she is due.'

Jenny will pull away from Tom, her smile fading. 'Don't you think that's a bit morbid, Dad?'

'Please, Jenny. There's bound to be so much of her in the baby. It would mean so much to me. It would mean so much to her too.'

'Mum's dead. This baby won't bring her back. I'm sorry, Dad. I really don't think Rashid will go for it, anyhow. But whatever we call her, you've got everything to live for,' she will whisper. 'Now make me a promise.'

Tom will turn his face away from her and lie quietly for a moment or two. More promises? More deals? Does everything have its price?

'Anything,' he will say, a feeling of dejection slithering through him.

'When you get out of here, no more drinking, OK?'

'Never again,' Tom will say. 'I'm going to make the most of this chance. You've made me so happy, Jenny. You've given me reason to live again. This promise is unbreakable. I will do anything to convince you that I mean what I say.'

Twice he will have seen his daughter's face glow with happiness in the space of minutes. More dark thoughts will pervade: How could I have forgotten her? How could I have been so keen to leave this earth without giving her a thought? It was all Daniel, me and my fucking problems. I sidelined her all these years, hardly considered her. She is my link to Daniel, to Alison, to myself. Now she will be my link to the future, to life, to new life. It is impossible to see why I'll have this second chance. Have I been released from the diabolical deal I've made? Have I finally done my penance?

Somehow, he will not believe that he has. Something nasty will be waiting down the line. Will this be another poisoned arrow to teach him the lesson of failure to consider what is important? If this is what's on offer, he will take it. He will accept whatever stay of execution this represents.

Fuck God, fuck Lucifer, fuck whatever powers that are controlling my fate. He will take this on whatever terms it means. In some way, Alison is being given back to him, even if it will just be a tiny part of her, a mere inkling. To see even a faint notion of his wife in his granddaughter will make these last purgatorial years worthwhile, of that he will be sure.

Jenny will blow him a kiss as she leaves his hospital room. He will do his best to reciprocate, but will push the oxygen mask back to his mouth as soon as she has gone. Deep inhalations will seem to make no difference, and a growing panic will exacerbate his shortness of breath. He will press the call button by his side and watch the light above his door illuminate like some beacon of hope. 'Come quickly!' Death will be so wrong now. His heart will beat faster than he can ever remember. The room will spin. The thoughts that form, as he begins to black out, will be despondent.

I am dying. Here is the ultimate punishment for this awful misspent life. How fitting that He should deny me the chance to see my beautiful granddaughter.

An angel will enter the room, clad in blue scrubs. She will take his pulse, her other hand on his forehead. Tom will feel a slowing in his chest, and a calmness will gradually return.

She will say, 'Just a panic attack, my love. I'm going to increase the flow to your mask, alright? You'll be fine.'

Tom will feel the rush of oxygen in the mask and chide himself. You fool, you idiot; this bastard gets you every time, doesn't he? Stop letting him rule your life. What will be, will be. Second-guessing Satan won't change anything. Live. Be alive. Enjoy it while it lasts. Breathe. You've done the deal. Take whatever is offered now.

He'd given his wife, his son. He'd given himself. Enough is enough. There has to be some reward, doesn't there? No more. Just take what is on offer and be grateful. Tom will be grateful. He will have a granddaughter. A second chance.

Rain will fall. Tom will keep little Alison dry under his big red golfing umbrella. She will be chattering away about her school friends, her gym class, the fact her latest painting has pride of place on the classroom wall. Grandad will respond exactly as she will expect him to and his reward will be a big blue-eyed trusting face at every word he says and an abundance of smiles, more than he will ever be able to believe he deserves. They will have to get a move on or Alison will be late for school. Alison will yank at his arm and tell him to stop. Mummy will be calling them.

Tom will hear Jenny's voice some way behind and look back. His daughter will be waddling as fast as she can go, carrying a lunchbox in one hand, and waving wildly with the other. By the time Jenny reaches them, she will be clutching her protruding belly and extending a lunchbox to Tom with her free hand.

'You two will be the death of me,' she will gasp, thrusting the lunchbox at Tom. 'I've been calling after you both for the last ten minutes.'

Tom will laugh. 'Did we forget again?' He will look down at Alison. 'You promised to remind me when you went to bed last night, didn't you?'

'Sorry, Grandad,' she will reply. 'I forgot.'

Tom will tousle her hair and say, 'My fault, titch.' Then to Jenny, 'Jesus, you shouldn't be dashing around in your condition. I could easily have gone back with it.'

'You're not getting any younger, Dad,' Jenny will say, sheltering under his brolly. 'But I could've done without getting soaked.' Her look will have turned frosty. 'You smell very… minty, Dad. Have you been drinking?'

For fuck's sake. One small snifter of scotch to take the edge off the morning. Call the fucking prohibition police, why don't you?

'Walk with us,' Tom will say, putting his arm around her. 'Not far now and you can keep me company on the way back. Don't worry, we can take it slow.'

'Sure, Dad. I could do with the exercise. The doctor says it's the best thing for my blood pressure.' Jenny will rub her tummy. 'And maybe some pounding of the pavement will get this one out and into the world… Dad, you promised to lay off the booze. You've been doing so well. What's changed?'

It's the fucking weekend. Can I not have one tiny drink once in a while? 'Bloody hell, Jenny. It's mouthwash you smell. Stop being so suspicious all the time. I told you I've stopped and I have.'

Jenny will glare at him as Alison says, 'Grandad said a bad word, Mummy.'

'OK, Dad, whatever you say. Let's get this one into school and get home. I can feel the bump struggling to break free.'

'At least wait until you get home, will you? Rashid can deal with it then. I'm not your man for maternity duties.'

'Like I'd even want you to be,' Jenny will laugh.

The rain will have stopped by the time they reach the school gates. Tom will stoop and kiss Alison on the cheek and watch her run into the playground, swinging her lunchbox as she goes.

'Bye bye, Grandad. Bye, Mummy,' she will call without looking back.

When Tom turns back to his daughter, she will look pained. She will be clutching her stomach.

'I think I spoke too soon,' she will say, through short breaths and gritted teeth.

Tom will start to panic. 'But you're not due for another fortnight. You'll make it home, won't you?'

Jenny will sit on the little squat wall at the side of the school gates, in spite of it being rain-soaked.

'You can't tell because the pavement is wet but my waters just broke, and the contractions are coming quite hard and fast,' she will gasp and clutch her belly. 'I didn't want to admit it to myself, but I've been having small contractions since the early hours of this morning. Call an ambulance, Dad.'

Tom will scrabble in his pockets for his mobile and will shout too loudly at the emergency operator when the call connects. Other parents will come to help and comfort while they wait for the ambulance to arrive.

The cherry tree will no longer be a sapling. The trunk will be thick and sturdy, covered in a heavy, beautiful, rough bark. Blossom will cascade from its branches, and a soft carpet of pink will cover the grass around it. Tom will put his bag down on the ground and smile at the scene. He will pick up a handful of blossom and hold it to his nose, breathing in the delicate scent. Thank you, Alison. The bag, a black leather attaché case from Asprey, with a glimmering gold hasp, will look incongruous on the carpet of pink. Tom will fiddle with the handle and gently touch the clasp. It will have taken the longest time to work up the courage to do this. *Not yet*, he will tell himself.

The dense branches will be silhouetted by a deep-blue cloudless sky and they will spread over what must be other graves, offering them gentle shade. There will be other trees nearby, mostly saplings, ash, birch, sycamore – loving tributes of the bereaved – but none of them will stand as tall or as majestically as Alison's cherry. Hers will be the healthiest in the whole setting and stand out like the centrepiece of the wood, a beacon of hope, renewal, life. Tom will be grateful that there will be no one else there. Only him, only Alison, only Rufus, only Daniel.

He will pick up the bag and kneel down, placing it on his lap. Undoing the hasp and opening the flap, he will pull out a small wooden box that will be held closed by a yellow satin ribbon, tied in a bow. Attached to the ribbon will hang a blue paper tag, upon which will be written in black ink, 'Rufus'.

Tom will finger the label for a moment or two before pulling at the bow. The yellow satin will fall on the grass, giving an added cheerful splash of colour to the fallen pink petals, and he will gently lift the thin lid from the box. Standing up, he will scatter the dust from inside the box around the base of the cherry tree.

'Now Rufus is here to keep you company, my darling. You are together again. Let him purr and rub against you until I join you.'

Tom will reach into the bag again and take out a silver urn. He will lay it on the grass and kneel down in front of it. It will look small and insignificant against the thick trunk of the tree, but it will glisten and catch the flickering light through the leaves.

'Here he is,' he will say. 'Our baby boy, our firstborn. I'm sorry it's taken me so very long to let go of him and give him back to you. It took a long time for me to feel ready. Do you remember how happy we were when you found out he was coming into our lives?'

Tom will pick up the urn and hold it to his chest. The grass will feel damp beneath his knees, so he will stand upright again, facing the tree. He will brush petals from his dewy trousers.

'We could never have imagined having to do this, could we? Experiencing the death of our child – well, that was a punishment that was mine alone, thankfully. Thank God you never had to go through this. God knows, you suffered enough. Maybe, if you'd lived, Daniel would still be here too. He loved you so much, much more than he loved me. You would love our beautiful grandchildren, Alison and Danesh.'

Tom will cling to the silver urn as if it is a part of him that he doesn't want to relinquish.

'But, Daniel. Without him, I would never have survived your loss. I'm here now because of him. I just don't know what happened, darling. I don't know how I lost his love. I was a drunk. That's when we started to drift apart, Daniel and me. He hated that about me. I'm not going to let anything spoil things between me and those two little ones. I have the chance to get things right again. Make amends. Pay my debts.'

Tom will take the lid off the urn and look inside. His eyes will fill with tears that he will be unable to stop flooding out. Some will mingle with the ashes, inside. 'This is all we have left of him. Our boy. I brought him here to be with you.

Safe from all the haters. Those people hate a different Daniel. They hate the boy who was changed, brainwashed, lost and misled. That wasn't our Daniel. Our boy wouldn't have wanted to put us through this. So I give you our son, pure and innocent. Cleansed. At peace now with his beloved mother. Look after him, darling.'

He will scatter the ashes around the tree trunk and pick up a handful of blossom, covering the grey dust with pink petals. A feeling of relief, or perhaps release, will begin to wash over him as he pushes the silver vessel and the box back into his bag. For the first time, in as long as he will be able to remember, he will not feel sad. It won't be happiness, exactly. More a feeling of having turned a corner and taken a better path.

'Goodbye, Alison. Goodbye, Daniel. Goodbye, Rufus. For now. I'll be with you all soon.'

Tom will pick up his bag and leave the woodland

graveyard. He will take a long walk to Daniel's old flat and will cry again as he looks at the cheerful curtains hanging at the windows, put there by whoever lives there now. During the walk to look at his old house in Cherry Lane, a sharp pain in his back will make him buckle. It won't be the first time he will have felt this pain, and it will not be the last time either.

His oncologist will have told him that the cancer in his liver will have metastasised and will be invading his lymph nodes. Although he will ask not to know the prognosis, the doctor will tell him that it will reach his lungs, bones and who knows where else within a matter of months and that he must plan for the end. A liver transplant could be a possibility that might save him, and chemotherapy and radiotherapy will have the ability to delay the spread until a donor can be found, but Tom will not agree to undergo any form of treatment other than palliative care. The deal will have to be settled, and by this point, he will be ready. All his fight will have fled. He will realise that he has been prepared to pay his debt ever since the day he said goodbye to Alison.

He will decide not to tell Jenny to spare her the misery of waiting for him to die as she had her mother, and he will spend as much time with his grandchildren as he can until the pain starts to resist the drugs. Then he will kiss them all goodbye, and he will go to his house alone, telling them that he is going away for a few days.

He will congratulate himself on his selflessness. Tom will write a long, loving letter to Jenny and explain his reasons, and he will leave notes and presents for Alison and Danesh. 'Hallelujah' will play as he drinks from the bottles of wine he has hidden away so carefully from Jenny. This time, he will swallow down many pills, gradually, and make sure he keeps them down. The pills will be in boxes that bear his name. His body will not fight against the onslaught this time.

Alison, Daniel, Jenny, little Alison, Danesh and Rashid will never be his again. Tom will have learned by this point that deals such as he has made don't work that way. All he will hope for is that his fate will be darkness, silence, infinite nothingness. As he breathes his last few breaths, he will wonder if all lives have the same outcome. All fear will be gone when his heart stops and his blood starts to congeal in his veins. If anyone thinks to ask Tom how he feels about dying, maybe his oncologist or one of his nurses, he will tell them that he is ready for it and that it holds no dread for him.

Chapter Twenty-Seven
Today, Friday

'We're losing him, Trevor!'

'I'll get the pads, Bill. Hang fire,' says the other paramedic.

Vince feels helpless. Benny stands near the archway to the living room looking as if he's in a trance. The one called Bill has torn Tom's shirt open and is pumping at his chest with both hands.

'Keep doing the compressions. I'll work around you,' says Trevor.

He sticks electrode pads onto Tom's upper body as the other man pumps furiously. A low-pitched rising tone sounds from the machine that Trevor has placed by Tom's side. When it stops, he says to Bill, 'Stand clear.'

He presses a button on the machine and Tom's body jerks. Bill recommences pumping at Tom's chest as Trevor presses another button on the unit. The tone begins to sound again, and the whole process repeats.

Vince turns to his colleague and says, 'Go back and look after the desk, Benny. We've left it unattended too long. I'll stay here.'

Benny mumbles something and shuffles out of the flat, looking glad to be released from this scene.

When Vince looks back to Tom and the two paramedics,

the one called Bill is pulling the pads from Tom's chest, and the other one is looking at his watch.

'Time of death: 23:57 hours,' he announces, gravely.

'He's dead?' asks Vince, a sick feeling spreading through him. 'But he had a pulse when you got here. He was breathing. I cleared his airways.'

'He was already in cardiac arrest when we arrived, mate. Sorry.'

The two paramedics are already unrolling a plastic zipper bag and assembling the stretcher gurney.

'We don't normally take them when they die at home,' says Trevor. 'But given that he lived alone, we'll take him to the mortuary at St Thomas's. There'll have to be a post-mortem, but it looks pretty cut and dried. Do you know if he has any next of kin?'

'Yeah,' says Vince, 'a daughter. I can call her and tell her what's happened if you like.'

'Thanks, mate,' Bill says as he helps manoeuvre Tom into the plastic body bag. Tom's face looks ghoulish, his head bent to one side and his mouth agape in a silent scream. Vince shudders as Tom disappears behind the metallic '*zzzzzup*' of the zip as it reaches its closing point. The two paramedics bundle the body onto the gurney and start wheeling him down the long hallway.

Vince opens the grand double doors and races ahead to the service lift and pushes the call button. When Tom is in the lift, he heads back to Flat 67 to turn off the lights and close the doors. As he is about to switch off the hallway lights, he notices the wooden cat again, still lying on its side. He stands it upright and reads the inscription on the silver Tiffany tag: I

SAW THIS AND THOUGHT OF YOU. ALL MY LOVE, ALWAYS, T XXX

Vince smiles sadly. Who was that meant for?

'What a fucking waste,' he mutters as he runs his hand along the deep shiny red of the Venetian plaster. 'You had it all, Tom McIntyre. You had it all and you threw it down the plughole like it was nothing.'

He gazes down the hallway to the dim dining room and the twinkling of the London Eye through the windows. Three or four versions of Vince's flat would fit in this hall and dining room alone. What a fucking waste. All he had to do was wait until the grief passed. Some folk just don't value what they've got. Such a shame. One of the nicest residents in the building too, and gone, for what? None of it was his fault.

'That poor girl. What on earth am I going to say to her?' he mumbles. He switches off the light and closes the door.

Epilogue

Perhaps Tom's moment of truth will be different. Infinite nothingness should not fulfil the payment for such a diabolical deal, after all. Who knows? Perhaps the doorbell will ring at four a.m. just as the last breath rattles from his chest, and he will awake to the buzz of the music system back in Buckingham Court. Who will know what part of purgatory each of us will enter after every death we will be made to endure? Daniel will already know this, or will at least have a sense of déjà vu as his face presses into the red tartan rug, or as he raises the sword in the desert. One thing will be sure: his yearning for Waqar, or some version of Waqar, will be eternal.

And Waqar? For him, the violence he will continually endure from his father may destroy him and allow someone else to inveigle their way into Daniel's soul as he seeks out a different purgatory. Maybe, each time Tom, Daniel, Waqar and all the other wanderers wallow in their misery, they will turn to one of their gods and believe again that their version of God will save them and release them from their awful existence. There will be no god to answer them. The faith they will invest all their energy in will be an eternal echo in a vast chamber of emptiness. The irony will be forever lost.

Ah, he serves you well, indeed!
He scorns earth's fare and drinks celestial mead.
Poor fool, his ferment drives him far!
He half knows his own madness, I'll be bound.
He'd pillage heaven for its brightest star,
And earth for every last delight that's to be found;
Not all that's near nor all that's far
Can satisfy a heart so restless and profound.

'Prologue in Heaven' in *Faust*, Johann Wolfgang Goethe.